Praise for *The Lady in Residence*

"Visions of a spirit that reside in a historic hotel are always on the top of my list for haunting heaven. *The Lady in Residence* will leave the reader turning pages faster than they can drift away into the darkness of the Menger Hotel. The vivid mystery is delicious and a few goosebumps might even find their way onto the reader's arms. A high recommendation from me!"

–Jaime Jo Wright, author of *The Haunting at Bonaventure Circus* and the Christy Award–winning, *The House on Foster Hill*

"Allison Pittman's newest novel is hauntingly delicious. I savored every page, from the colorful descriptions of San Antonio and the historic Menger Hotel, to the entertaining lessons in magic. Readers are transported to the past in a unique way, leaving it hard to decide which time period and set of characters is my favorite. *The Lady in Residence* is a thoroughly charming read that I highly recommend."

–Michelle Shocklee, author of *Under the Tulip Tree*

"This fun dual-timeline romance is a must-read for proud native Texans and those who've always longed to explore the home of the Alamo. Fans will delight in Pittman's beautifully written prose, witty dialogue, and organically infused tour of San Antonio. As rich in history as it is in modern San Antonio's vibrant culture. Bravo!"

–April W. Garder, San Antonio author of Christian historical romance

"*The Lady in Residence* is that perfect blending of history with gothic story that pulled me in and wouldn't let go. Told in split-time, I was vested in each story and couldn't wait to flip the page to learn what would happen next. The weaving of the two worlds worked, with a sweet romance and intrigue that left me wondering what was real. A book that readers of split-time stories laced with mystery will love."

–Cara Putman, award-winning author of *Flight Risk*

"Open the door to a breathtaking read but beware! Do not start reading *The Lady in Residence* at bedtime, or you'll never get any sleep. Pittman's deft hand at weaving the twin stories of Dini and Hedda kept me guessing while the growing romance kept me smiling. This book is a keeper!"

–Kathleen Y'Barbo, *Publishers Weekly* bestselling author of *The Black Midnight* and *Firefly Summer*

The LADY *in* RESIDENCE

ALLISON PITTMAN

The Lady in Residence

Print ISBN 978-1-64352-748-2

eBook Editions:
Adobe Digital Edition (.epub) 978-1-64352-750-5
Kindle and MobiPocket Edition (.prc) 978-1-64352-749-9

Published by Barbour Publishing, Inc., 1810 Barbour Drive, Uhrichsville, Ohio 44683, www.barbourbooks.com

Our mission is to inspire the world with the life-changing message of the Bible.

ecpa Member of the Evangelical Christian Publishers Association

Printed in the United States of America.

Chapter 1

San Antonio, Texas
March, First Friday Night

The tour ended where it began—in the courtyard of the Alamo, the fortress bathed in white light, flags snapping in the night sky. Standing still after the nearly four-mile walk, Dini Blackstone felt the chill. The Victorian-esque costume she wore to lead the two-hour walking Alamo Haunting Spirits Ghost Tour of downtown San Antonio gave little warmth. Spring in this city was a meteorological frustration, and this was one of those nights when you could feel the temperature drop with every step. By the time they made it back to the plaza, those with coats were clutching them closer, and those without were stuffing their hands in their pockets and bouncing on the balls of their feet through the last of Dini's spiel.

"And so ends our tour of the haunts of the Alamo City. You may not believe there are such things as ghosts, and maybe you're right. But what is a haunting, anyway? It's something that stays with you. And I hope the worthy tales of our restless spirits will follow you home."

Like all of the tour guides with the Alamo Haunting Spirits Ghost Tour, she was allowed to embellish the narrative script with her own interjections, and Dini had been delivering the same lines for nearly five years. So comfortable was she with the patter that she sometimes drifted away, letting her mouth move along with her feet while her mind soared, only to come back midsentence—just in time for a spooky punch line. So she was now, her face frozen in a smile as she posed for the millionth tourist selfie, standing close but not too close, before happily accepting the folded bills of gratuity. These she dropped in the deep pocket within the fold of her skirt, keeping a mental tally. Within hours her face would appear on the social media pages of strangers, hopefully tagged with the company name. Somebody in the office had the unenviable task of tracking those things, and the walker with the most mentions got a bit of a bonus every quarter.

The last pic ("say, 'Boo!' ") finally taken and the final tip in her pocket, Dini made her way across the street and walked into the bar of the Menger Hotel. The welcome warmth touched her face and hands—the only parts of her body exposed. Once inside, her eyes adjusted immediately to the comforting dark. The Menger Bar was exactly this hue no matter what time of day, giving respite from a bright, hot afternoon and solid shelter on the coldest night. With its well-worn wood floor and sturdy columns and tables, travelers and patrons had been greeted with this exact same view for almost a century. As was her habit, Dini looked directly up at the portrait of Teddy Roosevelt.

Blustery one is it tonight, my girl?

"Yep, but just in the last half hour or so." The fact that she spoke aloud to Roosevelt's silent, imagined question drew very little attention, mostly because there was little attention to be drawn. While other bars and nightspots in downtown San Antonio might be pulsating on this First Friday night of March, the Menger Bar remained its accustomed, dignified, nearly empty self. One elderly couple at a table sipping wine and a gentleman at the bar, foot balanced on the brass railing, tie loose and shirt collar open, absorbed in his phone.

"Wind's picking up?" This time the voice was real, and happened in its uncanny way to echo the essence of Roosevelt's speech. Troy Gil—Gil, according to his silver name tag and all who knew him—stood behind the bar, already reaching for the carafe of coffee and a thick white mug. "Should've worn your coat."

"Spring is the season of should'a," Dini said, tugging at her bonnet string. She wasn't supposed to be seen bareheaded in public while in costume, but the thing was unbearable. How did women ever survive viewing their entire world through a tunnel? She combed through her liberated short waves—blond, but interspersed with various pastel curls, like she'd just walked through a cloud of confetti.

"People always want to make March out to be spring. It's winter still. Always more winter than warm. But I have a sweater in the back," Gil said, gesturing with the carafe. "You're welcome to it."

"Thanks." She wrapped her hands around the mug. "Any chance I could get this à la Hedda?" It was her code—*their* code—for an Irish coffee, and Gil raised one eyebrow in chastising amusement.

"You know the rule, Blackstone. Coffee's free if you're in costume. You'll have to present yourself a proper modern lady for anything else, and I'll have to charge you a proper modern price."

Dini thought about the folded bills in her skirt pocket. Plenty for her loose expenses. "I've earned it."

Gil reached in for the coffee and took a sip for himself. "Go on, then. I'll make you one fresh when you come out."

He handed her a key, and she went behind the bar, through to the employee area to a small room lined with lockers along one wall. Within minutes she had divested herself of the skirt and blouse and pulled on jeans and T-shirt, this one featuring a local band with images of popular sci-fi monsters. She put her walking boots back on because they were of her own choosing and as comfortable as they were cool. She'd probably walked the equivalent of the entire state of Texas in these boots. The rest of the costume, though, got shoved into the depths of her vintage brocade satchel. It was due for a dry cleaning over the weekend, as she didn't have another tour gig booked for at least a week.

There was only one garment hanging on the brass coatrack in the corner—a grayish-green cardigan that must be Gil's, though she'd never seen him wear it. Theirs was not a relationship that ever strayed beyond the Menger Bar. He was handsome enough, with a high brow and ready smile. He wore his hair in long, thin braids tied neatly at the nape of his neck. Their first conversation had felt like a meeting of long-lost friends. Three years before—she, newly twenty-one and he seemingly ageless—talked until last call about the Menger Hotel, its famous history, and its two most infamous women: Sallie White and Hedda Krause. He was a font of knowledge and endless stories.

Gil was expertly spooning thick cream over the top of her drink when she emerged. "By the way, one of the guys who took your tour tonight? He's staying here, and we talked a bit before you set out."

"Okay." Dini drew out the syllable, suspicious as she laid her money on the bar.

"I think you're going to want to meet him."

"Stop. You know better than to try to fix me up—"

Gil held up his hand in protest. "It's not a fix-up, I promise. Promise. And I'm not gonna tell you any more, because the best mysteries are the ones you solve yourself, right?"

"Right." She looked up at Teddy Roosevelt and recalled the faces of her tour group. Four women, six men. Mostly coupled up, but of the two single guys (one cute, one. . .not), neither seemed heavily invested in her ghoulish tales of San Antonio ghosts. "Well, I don't recall anybody *interesting* in my group tonight."

"That's because I told him to hang back, listen, and talk to you after. But if the idea makes you uncomfortable, I can kick him out."

"No." Dini took a sip of her coffee to counter the unfamiliar buzz of wary anticipation. Never, in all her nights of coming in for coffee after a tour, or coming in for nachos before a tour, or hanging out—alone—on a Saturday night with a book and her cards had Gil *ever* intimated that he cared about her social life. Then again, something in his voice sounded like this had nothing to do with her social life. "Mind if I hide upstairs until he gets here?"

He scooped up the money. "You are officially a paying customer. Do as you please."

Breaking with the tradition of playing 1930s swing music, and undoubtedly for her sake alone, the dark room soon flooded with the soft sounds of the seventies. Drink in one hand, her bag in the other,

Dini took the narrow staircase up to the second level and settled at the corner table where she took out a small timer—old-fashioned, with grains of sand—and a deck of cards. It was a new deck, the cards slick and stiff. In a fluid motion, she upended the timer and commenced to shuffling, counting under her breath, "One. . .two. . .three. . ." A mere fraction of a second lapsed between the *ffftt* of the cards arched between her palms and their *clack* on the table before the next interspersing *zzzip*. "Sixty-seven, sixty-eight, sixty-nine, seventy, seventy-one—" and the last grain dropped through the glass. She gave the deck a final, frustrated tap against the thick wood of the table.

"Table riffle's faster," Gil called from behind the bar.

"And if I were some Vegas table dealer, I'd use it," she said, giving the deck a series of soft overhand tosses. She glanced down and noticed the new arrival, recognizing him instantly from the tour. The cute one.

He lifted his glass—a dark ale, two gulps down. "I was only listening—but it sounded impressive."

"Thanks," she said, with the perfect amount of gratitude to seem polite.

She took advantage of the balcony to study him. "You were in the tour group earlier?" Phrasing knowledge as a question put people at ease, not that this guy seemed to be the least bit nervous.

"I was. You were entertaining and informative."

"In that order?"

"Maybe 'engaging' would be a better word."

She looked to Gil. "This the guy you were telling me about?"

"It is," Gil said.

"I am," said the guy. "Shall we continue the balcony scene? Or may I join you?"

She looked past him to Gil, who gave an oddly encouraging nod. He mouthed the words *Trust me.*

"Fine," she said.

Watching his first few steps away from the bar, Dini thought him to be cautiously aware of his physique, moving purposefully. His footfall on the ancient staircase was even. Precise. The back of her neck still fizzed, and she admonished herself. *Don't be weird, don't be weird.* She was comfortable leading a crowd around the city, telling ghost stories, and even more comfortable in front of an audience, holding them spellbound with close magic and card tricks. The average back-and-forth conversation, however, danced outside of her comfort zone.

By the time he was upstairs and at her table, whatever strength she'd gained from her pep talk had utterly dissolved. She barely managed to invite him to sit opposite her before asking, "Want to see a trick?" So much for not being weird.

He set down his glass. "I love card tricks."

She shuffled the deck three times, set it down for him to cut, then recommenced shuffling.

"What's your name?" She knew he would eventually introduce himself, but asking allowed her to control the conversation.

"Quin."

"Quin? So, you're a fifth?"

"How did you know?"

She tapped a finger to her temple. "It's what I do. Magic. Plus, you had a bit of a hesitation before you answered. Means you had a choice in what to tell me, and you went with the nickname, even though we don't know each other well enough for you to be so informal. Also, it's a nickname that needs explanation. Not like Bob, short for Robert. A lot of people aren't aware of the tradition. Sure, maybe a guy named Trey is just a guy named Trey. But maybe he's really Morton Snoddinghouse the Third. So, you know, Third. . .Trey. And if Trey Snoddinghouse had a son? The Fourth? Drew. Like qua*dru*ple. Fascinating tradition, right? Almost lost in the rush to name everybody after Western cities. Austin. Cody." There she was, rambling in an attempt to explain the man's own name to him, like there was some invisible audience in need of distraction. *So much for being normal.*

Shuffling blind as she spoke, the cards moved almost as quickly as her words, so she stopped—the shuffling, not the speaking—and studied his face. *Bemused* might be the best word to describe his expression. Bright blue eyes behind light-prescription lenses. A hint of red in his neatly trimmed beard, darker in his hair cut short with a sharp part on the left. A bit of gel to keep it in place.

"Are you from out of town?"

"I am."

But nothing more. She launched into the conversation she would have in a darkened theater in front of an audience even though they were just two people at a tiny table in a dark bar. "Okay, Quin from out of town. Where are you from?"

"Buckhall, Virginia."

"What do you do in Buckhall, Virginia?"

"I teach high school math."

"Ah, math nerd." She hazarded a look up from her shuffling to make sure he was smiling. He was. "Here for a conference? Those are usually at the Marriott."

"Nope. Spring break. Being a tourist. And a little business. Some research, actually."

Dini committed a tiny fumble in her shuffling at the word *research*. He said it with a lilt that almost made it a question. Given Gil's mysterious lead-up, she had a feeling she might be part of the answer.

She focused with a breath. "Count a number of cards off the top of the deck. Up to twelve. Don't tell me how many, and put them in your pocket." He was wearing an athletic fleece with a zippered pocket. "Now, count out the same number. Still don't tell me." She kept her eyes trained on his face as he did so, noting how—unlike most people—he didn't move his lips as he counted. When he finished, she held her hand out for the remaining deck and told him to look at the top of the stack he'd counted out and memorize the card.

"Got it," he said after a moment of mock concentration.

"Now give it here." She put the small stack of cards on top of the deck and made a show of shuffling—once, twice, three times—never allowing the top cards to be mixed in, but keeping her hands at a practiced angle to disguise her skill. She slid the deck back over. "Now, I want you to think of three names. Any three. Your first, middle, and last. Or your favorite actors. Anything at all. Spell them inside your head and take out a card for each letter."

He counted off six cards. "You haven't told me your name. Unless it really is Henrietta, like you said on the tour. But you don't look like a Henrietta." He counted off five more cards.

Clever, him using the same distracting technique she'd worked so hard to perfect. "I'm Dini."

He counted off five more cards. "Like the song?" And, completely unbidden, sang a few soft bars of the old Shaun Cassidy hit "Hey, Deanie, won't you come out tonight?" It was a pleasant memory; her mother used to sing that song to her all the time, and she felt a soft bit of connection to this stranger who so easily tapped into that memory.

Dini smiled and took back the untouched deck, then scooped up the cards he'd counted off and put them on top. "No. Dini as in *hoo*."

Quin's eyebrows rose above the frame of his glasses. "Your actual name is Houdini?"

"Marilyn Houdini Blackstone," she said with a grand gesture of introduction. "Give me the cards you took off the top." He did, and she counted them. Nine. She deposited them casually on top of the deck. "Now, you're going to tell me your three names, and I'm going to deal off the cards and spell them. If I spell them wrong, don't tell me, okay?"

"Okay. First, Menger."

"Well, that one I know. *M-e-n-g-e-r.*" She dropped a card faceup with each letter.

"Hedda."

"As in, Hedda Krause?"

"I wasn't sure how to spell her name."

An unusual, and unwelcome, tremor zipped through Dini's hand. *"H-e-d-d-a."*

"Oh good. I spelled it right." He seemed genuinely relieved. "Last one, Irvin."

Her finger was poised on the top card, but at the mention of the name, her hand dropped to the table. "Irvin? Why Irvin?"

"Does it matter?"

The tone of his question ran everywhere from teasing to—maybe, but probably not—flirting. "It's kind of a random choice."

A tiny shrug. "Not so random. It's my name."

To say that Dini froze in that moment would not be quite accurate. Breath moved in and out, she blinked, and her left hand closed on the deck of cards with a death grip. Still a jab of ice pick–sharp pain stabbed at her head, like she'd taken an ill-advised gulp of a frozen drink. She fought—and, probably failed—to keep a neutral expression on her face as it waned.

Quin mirrored her gesture of introduction. "Irvin no-middle-name Carmichael, the Fifth."

She'd get back to that later. *"I-r-v-i-n."* She looked up. "Do you remember your card?"

"King of diamonds."

"And you had nine cards drawn." She counted them out, dropping them face up on the pile. "One, two, three, four, five, six, seven, eight"—dramatic pause—"King of diamonds."

"Cool," he said and took a sip of his beer. "The trick I get—you put the cards down in reverse order. But keeping the stack intact while you shuffle? That was amazing."

Dini decided not to confront his condescension, even though it irked her.

"Do you know who you are?"

"Do any of us really, Dini? And isn't that question a little too existential for a first date?"

The response caught her so off guard she laughed and fumbled her shuffle. She put the cards away and took the cooling mug in her hands. "This isn't a date."

"A date is in the eye of the beholder."

"Dates don't have secrets, Quin Carmichael. And I have a feeling you're carrying one."

"Not a secret, exactly. More like a mystery. Here it goes." Quin shifted himself as if settling in for a long story. "A few years ago, we—my sisters and I—were clearing out my grandparents' house. It was originally owned by my great-great-grandfather. Built sometime in the 1890s. We all had a chance to go through and take whatever heirlooms or knickknacks or furniture we wanted, and I found this." Quin reached into his pocket, pulled out his phone, and began scrolling. He held it out to Dini, who saw a battered cardboard box, loosely tied with string. "It was at the back of the closet in the master bedroom. So far back that I had the feeling it was hidden."

"Feeling."

"Sixth sense, you know? And when I opened it. . .just this weird assortment of stuff. A couple of magazines, newspaper clippings, and"—he all but shuddered—"photographs."

Everything within her sparked. So much so, she imagined tiny lightning bolts shooting from her curls as she forced her voice to remain calm. "So how did you know to connect it all to here?"

"The newspaper articles mostly. About the, um—"

"The robbery?"

"Yeah. I did some googling and learned more about the place. And since I had some time on my hands, I finally decided to come and check it out. See what I could learn. I came in here for dinner and told the guy behind the bar—"

"Gil."

"—and he said he knew someone who could tell me the whole story inside and out. And that you'd be leading a tour. So I signed up. And here we are."

"Here we are." No doubt Gil was relieved that she had a new audience for her obsession.

"So, I'm here until Thursday morning. Maybe we could meet up again? And you could kind of. . . ? Because I have to tell you, some of it's pretty. . ."

He had that speech pattern that made statements sound like questions, allowing spoken thoughts to drift off into vague hand gestures. He was clearly a gregarious sort—instantly at ease with a stranger, a quality Dini never quite understood. She had no idea how much silence had elapsed since he stopped talking, but she knew her cue was to pick up the thread.

"You won't be able to understand any of it if you don't know the whole story."

"So tell me the story. You're an awesome storyteller. I listened to you out on the tour for, like, two hours. Excellent. Chills."

She wanted to tell him that most of what he heard was a script, memorized and repeated. Despite his apparent lack of historical intuitiveness, he seemed harmless enough. Her week was pretty empty, save a birthday party tomorrow and an afternoon event on Wednesday. And she might get a free meal or two—call it her fee.

Plus, he was the in-flesh descendant of the man who had vicariously broken her heart a thousand times over.

"What do you know about your great-great-grandfather?"

"Not much. Not as much as I should. He worked for the FBI? Back in the day before it was, you know, the FBI." He punctuated this with a *duh-duh-duhn*. "So much of my family followed him on that. My grandfather. And two of my sisters, but they're forensic accountants. I took the wimp route and went into teaching. Not that I haven't had my share of rough days there."

Dini filed all of this away the way she filed everything—neatly and without effort.

"What do you know about Hedda Krause?"

"Again, not much," he said. "There's a couple of pictures and newspaper clippings. I did some online searching about her too and didn't come up with any more than what you said on the tour. I mean, I don't even know if all of the stuff in the box is related. So, like I said, I was coming to town anyway and thought I'd—"

"You said you had time on your hands and decided to come here. That's not the same thing as *coming here anyway*."

"Does it matter?"

Dini looked at him, thinking about the story of Hedda Krause and Irvin Carmichael. A story she knew by heart. A story that her mother had handed down, that they had spent hours telling and retelling each other on long bus rides and in cheap motels while her father slept in the next bed. She wasn't about to recount this story to a stranger like it was one of her farfetched Alamo Haunting Spirits Ghost Tour tall tales, no matter how desperately she wanted to get her hands on what he tossed aside as a few photos and clippings.

"I suppose not. But when I say you need to know the whole story, I mean—I think you should learn it from Hedda herself."

"I have no idea what that means, but I'm game. So we can. . .maybe tomorrow?"

"Not tomorrow, I'm working. Besides, that won't give you enough time."

"Time for what?"

Dini took a deep, patience-affirming sigh. "Time to learn the story."

"How am I supposed to know the whole story if you won't meet with me."

"Give me your driver's license."

Quin actually sat back and gave a small shake of his head, like her request had jangled his thoughts. "My—what?"

She held out her hand. "Your license. I want to be sure you are who you say you are."

"Why would anybody lie about being Irvin Carmichael the Fifth?"

Still, he reached into his pocket to retrieve his wallet. Simple, black leather, thin. He opened it to reveal his Virginia license, and the name he claimed. Besides his address, Dini's quick mind scanned the photograph. He must have weighed a good twenty pounds more when this picture was taken. The lack of beard alone wouldn't explain the round, soft face. That explained the certain edge he carried.

"Here's my deal," Dini said, opening the bag beside her and rummaging around beneath her costume. There, at the bottom, she found the quilted zippered pouch, which she opened to withdraw her greatest treasure from.

"You're going to read to me?"

"No. You're going to read for yourself."

The title, *My Spectral Accuser: The Haunted Life of Hedda Krause*, was stamped in gold lettering on the front cover of the thin green volume. Her mother had fished it out of a donated books bin at the library, and the way she clutched it made young Dini love it before she ever heard a word. Mom said she'd actually met the author, the subject of the book, who was a very old woman at the time. Since then, there was rarely a day when Dini didn't have it in her bag, or purse, or satchel—for comfort as much as anything. Even her mind, sharp as it was for numbers and patterns and memories, couldn't begin to calculate how many times she'd read it. Hundreds, easily. Some passages, thousands. And now, in a gesture that she would have deemed impossible only an hour ago, she handed it across the table to a stranger.

"You have to read this."

Quin took the book in his hands with what could be seen as either reverence for, or unfamiliarity with, such a thing. "Someone wrote a book about her?"

"She wrote a book about herself."

A smile spread on his face—one of pure joy and discovery. "Is Irvin the 'First of His Name' in here?"

Dini caught the *Game of Thrones* reference and tucked it away as another detail. "He is, but there's so much more. You have to know her—Hedda—and her story. The only way to really do that is to read it in her words. She only had a hundred copies printed. I don't know how we were lucky enough to find one."

"I don't believe in luck. There's a reason, a plan for everything."

He'd opened the book and was gingerly fanning the pages with his thumb.

Dini resisted the urge to leap across the table. "Careful, there. I haven't torn a page yet, but it's delicate." Indeed, the pages were soft, almost cottony around the edges.

Quin opened the front cover carefully and turned the book so Dini could see the displayed page. "I have this picture. The print of it. I could go—"

"No." Again, self-control. "Before we talk any more about her, you have to know her voice. Before we talk about your great-great-grandfather, you need to hear *his* voice. This is your family history. This is why you found a box hidden at the back of a closet. So read it."

"All of it? I mean, I don't have a problem reading, but. . .I'd like to see you again. Soon. To talk, I mean."

Dini felt the slightest and most unfamiliar frisson pass through her as he stumbled through the last sentence. "Not the whole thing. Wait here a second." She scooted out of the booth and walked down the stairs to the bar, allowing her body to loosen up and her lungs to exhale a breath she'd been half holding since Quin invited himself to join her. Gil was trying awfully hard to look busy, wiping a perfectly clean glass, as Dini picked up a napkin and asked for a pen. She probably had a dozen pens somewhere in the vastness of her bag, but this would be quicker than finding one.

"I know this is kind of a new deal for you," Gil said, his voice deep and rumbly with friendship, "but these days the kids just put their numbers straight into each other's phones."

"Actually, my phone is dead. Would you mind using yours to call me a Lyft? I'll pay you back."

"You could pay me back by returning my sweater."

She tugged it closer around herself. "You know that won't happen."

Gil had his phone. "You want me to order it now?"

"In the next few minutes? Please? I'm ready to go."

"Hey, Dini." He beckoned her close. "For what it's worth, I think he's a nice guy. This could be good for you."

Dini left without comment, keeping her face expressionless against the real pleasure in watching Quin watch her. "Do me a favor?" she called up. "Bring my bag down to me? I can't do those stairs again."

This was only partly true. Yes, there was a bit of a wobbliness in her thighs, but most of that could be attributed to the fact that she'd been a little bit in love with the ancestor of the man walking effortlessly down the stairs, carrying his glass and her cup, with her book tucked under his arm and her satchel cradled in the crook.

"Sunday morning. Brunch," she said once he was next to her.

"I was going to try to find a church to visit."

Church. Filed away. "You can find one that meets early. Then, we'll say eleven. A place called Mi Tierra. Sound good?"

All this she wrote on the napkin and drew two lines, solidifying the plan.

"Two minutes, Dini," Gil said. "Gray Honda Accord."

She thanked him again and said to Quin, "I don't drive in the city if I don't have to. Getting a Lyft is cheaper than parking."

"Do you live nearby?"

"Sort of. So, let me tell you two things real quick. First, that book means more to me than you can even imagine. Please, please, be kind."

"No reading in the tub. Got it."

Dini pushed the image out of her mind. "And two: if anything *does* happen to it, or if you choose to abscond with it, I will hunt you down and haunt your life."

"Well, I don't know how impressed I'd be with your hunting. Because, you know, I'm right here. Staying in this hotel."

"No, I mean I'll come to your house." She named the address, amused at his look of incredulity.

"You—you looked at my license for a millisecond ten minutes ago."

"I'm that good."

They'd been walking across the bar together, and not until they reached the door did Dini remember the cold wind waiting outside.

"I'll stay with you until your car gets here," Quin said, opening the door.

"You don't have to. It's freezing."

"I'm not going to let you stand out on the street by yourself. Looks like tomorrow might be a good day to stay inside and read after all, if it's anything like this."

Already his nose was red, and the skin above his beard blotchy. He shoved his hands in the front pockets of his jeans, and Dini was about to insist he go back inside, really, when a gray car with the Lyft logo in its window turned the corner.

"There's my ride," she said, lifting a hand to flag it. "I'll see you Sunday. Do your reading."

"I will. I promise." He opened the back door, leaned in, and verified the driver. His solicitude seemed a second nature—opening doors, escorting, protecting.

She had one foot in the car when she called out, "Hey, Quin Carmichael." Unnecessary, because he hadn't yet taken his eyes off her.

"Yes, Dini Blackstone?"

"Do me a favor, and don't read the whole book. Okay?"

He looked quizzical. "Okay?"

"Just up to page"—she closed her eyes and scanned her memory—"fifty-one."

"Fifty-one. Got it."

When she was settled in the car, he handed over her satchel, told her to buckle in, and the driver to be safe. The car was warm, scented with a freshener meant to make you feel like you were inhaling fresh laundry on a line. The driver, a fortyish woman with long blond hair pinned on the sides with sparkly barrettes, commented on the sudden change in the weather. "I was running the air conditioner at noon."

"Yeah." Dini looked over her shoulder to see Quin, still standing on the street, watching them drive away. "It's crazy."

Chapter 2

Excerpt from

My Spectral Accuser: The Haunted Life of Hedda Krause

Published by the Author Herself

I will spare you, Dear Readers, from the sordid details of my life before I walked through the doors of the Menger Hotel. What matters is this: I arrived with a heart burdened by grief, my dead husband's words echoing in each beat.

"Promise me," he'd said. "Go search out a life where love will find you."

By some cruel trick, I cannot see his face, but the memory of his touch, his hand grasping mine, comes to me as a tangible phantom, a pressure against my pulse.

"There is no love waiting for me anywhere but here, my darling," I told him. "Where would I go?"

I could never seek any life other than the one he'd given me. His cozy hearth was my cozy hearth. His bed, my bed. Never mind that I was his third wife to share it, or that his sons would never grant me a place in his life outside of it. Their father died in that bed while I sat beside him. It was late in the afternoon, and their shadows filled the doorway within minutes of his last breath.

"Go, now," the older one said, his voice so like his father's that I wondered for a moment if he'd stepped back from the angels.

"Where would I go?"

"Anywhere." His voice colder than his father's lifeless touch.

How came I to San Antonio? What guided my steps to the Menger Hotel? Surely the same Divine Guidance that made me mistress of my late husband's parlor carried me over the threshold and dropped me onto these shining parquet floors. It was early October, cool, and sloppy with rain, making the crackling fire in the fireplace just past the desk a welcome sight indeed. I made my way straight to it, holding my hands out to its warmth. With no idea how long my bit of pocket money would hold out, I'd had to choose between transport for my trunk and transport for myself. Thus, having been assured my luggage would arrive within a few hours' time, I'd walked from the station, feeling the cold seep in one step at a time.

The heat from the fire dried the thin layer of damp on my skirt and cloak, though my feet remained numb within shoes too thin for a walk in such weather. In time, my face grew uncomfortably warm, and when I turned to enjoy the warmth on my backside, I realized I'd caught the attention of a copse of gentlemen seated nearby.

I knew my skin glowed with a radiance brought on by flame rather than youth, though at twenty-seven my youth was not totally spent, and through no conscious pains I had my figure displayed quite artfully. There is simply no other way to stand by a fire. Though decorum at the time would never allow an unmarried woman to strike up a conversation with a man—let alone a small gathering of them—in a hotel lobby, I returned their murmured salutations with the slightest nod and a "Good evening, gentlemen," spoken with the controlled lilt I'd learned on my late husband's arm.

I was spared any further conversation when the station's porter approached the front desk, my luggage in tow. Even if I hadn't recognized the porter, I would have spotted my trunk from a mile away. It had been a wedding gift, crafted to withstand the travels that marked the early days of our marriage. The distinct aquamarine leather made it stand out in any cargo hold. Its gold-embossed latch was fashioned to look like two swans facing each other, the lock peeking through the heart-shaped space formed by the curvature of their necks. Instinctively, I raised my hand to touch the outline of the key, tied with a ribbon and nestled next to my heart. Everything I owned was in that trunk, and maybe a few things where ownership was a matter of opinion. But when one is given only a few hours between a funeral and sundown to pack up a life, some details must be swept aside.

The porter was using a hand truck, as the weight of my trunk—even empty—is prohibitive. From across the lobby I could hear him banter with the desk clerk. I couldn't make out all the words, but the porter rolled his shoulders as if injured. He would surely expect an extra tip.

I acknowledged my admirers (no other identifier would fit) and took slow, measured steps to the registration desk.

"I see you have safely transported my belongings, sir." I added an extra bit of warmth to my voice to counteract both the cold of the night and the unsuitable number of coins in my hand.

"Feels like you have all your house and home in there."

I initially bristled at his overfamiliarity but recovered with a small laugh. "I hope this will compensate the effort, along with the fare I paid at the station." He looked as if to say that, no, this bit wouldn't compensate at all, but there is no sweeter creature than a man entranced.

"Well, indeed." He pocketed it quickly and turned to the desk clerk. "Want me to take it upstairs?"

My eyes darted from the porter to the clerk. The porter looked like every other porter I'd ever seen: brawny and gruff, with two days' beard and a cap worn low. If I told him to be gentle with my trunk as it contained stockings made of spun glass, he would have been too inflamed at the word *stockings* to give any doubt to my claim.

But the front desk clerk was another animal altogether. I knew he'd been looking at me since I walked in, though his attention lacked admiration. He was tall and slight, with sleek dark hair and a thin moustache. His suit jacket fit a tad loose (I would have suggested a tailor take it in at the shoulders and maybe a nip at the back) but was of good quality. He made a show of opening the large, leather-bound registration book and running his finger down the page.

"I do not believe I see the lady's name listed among our guests."

I stood straighter. "How odd, given that you don't know my name."

He offered a smile that turned his moustache into something of a wavy line. "Forgive me. What I mean to say is that I see no reservation for a Mrs. . ."

"Krause," I supplied. "Hedda Krause. I wrote last week to secure a room."

"We have no reservation request for a Mrs. Krause. Or a Mrs. Anybody, for that matter. Furthermore. . ." He leaned over the desk and lowered his voice so only the porter and I could hear. "We are not in the habit of renting rooms to. . ."

A list of rejoinders filled my mind, but I responded with, ". . .to widows?"

He had the sense to look uncomfortable and muttered, "I am so sorry, Mrs. Krause. We simply have no record of a reservation."

"Is that to say that you do not have a vacancy?"

"Don't make me lug this back to the station," the porter said, leaning on the gleaming desk. "Wife's waiting supper for me at home."

Minutes passed as the clerk fussed with papers and keys, the porter drummed his thick fingers on the gleaming desk, the gathering of gentlemen moved to the edge of their seats, and I simply took one deep breath after another, trying to keep a soft composure while I gazed around the oval expanse of the lobby. No, not simply *around*, but *up*, as the ceiling of the lobby extended two. . .three stories above, with classically festooned columns throughout and an intricately carved balustrade surrounding the second- and third-story balconies. (I knew none of the terminology of these details upon my arrival, of course. My education came later after an informative dinner with a man who had carried out much of the renovative work.)

At last, the clerk stood straight and set a key on the counter. "Very well then, Mrs. Krause." A uniformed bellman discreetly emerged from some waiting wing, and the two conferred in whispers before the clerk leaned over the desk, drawing me in. "He will use the service elevator to take your trunk to this room." He tapped a long finger on the number embossed in gold on the leather fob. "Please wait here until he returns. You'll find it easily, top of the stairs, and then to the right."

"I appreciate your discretion, sir." I matched my voice to his in volume, offering a sidelong look of apology to the porter, who seemed none too pleased at having to wait for the return of his hand truck.

"Of course," he said. "Now, as a matter of payment. . ." This time his unwillingness to complete a sentence worked in my favor, and I allowed him to blink a dozen times in rapid succession before it became clear that neither of us intended to adjoin the phrase.

"I am quite tired."

"I understand. However, it is our policy to have guests planning to spend more than a single night pay their fee in advance."

"Will you arrange to have a late supper sent up to my room? Maybe a bowl of soup and toast. Or would it better suit for me to call from my room? Is there a telephone?" It is my particular talent to hide a wall of information until the moment a man stumbles against it.

"I—I, um, I suppose I could make that arrangement for you. Now, if you will please sign the registry."

"Wonderful."

He placed the enormous book in front of me. My name was to go on the top of a new page, and as I set the nib of the pen to the line, I noticed the admonition at the top.

Money, Jewelry, and Valuables must be deposited in the Office Safe.

Otherwise the Proprietors will not be responsible for any loss.

The clerk (manager, I would soon learn) noticed my attention. "Do you have valuables to deposit, Mrs. Krause?"

I twisted my neck for a quick glance to the gentlemen who had abandoned any pretense of hiding their curiosity. "Yes, Mr.—"

"Sylvan."

"Mr. Sylvan. I am in possession of quite a few valuable pieces, and while I am sure your accommodations are adequate for my own safety, I would prefer to keep them with me. Can you imagine, running down here every time I needed to choose which is best to accentuate my neckline? No, these were gifts, you see, and tokens from my late husband. I could not bear to part with them."

Mr. Sylvan drew back and looked at me, as if taking measure of my worth. It was for this moment that I was thankful for the trim of fur at my collar and the simple but flawless pearls in my ears. He cocked an eyebrow, unconvinced.

"Surely, Mr. Sylvan, you understand that I cannot travel—unaccompanied as I am—with any such valuable display."

"I'm simply wondering, Mrs. Krause, how long you are planning to stay here at the Menger? We do have suites for extended stays."

I could only imagine the expense of such a room. Fortunately, before I had a chance to respond, the bellman arrived, and I reached into my pocketbook once again, this time emerging with a full dollar bill, which I handed over with enough flourish to announce my status. The porter muttered something unsuitable for repeating and disappeared into the night. Key in hand, I turned to leave, but Mr. Sylvan repeated his question. "The length of your stay, Mrs. Krause? For my records?"

I had no answer. No, that's not quite true. I had several, and they all swirled around the limits of money and time. Meaning I would stay until I had either depleted my funds or found a new source. And given the appreciative looks of my fellow guests, time might actually be in my favor. I offered them a single smile but allowed my eyes to reach to each in turn, and there kept my focus as I responded to Mr. Sylvan's question.

"For your records, I will stay until I have some clear reason to leave."

Chapter 3

As far as piecing together a living with her very specific skill set, kids' birthday parties weren't the worst way to go. The hours were great—rarely before noon and never past dark. The food was plentiful and indulgent. Unlike her shows at the Magician's Agency Theater downtown, there were no drunks to deal with, and unlike the ghost tour walking scene, there was no. . .walking. No memorized script, no laughing at the same bad tourist joke time after time (*"Guess I'll really remember the Alamo after this."*). Sure, kids might give her a hard time, wanting to know how a trick was done, but they never shouted it out from the audience (*"Watch! She hid it up her sleeve."*).

All of this, plus cake.

She was still snug under her weighted blanket at well past nine on Saturday morning when the text alert sounded on her phone. She tapped the icon, hoping for a message that the sudden cold front had canceled that day's booking. She'd still get paid (acts of God were not part of her contract cancellation policy) and could reschedule for a time when her imagination wasn't piqued by a stranger with a box full of Hedda Krause mystery clues.

But, no. Just a chipper note from the hostess, a woman named Jessica Vanderkamp, informing her that they were still on LIKE DONKEY KONG :), but the party had moved indoors.

Dini tapped back, THANKS FOR THE HEADS-UP, and rolled over, burrowing deep. Her stage area was a trunk that she'd had custom made from the description of Hedda's in the first chapter of *My Spectral Accuser*. The only embellishment allowed to the craftsman was to mount a set of casters and an expanding handle so Dini could roll the monster easily from her Kia Soul to the stage. Otherwise, the trunk lived in the smaller of the two bedrooms in her bungalow, surrounded by the supplies of her trade: costumes, cards, silks—all neatly stored in perfect squares of Ikea shelving. Unlike most women her age, twenty-four, and relationship status, single, Dini owned her little house in King William outright. This, through no expenditure of her own. It was a property purchased by her great-grandfather and inherited generation after generation, in much the same way as Quin Carmichael described his own family home. The difference was, she could never, ever sell. Not that she didn't have offers. The neighborhood, like much of the San Antonio downtown-adjacent area, maintained a reputation of being simultaneously hip and historic. But for all the years her three-person family spent on the road, this was always home. Maybe only for weeks or months at a time, but a place where her father kept the key in his pocket, and she didn't have to wonder who slept in her bed the night before.

Coffee brewed while she took a shower. After, wearing sweat pants, her thick terry robe, and fleece-lined slippers, she sipped it from her favorite mug with a breakfast of peanut butter and jelly on toast. Normally, if she didn't have a gig, she'd cook up a hearty, complicated breakfast. But this morning her appetite felt pinched, and the second piece of toast got tossed out to the squirrels.

With a second cup of coffee, she reviewed the notes in her calendar. Nothing happened in her life without getting noted in the calendar. Her own memory might be flawless, but Dini couldn't ever be sure of anybody else's. Her calendar was her voice: multicolored notations and Post-it notes, stickers. Sometimes neat, bullet-point lists, some illegible, slanting scribbles. She opened to the next day, Sunday, and wrote, *Brunch w/Quin*. She held the pen aloft for a moment before adding, *Carmichael*. A bit of coffee sloshed as she wrote, and she wiped it up with her thumb, smearing the ink.

The soothing voice of the Waze app guided her on and off loops and highways as she drove to the party site. *Soothing* might be an exaggeration. Her pulse still pounded, her eyes darted constantly from the road to the mirror to the other mirror and back. Other people might listen to their favorite music or catch a podcast, but not Dini. She could take a stage in front of thousands of people (or dozens of children) and remain smooth and cool and in total control. But she hated—*hated*—driving. She clutched the wheel (at 10 and 2) and took solace only in the occasional comforting glimpse at the ring she wore on the first finger of her right hand. This was part of her brand, something distinctive and attention getting and, ultimately, distracting for the audience. A flash of a ring might bring their subconscious to focus on it rather than on the sleight of hand she was performing. Today, in honor of the party, she wore a miniature snow globe with a tiny princess caught midtwirl within the swirling flakes. It had been a gift from her best friend, Arya, who would be one of the moms at today's party, not to mention somewhat of a mother to Dini herself.

At the locked gates of the Carved Oaks community, Dini showed her ID to the real human guard and checked her pocket for business cards while he waited for the confirming text from the hostess. If even half of the guests came from this neighborhood, that could mean a slew of bookings. Waze led her past one sprawling property after another before declaring her destination on the right, where two young men—teenagers—stood next to a pyramid of pink and gold balloons. They were dressed in fairy-tale prince costumes, and the one who came to her open window could have been the model for Cinderella's beau.

"Are you here for the celebration of Princess Isabelle's birthday?"

"I'm the entertainment," she said, trying not to sound dazzled.

"Very good. If you don't mind, I will take your car and park it for you."

Dini motioned. "I have my things—my trunk—in the back."

"Not a problem at all, ma'am. My friend Charming will get that for you and deliver it wherever you please." She stepped out of the car and obliged the eager prince.

To Dini's surprise, her friend Arya opened the front door before the chimes completed their complicated tune.

"You're here early," Dini said after the two exchanged their traditional air kiss. This act of affection was a sacrifice on Arya's part, as she was a hugger by nature but had long since acquiesced to Dini's zone of touch.

"Three properties for sale in this neighborhood." Arya, one of the most successful real estate agents in San Antonio, was never one to miss an opportunity. "I made some visits."

"That explains why you're wearing an eight-hundred-dollar outfit to a child's birthday party." Dini had been with her when she bought the blouse and shoes.

"Well"—Arya looked Dini up and down and up again—"at least I have an explanation for my outfit. You look like a punk rock Tinkerbell."

"Exactly what I was going for," Dini countered good-naturedly. She'd chosen a multicolored toile tutu, black leggings, Doc Martins, and her well-worn leather bomber jacket over a hot-pink turtleneck. "Now, show me to the hostess."

Arya's daughter Beatrice (called Bea with two syllables—*Bee-yah*) came barreling into the front hall and wrapped her little arms around Dini's waist, burying her face in the tutu. Bea alone was granted such physical dispensation, and Dini patted her hair—all twisted up in a pretty princess do.

"I can't wait for Auntie Dini's magic." Bea looked up adoringly, her cheeks dusted with glitter.

"It's not magic," Dini said, prompted by Arya's familiar scowl. "Just illusions, remember? I play little tricks on your eyes. Now, go. I need to get back to the kitchen so none of the guests will see me before the show starts."

Bea ran off, up the stairs, with a confidence that spoke of a familiarity with the house. She wasn't merely a guest at the party, she was a friend of the birthday girl. The realization brought the usual pang, a reminder that Dini had no such memories of birthday parties or childhood friendships. The life she lived now began just eight years ago, marked by the death of her parents and, being alone in the world, given over to Arya and Bill Garner, who served as foster parents specifically for teens. She lived with them for three years, homeschooled by Arya. After earning her GED, the two of them enrolled in St. Phillips Community College, where their previous roles as guardian and child cemented into this unlikely friendship.

"There's a few other parents here too," Arya said, "and I'll introduce you to Jessica. She's a bit high-strung on any given day and is feeling some party pressure, so give her some slack, okay?" She led Dini past a pristine living room and through to an enormous family room where the furnishings had been moved to the edges of the space. It was decorated with streamers and balloons—all in the pink-and-gold theme—with the brick fireplace embellished to look like the outer wall of a castle. One end was screened off, and the young man from the front was wheeling Dini's trunk behind it.

"I've never been to a kids' party with valet parking before."

"Don't be too impressed. They're dispersing the cars up and down the block so the driveway doesn't look crowded. One of them is the older brother of the birthday girl, and the other is his buddy. I think Jessica is signing them off as school community service hours. Anyway, more important things. . . There's going to be a guy here, owns his own air-conditioning repair service, *divorced*"—this she whispered—"with the cutest little boy. His name is Marcus, the dad, not the boy, and—"

"Stop," Dini said, drawing the word out with a good-natured laugh behind it.

"No, really. This guy is maybe thirty-four? Thirty-five? Probably younger. And super handsome, in that blue-collar, manly man kind of way. I met him at the kids' Valentine's Day party and had to convince Jessica to make this a boy-girl party so he could come and meet you."

"Well, you shouldn't have." Dini was used to Arya's matchmaking attempts—men from her church, her gym, her monthly Do You Need a Realtor? seminars. Thus far, Dini had agreed to a handful of dates: Bea's pediatric dentist, the bass player in the church's praise band, and a widower finally ready to sell the house he and his wife enjoyed for their five-year marriage. But none got past a third date.

In fact, she wanted to tell her friend about Quin—not that Arya would appreciate the encounter. Her sole purpose was to find Dini the perfect man so that she could embark on Arya's vision of a stable, conventional life, and a few conversations with Quin Carmichael were not going to result in that end. Still, it was the first time in—well, maybe ever—that Dini had the words *I met a guy. . .* burning on her lips.

Jessica—thus far known to Dini only as Mrs. Vee in their email and text exchanges—was a tall, stringy woman wearing a powder-blue sleeveless jumpsuit despite the outside temperatures in the low 50s. She greeted Dini with a firm handshake before proceeding to lay out the agenda. The party started at 1:00 for mingling and free play time, lunch at 1:15, Dini's show from 1:45 to 2:15, absolutely not beyond 2:25, as the cake cutter was due at 2:30, leaving only thirty minutes for presents and gift bags and a 3:00 pick-up time for parents who would drop off their kid and use Princess Vee's party time as a free babysitting opportunity.

Dini smiled and interjected, "Okay," wherever necessary.

"And," Mrs. Vee said, "as adorable as you are, I absolutely do not want you out mingling with the children before your performance."

The screened-off area where the student volunteer had dropped off her trunk proved to be more spacious than she imagined and was outfitted exactly as she had requested in her rider. A four-foot table, over which Dini threw her most ornate purple velvet cloth, two bottles of water, and hand sanitizer with a pump dispenser. She opened her trunk and pulled out the flat craft supply tray, each of its squared-off compartments stuffed with balloons of all shapes and colors. Today's balloon offering would be princesses and swords, in accordance with the theme. She listened to the arriving children, making note of their names, keeping a running tally of how many girls, how many boys.

At 12:50 the room filled with a medley of Disney and Pixar princess songs, masking the sound of her balloon pump. She filled long silver ones for the swords, a variety of other colors for the hilt, so each boy (or girl, if she preferred) could choose. She also filled balloons for the princesses: various skin tones, pink, blue, purple, and green dresses. These would be entirely customizable—black hair, blond, or brown—and a cupful of sharpies to draw faces. This party marked the debut of her princess balloon doll, following hours of study from a YouTube tutorial and visiting a dozen elementary classrooms to hone her skill and speed.

"All set up?" Arya's face poked around the corner of the screen. "Are you hungry? The kids are eating pinkie sandwiches, but there's a great baked brie and quiche in the kitchen for the parents. You want me to bring you a plate? Or, I could have that guy Marcus bring it back to you."

"No, thanks, to both. But save me some?"

"I'll try, but I got to tell you, there's a lot of dads here using this time to do their fantasy baseball draft."

"Then, go. Make me a plate. I'll talk to you after—there's something I want to tell you."

Arya scrutinized her. "Some*thing*? Or Some*one*?"

Dini gave a cryptic smile. "Both."

The show, thirty minutes of enthralled children, included a few card tricks played with a Disney Princess deck (given to the birthday girl as a gift), plus the usual array of interlocking rings, objects disappearing and reappearing, toy rings with enormous plastic stones fetched from behind ears, and Dini's favorite—the little stuffed mouse that, seemingly on its own power, scampered up and down Dini's sleeve. Then the children lined up for their princesses and swords—swords first, so that the boys, growing ever restless, could beat each other about the head and shoulders while waiting for cake. Dini twisted and assembled the princess bodies after enlisting Arya to draw the faces (even though she insisted Marcus might be quite handy with a sharpie), and by 2:24 on the dot, the professional cake cutter had arrived to turn a frosting-pink castle into a mass of small square servings. Dini, assured she would get one of the pointy white turrets, took herself off to the kitchen and collapsed in one of the chairs in the breakfast nook. There waited a paper plate, covered with another upside-down paper plate on which was written, *Dini the Magnificent*. Arya joined her with an ice-cold Dr Pepper in hand.

"Good show, girl."

"Thank you." She clunked her aluminum can to Arya's bottle of water. "And how much are the parents going to love me for sending their boys home with those inflatable weapons?"

Arya laughed. "You might want to rethink putting your business card in the goodie bags. Might wake up to some angry emails." She leaned close and pointed—as if casually gesturing to the group of men huddled around the island—to a dark-haired man wearing cargo shorts and a Dallas Cowboys sweatshirt. "That's him. Cute, right?"

Dini feigned scrutiny. "Maybe?"

"Do you want me to go say hi to him for you?"

"Arya, I love you. But just because I never went to junior high school doesn't mean I want to start going now. He's not my type."

"You don't have a type."

"I have a type. Everybody has a type."

"So, what is it? Because I've never known you to embrace anybody."

Dini wound a slice of prosciutto around a small bit of cheese. "You won't believe this, but I met a guy last night."

Arya's eyes went wide. "And you're telling me now?"

"I haven't had a chance. It was late, and today's been crazy."

"Wait one second." She disappeared and returned with a cup of pretzels and two hunks of cake. "Now, tell."

"Okay. Well, I know you're going to think this is crazy, but. . .his name? Irvin Carmichael." She paused for dramatic effect and was disappointed by Arya's disapprovingly curled lip.

"Irvin?"

"Yes—but, he's *actually* Irvin Carmichael the Fifth. He goes by Quin."

"So his name is Quin."

"Yes." Somehow, Arya was slow to share her excitement. "As in, the fifth. Arya! He is a direct descendant."

"Of who?"

"Irvin Carmichael." She was tempted to shake her friend by the shoulders. "*Detective* Irvin Carmichael." She waited for the light to dawn, and when it did, she felt more let down than before. Arya went from dismissive to disappointed before her very eyes.

"Ah, Dini."

"What, *Ah, Dini*? Do you know how awesome this is?"

"I know I wish you spent more time with real people. Like people who are actually among the living."

"I'm around people all the time. It's exhausting."

"You know what I mean."

"Well, look here—I'm going to spend some time with this guy. And he is very much alive."

For the first time, Arya emitted a spark of approval. "Is he cute?"

"Very." Dini surprised herself with how quickly she answered, along with the flush she felt.

"Well, that's a start, at least. Is he as obsessed with this whole Menger story as you are?"

"Opposite, actually. He doesn't even know it. But he has—I don't even know what all. We're meeting for brunch tomorrow." She added quickly, "It's not a date."

"It's all right if it is, you know."

"It's not. He's not from here, doesn't live here. He's only in town for the week, so. . ." Dini let the sentence trail away in the guise of eating a guacamole-laden chip. Arya snagged a cube of cheese, and both used the silent chewing interval to cleanse the conversation palate.

"Does that mean you're not going to make it for the concert in the park tomorrow?" Arya asked.

"Can you promise not to try to fix me up with some random saxophone player?"

"I promise nothing."

Chapter 4

Excerpt from

My Spectral Accuser: The Haunted Life of Hedda Krause

Published by the Author Herself

I have never had the opportunity to think of myself as a lady of leisure. In fact, for most of my life, I don't know that I could have presented myself as a lady at all without a healthy dose of irony. If my marriage to my late husband gave me respect—a name, a home, a desk drawer full of monogrammed stationery and calling cards—then my life at the Menger gave me all of the same, with the added elements of desirability and intrigue. My friendships here were transient at best. Fellow lodgers in town for business or leisure might invite me to their table for dinner after light conversation in the lobby. I often accepted, as politeness required, and thanked them with profuse incredulity and sufficient protest when they insisted on charging my meal to their room.

I developed a thriving social life outside of the hotel, heavy with engagements and invitations. I learned of all the grumblings of the coming war while walking with an army officer through the Mexican Courtyard, his whispers no louder than the sound of the wind through the leaves. I joined a group on a walking tour of the surrounding Catholic missions—long abandoned but still holy enough to inspire a convicting reverence. Over the course of a week, a state senator escorted me to two concerts and a charity banquet before he—with great reluctance—informed me that his wife would be joining him for the remainder of his stay, and he would be removing himself to the Beverly Hotel across the street.

I'd also taken up going to the theater. Not to the shows, exactly. To buy myself a ticket remained beyond my budget. Instead, I'd don my finest evening gown (wishing each time that I'd thought to pack more than one) and take myself to the newly opened Empire Theater, timing my arrival to coincide with the show's intermission, where I could indulge in a glass of champagne and introduce myself to some of the local people of worth. Sometimes, if I lingered long enough, I had the occasion to meet a few actors who would go on to be silver screen stars, though I'll not name them here. Stardom, like youth, is fleeting.

One evening, during a run of the popular play *Sadie Love*, which would be the stage debut of the beautiful actress Thalia Powers, after some artful positioning I caught the eye of a burly, unkempt man who was maneuvering through the crowd. He wore a bulky camera strapped around his neck and hoisted it to beckon me closer.

I was on the fringe of a conversation, not quite invited in. Still, I excused myself with a touch of my gloved hand to a tuxedo sleeve and worked my way over.

"Mind if I take your photo, ma'am?"

"My photo?" I held my glass aloft. "Why, I'm nobody special."

"We can let the readers decide that, I think. I do freelance work for the *San Antonio Express*. They like pictures of the society people for the Sunday paper. Over here?" He indicated the wide staircase that led to the private viewing boxes. He walked backward, expertly, leading me. "The managers will only let me take one photograph—worried about the crowd and the flash, I suppose."

"And you've chosen me?"

"You're the only woman here alone. That's interesting. All the men look alike, and the other women wouldn't dare be photographed without them."

Spying the empty tripod at the foot of the stairs, I instructed him to move it. "You'll want me standing on the first step." I already knew how I would position my arm on the curve of the bannister. He had his camera mounted in a thrice and instructed me to hold still—very still—until he told me it was safe for me to move.

I was wearing one of my most exquisite necklaces—an intricate design of a brass chain and beads with a heavy topaz pendant positioned perfectly above my neckline. Knowing better than to hold my face in a neutral expression, I tilted my head, thus elongating my neck, and set my lips in an enigmatic smile that would rival that of Mona Lisa. I followed the instruction to look at the camera but focused my eyes beyond it, to the crowd that stood watching, wondering—I supposed—just who this woman was to have garnered such attention. Someone shouted an offer to hold my drink, but I ignored him. Instead, I lifted it higher, careful not to obscure my face, as if offering a toast to whoever gazed upon the photo.

"Three. . .two. . .one." A flash of light then the smell of the burning powder. I willed my eyes to remain open, my body rigid, until my vision cleared. Spots remained as I stepped down where the photographer waited with a small notebook and grubby pencil. "Can I get your name for the caption?"

"No," I said, mindful of my need for some level of anonymity. "Refer to me as Mrs. K., a widow. Newly arrived to the city, currently residing at the Menger Hotel until a more permanent situation can be found."

He looked up. "You want all that in there?"

"Of course. The titular character in the play is a widow, as am I. The detail will make the photograph more"—I paused for the impact of his own word—"*interesting*."

My photograph appeared alongside a tepid review of *Sadie Love*. I don't normally take the paper in my room, preferring to read one abandoned in the lobby. This morning it arrived courtesy of a sharp rap on my door at the ungodly hour of seven o'clock, folded open to the page, delivered by one of the messenger boys on a tray with my customary coffee and pastry.

"Why, thank you," I said to the boy as both of us tried to ignore my haphazardly belted dressing gown. "What an unexpected surprise."

"And there's this, ma'am." Avoiding my eyes, he handed me the small, familiar envelope. I say *familiar* because I knew immediately who'd sent it. Mr. Sylvan. He and I had taken to communicating through short missives. In fact, he had warned me about the state senator's visiting wife in such a manner a full day before the state senator himself did. This too was how we settled my bill. Rather than a common transaction at the desk, he weekly sent up a note with a figure written in his crisp, neat hand. I delivered said amount in the same envelope. What a comfort to do business with a man who understood how crass it is to speak of money to a lady.

"Here you are." I held out a nickel to the boy. "And be sure to thank Mr. Sylvan for the coffee."

I kept my smile frozen in place until the door closed completely, then tore into the envelope. Mr. Sylvan's usual billing, inflated, with this explanation: *We have added a $10 fee for creating undesirable attention.*

I felt my face flame, as if the man himself were standing beside me. Furious at the distraction from my first appearance in San Antonio society, I dropped Mr. Sylvan's note into the waste bin, picked up the paper, and opened the curtains to the piercing morning light. I would never describe myself as an unusually beautiful woman. Still, I can say confidently that the image on the paper was stunning. The photographer—one J. P. Haley—framed it perfectly, including the half circle of the crowd who stood with their faces turned to me. I captured the effect I sought, looking mysterious and inviting, glass raised in tribute. Somebody, an editor I presume, captioned the photograph thus: *While Miss Thalia Powers might have underwhelmed the audience in her tour as the widow Sadie Love, this widow captured everyone's attention.*

I caught my smile beneath my hand, as if there were somebody in the room watching. All across the city people would turn to this page and see me. Those who were there would look at each other over their breakfasts and say, "Do you remember seeing that woman?" Wives would bristle in jealousy at their husbands' raised eyebrows, but what did I care about that? I needed men to see me. Stately, eligible bachelors. Lonely widowers. Even a man living in the wake of divorce. Enough dining with businessmen and dignitaries passing through the city. I needed roots. A home. A means of support. I couldn't live forever at the Menger Hotel—a sentiment truer than ever as I pawed through my resources to satisfy Mr. Sylvan's demand.

My photograph did not bring throngs of curious men into the lobby of the Menger. I was not a showgirl or some other morally questionable young woman. I had not *advertised* myself as a good to be procured, merely as a woman with the possibility to be found. And, a few found me. Local men of quality, equal to those who took rooms on their travels, walked into the lobby, took lunch in the restaurant, took a seat at the bar—all with a roving eye that came to rest the moment it fell upon my person. Then, a tip of a hat, a lift of a glass, a feigned curiosity that began with the same question: "Haven't I seen you somewhere before?" At which I would laugh and say, "My goodness, that photograph has proven to be more trouble than I could have imagined."

One night in early December, my sixth week in residence at the Menger Hotel, I bid good evening to a man at the lobby door after a steak dinner that might have come from cattle on land he personally owned. He was a bit older than my preferred suitor (nearly the age of my late husband), and he confessed to have taken several whiskey sours at the bar for five nights in a row before summoning the courage to introduce himself to me. A sweet man, with florid cheeks and a hearty paunch, but by the time I was safely in my room, I'd set my mind not to see him under such circumstances again. It would be too cruel, I would tell him, to continue such a ruse when I was still in such mourning for my dear, recently departed spouse.

Safe within my room, I undressed, thankful to breathe deeply after such a satisfying meal, and unclipped my hair, letting it fall to its full length, just past my shoulders. Other women gave their hair full range to their waists and even lower, but such always smacked of a country hovel pioneer. I brushed and braided it loosely and ran a wet washcloth across my face and under my arms before donning a freshly laundered nightgown.

San Antonio, I'd soon learn, was not known for its harsh winters. That night was the first with a true chill about it—one that I felt along the edges of the room. This, and the fact that my nerves were still on edge from attempting to appear enthralled throughout the evening, took me to the small cabinet next to my washbasin where, tucked away from the chambermaid's prying eyes, I kept a decent-sized bottle of very good brandy from my late husband's cellar. I'd given precious trunk space to two bottles, from which I imbibed judiciously, just one glass a night, and not every night to be sure. But tonight I fancied a generous pour.

I didn't hear the scratching at my door. Not at first. Or perhaps I did but dismissed it, thinking even an establishment as fine as the Menger was prone to have a mouse. Or two.

But then again. And unquestionably at my door. Not a knock but a scratch. A series of three. Somebody wanting in but not wanting to be heard.

"So," I said out loud, hoping my voice would quell my misgiving, "it's not a mouse so much as a rat."

I'd been so careful, so very, very careful, not to give any of my suitors even a hint they would be welcome to my room. I never told them my number, or even which of the two floors I occupied, thus avoiding Mr. Sylvan's wrath and preserving my person. I know more than most the consequences of letting a man assume liberties you have no intention of granting. I will admit to being an unrepentant flirt—a woman in my circumstances never had any other means of survival. I may have laid a trail of bread crumbs to the lobby door, but I never dropped so much as a grain in front of this one where the scratching continued.

I took another sip of my drink and had decided to ignore the rat-like plea, but his persistence unnerved me. Intermittent assaults upon my door: *scratch, scratch, scratch.* Then a pause before trying again: *scr–scratch, scratch, sc–scratch.* So purposeful, so unrelenting. Soon, I feared, one of my neighbors would hear and be bound by curiosity to investigate.

Taking careful steps across the room, I stood at the corner of my bed and stared through the slatted vent at the bottom of the door. Where normally I would see the spit-shined shoes of one of the bellboys (or, in this case, the ill-fitting brown monstrosities with my escort's fat ankles spilling over), I saw only the pattern of the carpet in the hallway. This detail shook me, robbed me of my balance, and I gripped the footboard for support, breathing deeply until I felt my balance return.

One step, and I pressed myself against the door to hiss through the narrow crack. "Stop that. Do you hear me? Go now, or I shall call down to the desk and have someone sent to remove you."

Why I hadn't thought to do that in the first place I don't know, other than the fact that it would bring an unwelcome blot to my unblemished residency.

I held my breath, hoping to hear his. It had been loud enough at dinner—wet and wheezing in between listings of his properties. But nothing. It occurred to me to open the door wide enough to glimpse him in retreat never occurring to me that he might be holding *his* breath too. Waiting for my moment of weakness to push his way through. Instead, I said, "Do you hear me?" with more authority than I felt.

Silence.

More silence.

Until. . . "Something for you, Hedda Krause."

Even now, all these years later, I cannot forget, nor can I easily convey, that voice. It was at once like someone speaking from the bottom of a tureen, while simultaneously like a creature nestled in my collarbone, hands cupped against my ear. Tinged with echo, the words sounded like they were dragged across a dry streambed, each syllable caught on a pebble. It struck me like a splash of icy water, taking my breath as if I'd plunged below a frozen surface. My lungs burned with it and, in weakness, I fell against the door spluttering, "Who is this?" with considerably less strength than I'd had when I shooed away my suitor.

Nothing for what seemed an eternity but was likely only a few moments before it repeated.

"Something for you, Hedda Krause."

A new burning set itself loose, one fueled by anger rather than fear. Mr. Sylvan, of course. The night manager must have phoned him, told him about my late arrival on the unsteady arm of a would-be flesh profiteer. Mr. Sylvan with his filthy mind and prudish demeanor. He who sent missives to my room at all irregular hours. Notes about my rent, about my accumulated restaurant bill, messages from callers, accounts of how many cups of coffee I'd consumed in the lobby and how many brandies I'd sipped in the empty bar. Here, almost midnight, and he'd sent some poor, sick boy with a note.

"Just a moment, please." I made no attempt to disguise my irritation. I tugged on my dressing gown and cinched the belt before sliding the chain lock into its groove. The chain allowed little more than three inches, but enough to give some pubescent boy the sight of an attractive older woman in dishabille. I had barely enough room to snake my hand outside and say, "Give it here," before noticing there was no one on the other side of the door.

I snatched my hand back inside, slammed the door, and leaned against it—chained and all. And then—

"Something for you, Hedda Kraus."

Of course. My own unspoken thoughts sounded shaky even to the sole audience of my own mind. *Of course, he would step aside, knowing the lateness of the hour. Knowing I might be undressed. And I'd reached my hand out empty. These boys. Merciless pursuit of gratuity.*

My hand shook as I reached into the dish on the large dresser and took out a dime. Two, in fact. Then opened the door.

"Here, take this." I clutched the money between my thumb and first finger, peering out, waiting for the sight of an open hand. I held back an irrational sob, though a small whimper escaped, because more and more it seemed there was no one there. Nobody to have scratched. Nobody to have summoned. My hand remained alone, suspended, until something brushed against it. Weightless, like a breath. A feather touch. From my angle behind the door, I saw nothing, only *felt*, and the feeling lingered long after, like sparks of cotton crawling up my skin. In the shock of it, I dropped the dimes, pulled my hand back through the door, and slammed it. What game was this? If Mr. Sylvan had enlisted his night staff to frighten me, he had more than accomplished the task. Tears burned at the back of my throat, not only at the immediate circumstances, but at the shame of my movements being so cruelly scrutinized.

Throwing caution to the wind, and eager to put this incident behind me, I unchained the lock, threw open the door, and peered out to see—nothing. Only the emptiness of the hall, dimly lit by strategically placed sconces.

I looked down, and my dimes had disappeared.

I spent most of the night sleepless, pacing the room, a damp cloth on my hand, red with a rash that traveled up past my sleeve. I'd taken down the last of my brandy in three great tumblers, and perhaps this is what finally allowed me to succumb to slumber. I awoke far later than my usual hour, mouth dry, skin slack, and my housecoat still bound haphazardly around me. At some point, I had moved from the chair to my bed, the sheets so entangled that I experienced a moment's panic trying to free myself from them.

I brushed my hair, pinned it in a simple fashion, and dressed in my most serviceable day dress. I could do little about the puffiness of my eyes without an hour's treatment of a cold washrag. No matter. I wanted Mr. Sylvan to see the toll his reckless prank had taken on my natural person.

I descended the stairs, took a fortifying pause where they turned, and strode straight for the desk, my eyes trained on the irregularly shaped bald patch on the top of Mr. Sylvan's head as he bent over some paperwork. Not until I cleared my throat and rapped on the wood did he favor me with his attention.

"Good morning, Mrs. Krause." He granted me a supercilious smirk.

"That is a matter of opinion, Mr. Sylvan."

"You seem agitated."

"Do I? I suppose I am, given the circumstances of last night."

The smirk disappeared as one eyebrow lifted. "Last night?"

"Your prank."

"My. . .*prank*?" He whispered the word, as if speaking of something vile.

"I don't know what else you would call it, sending a message to my room in the middle of the night." I'd dropped my voice to a hissing whisper too, but seeing the postman at the end of the desk, resumed a normal volume to add, "And, there I was, a poor widow, all alone, scared nearly to death."

"I should be hard-pressed to think anything would scare you, Mrs. Krause. But even so, I can assure you, no message was sent to you last night. At least, not to my knowledge. Unlike yourself, I have a home to which I retire every evening at nine o'clock. If you kept decent hours, you would know that."

I hardly knew which insult to tackle first, so I simply stood in shock at his temerity. The caterpillar above his lip lay flat, utterly unamused.

"Well, then." The courage that fueled me thus far dissipated, exposing a remnant of last night's fear. I swallowed against the dryness of my throat and began again. "Well, then, I suppose you must have a stern talk to your night clerk, because I was awakened at midnight by a most frightful noise."

The caterpillar hitched. *"Awakened?"*

I leaned over the counter and stared him down until the moustache was once again supine. But now, something new. A flicker of his eyes, as if they might jump out from behind his lenses and speak a warning if he hadn't drawn them back in, corralling his gaze with a blink. "For your peace of mind, Mrs. Krause, I shall interview the night staff personally. But I would urge you to put the incident behind you. I'd be happy to send up a complimentary breakfast tray to offset your inconvenience."

I shrank back with each word, his kindness nearly as disturbing as last night's event. "What are you hiding?"

"Nothing." He used his cuff to wipe the already gleaming desktop. "Only what I assume to be the outrageous shenanigans of a night staff with nothing better to do."

I took an unsteady comfort in his words and acquiesced to eggs Benedict and rye toast accompanied by a grapefruit half and coffee with cream and sugar.

I spent the day in seclusion, catching up on the night's lost sleep with lazy catnaps snatched between chapters of my reading. I penned a letter to my late husband's sons, which upon signing it "Your Father's Grieving Wife," I filed away with the others until I could find the courage to post them. I straightened the dresses in my wardrobe, summoned the hotel's laundress, and entreated her to give some a fresh steam pressing. I sorted my stockings, lined my shoes up in neat pairs. Between bouts of activity, I took stock of my room. The comfort of it. The elegance. Nothing gaudy or ornate, like some of the places I have known, where velvet and brocade were used to create a false sense of class. Here I felt like a guest in a welcoming home. The walls were a cheerful yellow—the color of fresh butter. The ceiling vaulted tall above me—three acrobats could stand feet on shoulders beneath it. A sturdy dresser with enough drawers that my trunk need only hold my most valuable possessions, and a well-stocked desk where I could sit and complete correspondence, if I ever had the opportunity. I had a bed with a headboard and a footboard—and all of it in heavy, polished wood. More than being a guest, I felt as if I could walk out the door and down the hall to my own parlor. The staff knew me by name.

Something for you, Hedda Krause.

By evening the growing shadows and enveloping gray unsettled me, and the four walls that had seemed a cocoon during the day loomed like a trap in the night. I changed into a dress suitable for the evening, one with sleeves long enough to cover the raised, red rash that persisted above my wrist. I pawed through my jewels to find a piece with the perfect understatement, but nothing seemed to suit my mood. Finally, I chose my simple pearl earrings and my wedding band. Nothing else. It somehow seemed fitting not to be weighed down by my worth.

I dined alone, surrounded by empty tables. It was midweek—a slow night in a slow season, and I ate my supper slowly as well, savoring each bite. Biding my time, delaying my return. As I lingered over the last crumbs of cream cake, the staff began clearing the tables and running a sweeper over the carpet. Boisterous laughter came from the kitchen, accompanied by the sound of clinking dishes. The waiter assigned to my table, Kenneth, had rolled up his sleeves and loosened his collar but still spoke deferentially when he came to clear my plate and take my glass.

"Have a good evening, Mrs. Krause."

I tuned my ear to see if I detected any of the malevolent tone from the previous night, just as I'd done all evening, but found none.

"Yourself as well, Kenneth."

I left the dining room and walked toward the stairs, my body in gradual rebellion with each step. The whole of the Menger felt cavernous. Silent and dark. I could not will my foot to touch the first stair, could not bear the thought of ascending the next. I glanced at the clock. Not quite ten. Still early enough for a cup of coffee. Or tea, perhaps, to be less jangling to the nerves. And while I could have such sent to my room, I chose the only other option.

The bar.

It seems unconscionable to be this far in my tale and only now bringing Bert to life, especially given the role he will play in my troubles. And my salvation. I do not want to give the impression that this was my first visit to the bar, nor to imply that my visits were a regular occurrence. Never mind that Theodore Roosevelt himself had been a regular patron. A lady simply didn't hoist herself on a barstool or lounge in a booth with a drink.

And yet there had been nights like tonight when there were no prying eyes, no one to pass judgment other than Bert, who proved himself instantly to be a trustworthy friend.

"Good evening, Mrs. Krause." He smiled in a way that no other man in this place ever smiled at me—as if he'd been anticipating my arrival and was genuinely glad to see me. "Looks like you can have the seat of your choice." At this, he gestured expansively, a coded message that I was, indeed, alone. No patrons lurking in the dark corners.

"Good evening, Bert. This will do." I took a chair at the table closest to the bar, out of the sight line of the door.

"Coffee? It's a cold night. It's fresh."

"That sounds lovely." Though covered neck to wrist to toes, I felt the chill.

"I could heat it up for you, if you like."

"That sounds even lovelier." More code. Heating up the coffee had nothing to do with the temperature, only the added ingredient. Whiskey.

I anticipated the warmth of it even as he walked out from behind the bar, carrying the steaming white cup. He set it down on the table and lingered at my side in a way none of the waiters in the dining room would ever dare.

"Is there anything else I can get for you, Mrs. Krause?"

His voice was deep, dark, and smooth—matching the taste I anticipated from my drink, nothing like the rasping, grating speech of the night before.

"Would you join me, Bert?" The question was out before I could even consider the consequences, but by the time I asked, I found myself desperately wanting him to comply.

He looked to the door, seeming to gauge the probability that one more lost, chilled patron might arrive. Then, without a word, he strode across the room and locked it. Then back again to lock the street entrance, turning the sign to CLOSED. All of this, wordlessly. Clandestine. Soon he was seated across from me with his own steaming cup. Straight—I watched him pour. A single candle burned in an amber glass between us. I studied his face, boldly. No coquettish glance. He did the same, and I thought, *He knows*. He knows that despite my demeanor, my speech, my jewels, my *person*, I'm no better than he. Born no higher—even lower, I would have wagered at the time.

Finally dropping my gaze, I sipped my coffee, savoring the burn of it down my throat. When I looked up, he was still watching.

"Is it to your liking, Mrs. Krause?"

"It's perfect." The resurgent heat kicked. "Strong."

"You seem. . .not quite yourself. Lost, tonight."

"And you think this will help me find myself?"

"I don't think it can hurt."

A companionable silence followed, and I realized how long it had been since I shared such a moment. Before my husband died, in the lingering days of his illness, there had been long stretches of quiet—he in the bed, me sitting beside it. All the time after, with his sons at the table, or in the lawyer's foyer, the silence had been stifling. Condemning. My survival in San Antonio conditioned itself on conversation. Chattering, stringing one mindless word after another to keep a man's attention. Here I took the time to study Bert—his handsome face, beautiful almost, clean-shaven with a rounded jaw and soft mouth. His eyes were something close to bronze, his lashes—dark and dense enough to look almost kohl-lined—curled up along the top. I'd spent enough time in the Deep South to recognize the coloring, the close-cropped dark hair. The realization brought a new thrill to the idea of the two of us sharing a dark table in an empty room. It was a thrill that might have been a fear under other circumstances, but I'd had quite enough of fear already.

"How long have you worked here, Bert?"

"At the Menger?" He looked up, calculating. "I'd say close to thirty years."

I nearly choked on my drink. "*Thirty years?* But you, you look—"

He laughed, rich and rolling. "I started when I was a kid, back with the brewery. Not even ten years old. Runnin' errands and such. I carried bags of barley as soon as I was old enough to lift them, carried blocks of ice as soon as I was strong enough to do that. Worked in the laundry, the kitchen. Pretty much wherever I was needed."

"How did you end up behind the bar?" It was a reasonable question. A good bartender is a prestigious position, not usually attained by the kitchen help, and never, in my experience, by a man of any color other than white. Bert cocked his head and nodded, understanding the essence of my question.

"One day a few years back, I carried in a keg. It was middle of the morning, not a soul around, so I set it up, tapped it. Manager at the time came in, and I think was ready to tear into me, and I asked him if he wanted a beer. Nice and gentlemanlike. *"Can I draw you a beer, sir?"* And he looked surprised, like he didn't know I could speak beyond 'Yassuh, Mr. Boss-man.' "

He broke off with a rueful laugh, but I did not join him. In that single fragment of speech, he'd transformed himself from the elegant man behind the bar to something unrecognizable.

"The power of vocabulary and syntax," I said, knowing my own past was riddled with simpering, cooing phrases.

"That, and a perfect pour. And silence about havin' a drink before noon. He advanced me five dollars to buy a suit, get a good shave and a haircut. Told me if a single customer ever had reason to complain about having a Negro behind the bar, I'd be fired."

"And what," I said after a beat, "do you think he would say to finding you sitting alone, late at night, with one of your more desirable guests?"

He shrugged, letting me know he appreciated the humor of the question. "What do I care? He died years ago. Then Sylvan came, and he and I haven't met but twice."

"He doesn't drink."

"Not a drop."

"And he leaves you to yourself."

"I have it well under control."

"I envy you." My guard dropped enough to let a hint of wistfulness come through. His brow furrowed, and he reached a hand across the table. Close to mine but not touching. We both knew better than that. The inch of space between us carried the burden of centuries.

"Why are you in here, Mrs. Krause?"

I tapped the rim of my cup. "I wanted a drink."

"You can drink in your room."

"I can't—I wasn't ready yet to go to my room."

"Why? Tell me."

At that moment, everything that should have been a barrier between us dissolved, washed away by waves of tears. I wept as I hadn't since my husband's last breath, when I wept not only for the loss of him but because no one would truly believe my mourning. I wept then too as I did in this moment, for the woman I'd become. Lost, alone. I wept for what I couldn't face the night before, for being frightened to the core and having no one to protect me. To soothe me. To reassure me that I was safe. I brought my hands up to cover my face, as if that alone could hide this horrific emotional display, and then I felt them—his warm hands wrapped around mine, tugging them away.

"Mrs. Krause? Did something happen?"

I opened my eyes and took in our grip. His finger grazed across my knuckles, stopping before touching my wedding band. The sight was mesmerizing, like a tiny ballet. My pulse eventually slowed, matching the pace of his touch. My breath grew steady, my eyes dry. My sleeve had hitched up, exposing the rash. This too he touched, a sensation as featherlight as the one that brought it.

Regaining my senses, I took my hand away and answered his silent question. "It's nothing."

"It's not *nothing*, Mrs. Krause. I don't know everything, but I do know that. Something happened."

The way he spoke made it seem as if we had a history of confidence between us. So I told him. Everything, starting with the scratch on my door, the invisible touch, the voice. When I tried to replicate its sound, however, the chill of memory overtook me and I grasped my throat, unable to continue.

"What did she say?" Bert prodded.

"She said, 'Something for you, Hedda Krause.' " Then a thought nudged. *She?* "It wasn't a woman's voice."

"Are you sure?"

"I've never heard a woman's voice like that before."

Bert steepled his fingers and propped his chin on them, waiting. For what, exactly? For me to remember, to recall, to bring back the voice. A woman? Certainly not. But then—

A memory. When I was a young girl, my mother still alive, we lived in a house populated by many other women. There was one, much older than my mother (so I thought at the time), whose voice carried the same quality as that of my visitor. I conjured it, right there at the table across from Bert. I heard her speaking, beckoning, even laughing. Some of the younger women called her "Froggy," and I did too, once. But Mother chastised me, telling me that she'd been badly hurt years ago at the hands of a bad man, and that was why her voice sounded broken. It *was* broken. And so was she.

"I suppose. . ." I left the conclusion to trail. "But that doesn't tell me who she was. Or why she would want to inflict such torture on me."

I may have imagined it, but I would swear I saw a hint of a smile tug the corner of Bert's lip. "So, no one's told you?"

"Told me what?"

Now he did smile, broadly and engaging. "Are you telling me the whole time you've been here, nobody's said anything to you about Sallie?"

Without knowing why, only that his levity brightened me, I found myself smiling too. "No. Who is she?"

Bert made a small, secretive sound. "Finish your coffee." Then he stood, hand outstretched, waiting. By now the drink had cooled to where I could take it down in a few satisfying gulps. He took our cups to the bar, set them behind, and came back to help me with my chair.

"Now, Mrs. Krause," he said, placing my hand in the crook of his arm, where it felt instantly at home, "if I were any other man, I would escort you right to your room. But I know neither of us wants that kind of trouble."

My latent tranquility vanished. "I can't—"

Bert pressed my hand. "Trust me when I tell you this is not a conversation to have tonight. Not at this late hour. And not with so much. . .coffee."

"Please," I said, not even sure what I beseeched.

"Just walk yourself right up there. Keep your eyes focused on the floor. Walk like you can't stop, and then—" We were at the door. He looked out into the lobby, checking the path to be clear before dropping my arm, taking my face in his hands.

"Bert," I said right before he placed a single, soft kiss directly on my waiting lips.

"Think of it as a charm."

I had nothing in me. No response. No words. No breath. My feet, numb with disassociation, stepped into the hall, but at his voice I turned.

"One more thing, Mrs. Krause?"

"Yes, Bert?"

"Once you're in your room, shut the door. Lock it. She don't like to go inside."

Chapter 5

Excerpt from

My Spectral Accuser: The Haunted Life of Hedda Krause

Published by the Author Herself

I shall now pause in my own narrative to tell you the story of Sallie White. What you are about to ingest in only a few minutes' time is the product of hundreds of hours of conversations on my part. Idle chat with the chambermaids along with brandy and cards in the lobby with guests who have been patrons of the Menger Hotel nearly since its opening day. I never exchanged a word on the subject with Mr. Sylvan, but I'd taken to the more than occasional hot toddy with Bert in the late evenings. I could tell how reluctant he was to share details about Sallie White, and he did so only at my insistence.

"It's never a good idea to plant a ghost in someone's mind," he said, wiping the cherrywood bar with a clean white towel. "Muddles it all up if there's an expectation."

As for you, Dear Reader, if you are faint of heart, if you are profoundly disturbed by stories of violence and murder or fearful of tales of an otherworldly nature, I invite you to bypass the rest of this chapter and go to the next. I intend to spare no detail, nor shall I embellish beyond what was told to me. There are lessons to be learned in the most tragic of lives, and none could be more tragic than that of poor Sallie White.

Death of a Chambermaid:

The Sad Fate of Sallie White

Sallie White arrived in San Antonio a free woman. Independent. Alone. A mixed blessing to be sure, as there has never been a time when such was advantageous for a woman. Her place of birth, her origins, her people—none of it is known, nor is there a path-print to tell us how she happened upon the bustling streets of this city. She comes to historical life established as a chambermaid at the Menger Hotel.

By all accounts, Sallie White loved her job and took great pride in performing it well. She was always fastidious in her appearance—dark hair tucked neatly into her cap, her face and hands always scrubbed clean. Guests said she moved in and out of rooms like a whisper, leaving everything neat and tidy with no disturbance to their presence. She fielded requests with a soft-spoken "Yes, ma'am," or "Certainly, sir," and then tended to the matter with all required discretion.

If history could rewrite itself, Sallie might have fallen in love and settled down with a man well-matched to her work ethic and good nature. No doubt there were shopkeepers and livery drivers and carpenters who would welcome a woman with her heart to share their own. Instead, she fell into the arms of Henry Wheeler, and later would die at his hands.

Little is known of Henry Wheeler either, other than he had a jealous nature and a violent temper. Of course, that could be because he is known only as the man who murdered Sallie White. Before that, he must have had some quality to attract her to his side. Perhaps a sweet tongue or a slick charm, a gaiety that promised respite from long hours of hard work. After a time, she moved herself into his house. Theirs was a common-law marriage; such arrangements are more common among the poor. Nobody cares to scrutinize the morality of the powerless. She loved him enough to entrust him with her life, but there is always a precariousness to a union without marriage. After a matter of years, the balance of trust tipped—and not in Sallie's favor.

The Menger Hotel continued to grow in reputation, attracting an increasingly wealthy clientele who knew no boundaries to their privilege. Men of business, high-ranking officials, wealthy tourists—all were frequent guests, and while most were probably perfect gentlemen, there were the occasional few who thought her services should extend beyond turning down sheets. Wise enough to understand the importance of their favor, Sallie laughed off their advances, and if the occasional tussle occurred—a door closed behind her, a strong hand gripping her arm—rest assured Sallie would emerge unsullied and victorious.

Through the gossip chains of kitchens and streets and taverns, word of Sallie's popularity reached Henry Wheeler, and his rage enflamed. At first he seemed ready to confront Sallie's would-be molesters himself, but like most bullies, Henry had a sense for finding a suitable victim and soon turned his violence on Sallie herself.

"I don' want you goin' back to work at that place no more," he'd say. To this Sallie would argue that her wages were good, the work steady. She was given two meals with each shift, and she often brought home covered plates for Henry too. She'd pet him and kiss him to ease his fears, reassuring him of her devotion to him, and him alone. This worked for a while, until the stories continued, his fellows laughing at his expense, and the quarrels between Henry and Sallie rang in the streets.

Soon evidence of Henry's anger began to show on Sallie's face. She often had deep shadows, which she attributed to fitful sleep, but then came the day her left eye was swollen shut—the bruise lasting for more than a week. She took to a particular way of carrying stacks of folded towels, balancing them on a swollen wrist. The light faded from her countenance, her smile all but disappeared, showing itself only when politeness demanded. She aged twenty years over the course of her time with Henry Wheeler, and why she did not take advantage of the freedom she so desperately prized and walk away from him is a question for the ages. She did, however, give an account of his violence to the courts, and enjoyed a few nights' respite while Henry slept in their custody.

It was, perhaps, this action that sealed her fate.

Henry's rage roared from the moment the cell door opened to release him. He stormed into the street screaming Sallie's name with strings of unflattering epithets. He found her at home and took to beating her with such severity, neighbors finally came to her rescue. Henry fought the grasp of four men, screaming all the while, "Set my hands free! I'm go'n kill the slut for who she is!"

Sallie took nothing with her, only seized the opportunity to run straight to the police station to beg for refuge.

"He has sworn he will kill me," she said to the officer on duty. "He has sworn so, and I believe him. Please, arrest him and protect my life."

The officer had no reason to inquire her name, or request his, as the turbulence of Henry Wheeler and Sallie White was well-known and documented. Still, he insisted, he could not arrest Henry for such threats. After all, if every man who threatened such murder upon his wife were arrested, there'd be no room in the jails for those who actually followed through. As a compromise, the officials agreed to take Sallie herself into their custody, to let her sleep the night in the courthouse, safely locked away while Henry's temper burned itself out.

In the early morning hours, Sallie asked to be released and made her way home. Did she hope to bring Henry to his senses? Or, one might wish, she meant to leave him once and for all, preferring a life on the street in peace over the weight of his constant fury. Whatever her thoughts, they galvanized into one of heart-stopping fear when she saw Henry on the sidewalk.

"Sallie," he said, and only this as he approached. Whatever hold he had on her all those years kept her feet planted to the sidewalk. His hand reached for her, and she stepped into the familiar embrace, raising her lips to his for a reuniting kiss.

"I promised to kill you," he said, breath sour with whiskey, "and so I will."

She felt the gun pressed into her as he held her tight against it. The shot was muffled by the closeness of their bodies. Sallie stepped away and looked down to see her uniform—that which she wore with such pride and care—blossoming red with blood. She instinctively doubled over in pain and, calling on a strength supernatural to her own, turned and ran. There were men and women aplenty in the streets, but none gave aid. It was only Sallie and Henry, after all. Rather, they took to sheltering themselves once Henry gave chase.

Where could she run? Sallie felt her body growing weaker with each step and heard Henry's shouts closing in. To the police? But they'd shown her such disregard. She paused long enough to take into account her location. Steps away from the Menger, her first home. If she could only get inside—Henry wouldn't be allowed, a black man not in their employ. If she could only—

Two more shots, and a third that brought her down right outside the brewery's entrance.

Not close enough.

Trusting the strength of her Creator, Sallie grasped what she could and brought herself to her feet, calling out for help, shocked at the weakness of her voice. How could she be calling and calling and hear no sound?

That's when she realized she hadn't brought herself to her feet at all. *He* had—Henry—and he held her now, his hand to her throat, her back against the wall, her feet kicking free in midair. She wanted to free herself, but one shattered arm dangled helplessly, the other was pinned behind her. Sallie felt life streaming out of her, like a towel wrung out in the wash, Henry speaking words of hate into her face until everything went dark.

It would take three days for her to die. Three days during which her spirit hovered between her life in this world and whatever lies beyond it. Thus, she remained. A spirit. It is, perhaps, this restlessness of waiting that so unsettled her. There are those who have told me that she haunts this place because she fears to leave, lest Henry be waiting to kill her again. Others say her spirit stays because she fears she will fall under his spell and forgive his murderous cruelty. One minister told me she is simply evading judgment for her sin of an unsanctioned union.

I learned I was not the first to receive her attention, and that the hotel was earning a reputation for her presence. Nothing to be discussed in polite society, thus I had to experience the presence of Sallie White before ever knowing her name. Little by little, over the course of several weeks (and by now, of course, years) I heard testimonies of sightings—mostly shadows and whispers and otherwise softness of apparitions. A twisting doorknob, a snuffed light in the hallway. A spoon dropped from an ice-cream dish. One maid told me of a time she went to deliver towels to a room only to find a stack, clean and neatly folded, waiting at the door. No one else on staff would attest to having left them.

Her scratches on my door (for I never sought any other explanation) recurred, sometimes multiple nights in a row, sometimes with more than a week in between. I would hear an occasional odd footstep in the hall during the hours when no one should be about, but I refused to open my door in the slightest. We had a silent agreement, Sallie and I. She stayed in the hall, I stayed in my room. From time to time I would awake to the sound of my name, *Hedda Krause*, floating through the keyhole. The first time (after that *first* time), I opened my eyes only to remain frozen in fear, even as a wave of heat rolled through my body. Oh, how she teased. How she beckoned with that broken throat. I'd reason that I must have been dreaming, since I heard nothing once I was fully awake and aware. Or perhaps it was merely the growing sounds of winter, bare branches and dead leaves scratching against the sidewalk beneath my window.

Once, when I awoke to hear her call me three times in succession, I clutched a pillow to my breast to break the fear-formed ice in my lungs and answered back, speaking, "Sallie White," into the darkness. We went back and forth a few times, she and I, calling to each other until she emitted a sound so awful it could only be laughter.

I did not sleep again that night, nor did I tell Bert. The public might not doubt the sanity of one who claims to hear a ghost, but I'm not sure such grace would be extended if one admits to speaking back. Already I sensed a certain aura—a marked change in how the staff attended to me. Whispers, sidelong glances—I wasn't sure if Sallie's attentiveness made me a favorite or a pariah. Mr. Sylvan ceased to send my bill to my room; rather, he called me to his desk every Friday evening to present me with the charges for my meals and for the coming week of lodging, should I choose to stay. I felt myself becoming more and more withdrawn, preferring to dine alone, to keep my eyes trained to a novel or magazine as I sat in the lobby or along the second-floor landing. I still accepted the occasional invitation to the theater or to dinner, but those invitations became frustratingly infrequent.

Thus, a new fear. When I caught glimpses of myself in the glass, I saw a woman beginning to look her age. Beyond it, actually, her face pale and puffy, eyes dull, expression drawn. The spirit of Sallie White had stolen the spirit of Hedda Krause, and I was determined to reclaim it.

Chapter 6

The music of a mariachi trio underscored the Sunday morning sounds of conversation and clattering dishes. Waitresses bustled by with big sloshing bowls of menudo, and Dini's stomach growled. Not for the traditional Mexican breakfast, not even really out of hunger. But nerves. There was a reason she glided through life alone—reasons like this. What if Quin didn't show up? What if he thought it was a date? What if he didn't?

When she finally spied him at the check-in stand, all questions were put to rest. He was here, and it wasn't a date. Because, as out of touch as she might be with what the kids on the dating scene were doing these days, she was pretty sure they weren't showing up in running gear.

For the moment, she had the advantage of the crowd while she assessed. Running pants, expensive shoes, and a close-fitting top that gave evidence to a regular upper-body workout. Thinking back to the picture on his driver's license, the beard was meant to accentuate, not create a thinner face. His was a purposeful body, not one merely maintained.

She was ready with a welcoming wave when he caught her eye, thanked the hostess, and made an easy way over to the table.

"I'm going to go wash my hands," he said, barely slowing momentum as he shrugged a string pack from his back.

"Should I order you coffee?"

"Just water, thanks." And he was gone.

There was something unsettlingly familiar in the exchange. Like they'd been doing this forever. Looking around at her fellow patrons, she saw one couple after another, some who had probably spent decades ordering for each other. She'd rarely ever shared a table. Most mornings here, she'd scoot back into a booth and hide away. Now she was supposed to order a glass of water for someone else? How weird was this?

Quin was back at the table before she had the chance.

"You ran here?" She sounded accusatory. Small talk had never been her strength.

"I had to get here somehow." He caught the waitress's attention and ordered water between words. "You know, two birds, one stone."

"I thought you wanted to go to church?"

"First Baptist on McCullough. 8:30. Beautiful service."

"So you've had quite the productive morning?"

"I have." He worked the opening of the bag and brought out *My Spectral Accuser*, wrapped protectively in a towel. "And, you'll be happy to know, I finished my homework—"

"Stop there."

Quin sat back.

"We don't talk about important things until after we order," she continued. "Otherwise it's all interruptions and questions. Takes you off track."

"Okay. So, tell me about this place. Why did you choose it?"

"Ah, this place. It's a San Antonio microcosm. You go either every Sunday or once a year. Lifeblood, or special occasion." She paused for a moment to look around, inviting him to do the same, leading his gaze to the mural depicting the images of dozens of men and women that dominated one wall. "It's called *American Dream*—great leaders of Hispanic industry and culture."

"Do you know who all those people are?" His eyes tracked the sea of faces.

"No, but I should. It's been a work in progress here forever. From before I was born, at least. If you look close, you can see that some of it is three-dimensional."

He turned his head and squinted a little. "I see that. Cool. So you're a magician, a tour guide, amateur historian, *and* restaurant mural docent?"

"Something like that. The paper flags hanging from the ceiling?"

"The ones that make it look like a piñata exploded?"

"Those are called *picados.* There. Now I'm a cultural liaison too."

The waitress turned up at that moment, set a glass of water in front of him, and pulled her ordering pad out of her apron pocket. "Do you know what you want? Or do you need more time with the menu?"

Dini said, "More time," just as Quin said, "I'm ready—" and he prevailed, ordering four eggs scrambled soft and two pieces of toast.

"Stop," Dini said, this time to the waitress, who kept her pen poised. "You cannot come in here and order four eggs and toast. Not *here.* You can order that anywhere. You can cook that at home."

"It's what I eat for breakfast."

"Every day?"

"Every day."

The waitress followed the conversation, head turning back and forth, obviously amused.

"He's in San Antonio for a week. He has one, maybe two shots at getting a decent breakfast. He's *here*, where breakfast comes to life. Promise me"—she glimpsed at the girl's name tag—"Crystal, promise me you won't let the kitchen cook his stupid eggs and toast."

Crystal, a sweet girl with doe eyes, smiled and tapped her pen against her dimple. "How about we scramble them up with some steak fajitas and onions? Tortilla strips and peppers?"

"Exactly," Dini said, decided. "Those are called *migas,* my Virginia friend. Beans and potatoes on the side?"

"Do I have a choice?" he asked.

"Not really. And, since it seems like you might be wanting to keep the thousand or so calories at bay, I'll happily split with you." She looked up at Crystal. "Divide it between two plates? We don't really know each other that well."

"Of course."

"And six flour tortillas."

"Six?" Quin sounded genuinely appalled.

"What? They're small," Dini said, scooting her coffee cup to the edge for a refill.

Crystal dispatched, Quin once again reached into his backpack, only to be stalled again by Dini.

"Not until after the food gets here. Otherwise it's all 'Careful, hot plate,' and, 'How does everything look?' and 'Do you need anything else?'"

He studied her. "This really isn't your thing, is it?"

"What isn't?"

"*This.* Talking. Socializing. Conversation. Because it is possible, you know, to have a natural flow. Little interruptions and then right back to it."

"Sorry," she said, not feeling nearly as self-conscious as she knew she ought. "I haven't done anything like this—haven't *had* anything like this for. . .I don't know how long. I don't remember."

"Since you've had a date?"

Now it was awkward. "A *date*? No. I mean, sure, that's been a while too, but I meant a talk about Hedda Krause. New information, new—anything. I've exhausted my resources." A soft laugh bubbled out. "And I've exhausted my friends talking about her. You're new territory."

"So you're using me for my. . ." His voice trailed, and she rushed in to fill it.

"For whatever you have. My friend Arya thinks I'm obsessed."

"And are you?"

As an answer, she filled him in on everything he might not know about the Menger Hotel. How it was initially a brewery and eventually one of the most prestigious hotels in Texas. Its famous guests—Babe Ruth and Teddy Roosevelt the only names he recognized—its scope and renovation. And, of course, its reputation for ghosts. "But you learned all about that on the tour."

"So, after talking for five solid minutes, do we conclude that you're *not* obsessed?"

His delivery didn't carry a bit of malice, so she took no insult. "There's something. Something I don't know. Which means there's something *nobody* knows, because I know everything. You're going to give me that something."

He was laughing now, soft and affirming. "So, clearly, this is not a date."

She was spared a response when the trio of musicians stopped at their table, the tenor singing a mournful song, drawing out the notes like a stream telling a story. She couldn't understand a word of it and suspected Quin couldn't either, but the way the singer's eyes twinkled as he enunciated *amore*, sweeping his guitar as if binding them together, made it impossible to focus on anything other than the ornate stitching around the brim of his wide hat.

The three took their leave as Crystal approached. She gave the customary warning about the dangerous hotness of the plates and the cheerful invitation to enjoy. A tiny strip of tortilla poked out from under the lid of the warmer. Dini lifted it and bounced the steaming, piping-hot disk on her fingers, cooling it. "Have to be careful you know," she said. "These hands—they're my life. But"—she rolled the tortilla and dipped it in the mass of beans and took a bite—"totally worth the pain."

She chewed, watching Quin use his knife and fork to cut through the near solid mass of cheese-covered egg and meat and peppers then spoon the refried beans and diced potatoes into its midst, giving everything a swirl before taking one forkful that miraculously contained a bit of everything. His eyes closed for a brief second in appreciation. She kept her own open to experience the deliciousness of the moment vicariously.

"I've never seen anyone do that before," she said.

He lifted a questioning brow.

"Mix it all together, like a casserole."

"I eat everything that way." He lifted out a tortilla. "And this, by the way, is amazing."

"But you don't get to isolate the flavors." She used her fork to spear a perfect piece of steak. "You'll never know how amazing this—"

"Let's talk about Hedda." He offered it like a distraction. "It's time now, right?"

She moved to the edge of her seat. "How far did you read?"

"Just as far as you said. The voice at the door."

"And the conversation after."

"And the kiss."

Dini studied her food closely. "Yes. I love that. There's a sweetness to it. An innocence. And it shows that a kiss doesn't always have to be from some huge romantic buildup. Sometimes, it's an acknowledgment of a moment."

"But most people don't kiss each other unless there was something building up before, right? And some promise—some hope, I guess—of something to happen after."

"Something to happen?"

"A relationship, I mean. You don't think a kiss is a promise for a future?"

"I don't know, Quin. Have you had a future with every woman you've ever kissed?"

He tore off a portion of his tortilla. "No, I have not." He chewed, trying, she was sure, to hold an air of nonchalance, but something had changed. For the first time since he sat down, he wasn't looking at her in the way that made it seem he was trying to figure her out. Like the rare equation he couldn't solve.

"How about we move on to a safer topic?" she said, before he could ask about *her* kissing history.

"Okay," he said, swallowing, recovered. "You don't look like a magician."

She was expecting the conversation to veer back to Hedda, but the comment took her pleasantly by surprise. "What do magicians look like?"

"Old men with top hats."

"Well, it should please you to know that I actually do have a top hat and have been known to wear it on occasion. With a tuxedo. Arya calls it my sexy penguin look." It was out before she could stop it—such a well-worn, common joke between herself and her friend. She was rewarded for her gaffe by Quin's outburst of laughter, and further with the distraction of Crystal, who chose that moment to come by and pour coffee. And water. And to ask how everything was. And if they needed anything else. Dini hoped the air would be clear by the time the waitress left, but no.

"Sexy penguin?"

Dini squeezed her eyes shut. "I should have just showed you my tattoo." And then, at the invitation of his raised eyebrows, she did. It sat on top of her right shoulder and needed only the slightest push of her wide-necked sweater to reveal the black silk top hat with two bunny ears peeking out. "Now, on to you."

"I have a feeling I might die as the last un-inked man on earth."

"I mean, you don't look like a math teacher."

"What do math teachers look like?"

She busied herself, isolating three pepper strips and spearing them to a chunk of potato. "I guess I don't really know." Looking up, she saw nothing but kindness and logic in his eyes and thought, truthfully, she'd never seen anyone *more* like a teacher. "I never actually went to school."

"What?" Were it not for the music, the echoes of a hundred people speaking, the shouts of orders and instructions, the distant "Happy Birthday" song in the corner, his outburst might have been embarrassing. "How? Wait, homeschool?"

She nodded. "But not, like homeschool homeschool. My dad was a magician too. Old-man-top-hat kind. And he traveled all over, Mom with him. And me. So I just had books and stuff in the back of the bus or on the train or whatever we were doing at the time. Backstage dressing rooms, places like that. Mom didn't follow any kind of actual curriculum. I just, you know, learned stuff." She turned the focus back to Quin. "Come to think of it, I'll bet you're a great teacher. Sleeves rolled up. Tie loose."

"I don't wear a tie."

"Sitting on the edge of your desk. Letting the kids call you by your first name. Playing Led Zeppelin music while they take a quiz."

"So you've never been in a classroom, but clearly you have seen them on TV."

"I spent a lot of hours alone while my parents were performing. Mom was his glamorous assistant, folding herself up in the box and getting sliced to pieces every night."

"Fun." He scraped at his food. "Do you ever perform with your dad?"

"I did, some, when I was little." And then, as she feared would happen, her throat closed. What was it about him that made her forget to plan her words ahead? Silently she begged, *Please don't ask. Don't ask. . . .*

"How about now? Is he still performing?"

She could simply say no and change the subject. They were still strangers after all, and this was far too deep a wound to invite him to step in. Usually she was much better at keeping up the guardrails, cutting off any talk that would bring her to this point. But he had lulled her, bringing her to some place where bits of herself were floating, disconnected from the moment, and fair game to be rescued and brought up in conversation.

The pause had been overlong. "Hey," Quin said, "it's okay. You don't have to talk about it."

She took a sip of coffee—a test to see if she could swallow. If she could swallow, she could speak.

"When I was sixteen, we were part of a big traveling talent

showcase. Booked little theaters all over Nevada, California, Colorado. Months on the road. We were on a mountain pass in this huge rainstorm, and the road—the ground—just sort of slid out from under the bus. It killed almost everyone on it." She put her coffee down. "I'm one of the *almost*."

"Oh, Dini. I'm so sorry."

She'd left her hand, warm from the coffee mug, sitting on the table. He reached across, covered it with his own, and she let him. Neither spoke, and he sent the ever-attentive Crystal away with a glance. Dini loved whatever intuition led him to stay quiet with her, where others would pepper her with questions. "Were you hurt at all?" "Where did you go?" "Did you sue?" Instead, there was only the protective cloud of restaurant noise—forks against plates, the rumble of the bus cart—and over it all, the mournful trumpet of a Mexican love song.

At his elbow, Quin's phone vibrated, and his eyes immediately glanced at the screen.

"Go ahead," Dini said, grateful for the interruption. She watched him swipe the screen, read it with a bit of a furrow to his brow, and then type out a quick message before setting the phone, screen down, next to his empty plate.

"Okay," he said, rubbing his hands together. "Back to Hedda. What do I need to know?"

She was recovered, ready—at last—for this conversation. "It's more like what I need to know. From you. Do you believe her?"

"What do you mean?"

"Just from what you've read so far. Hedda's account of that night. What she said she heard. That voice, the touch. Do you believe her?"

"I believe *she* believes."

"That's not the same."

Quin took a tortilla out of the warmer and tore it in half. "These are amazing. I've lost track of how many I've had."

"That is your third. And don't change the subject."

"Why does that matter?"

"Because it does." Dini knew she sounded. . .crazy? Obsessive? Basically everything Arya accused her of being. She didn't want to scare Quin off. Not yet anyway. Not before she'd seen what he'd brought from the rest of the story. Without asking, she took up the other half of the torn tortilla and softened her tone. "Because it matters to Hedda."

"My first instinct then, quite frankly, is to say no. I don't believe her, because I don't believe in ghosts. We are all susceptible to suggestions and fears. She was a woman in a precarious situation. She needed sympathy? Attention?"

"Sallie's throat was crushed. She didn't speak a word for three days. Hedda is the only person who ever heard her speak."

Quin's voice was low, his tone patient—as if explaining to a child for a third time that the monsters in the movie won't follow you home. "She heard *someone* speak, but it wasn't Sallie White. It's like solving any problem. Once you know what the answer *isn't*, you can go back to the beginning and start over, look for something you didn't see—some small miscalculation."

Dini chewed, thinking. He was right, of course. Not even she, if held to the fire, could confess an unyielding belief in ghosts. Always, the question wasn't *what* Hedda heard, but *who*. Dini knew the how of it: a phonograph most likely projecting a voice, a chemical blown like an air dart. But again, *who*? Dini had read the account so many times, she could quote passages without prompting. Still, she remained unable to solve the mystery, to put the torment to rest.

She brought her attention back to Quin, finding him once again tapping away on his phone's keyboard. Trying not to bristle at his distraction, she shifted her position in the booth, the squeaking of the vinyl seats louder than she anticipated.

"Sorry," he said, putting his phone back on the table. "Maybe talking through all of this with me will illuminate something new. Plus, who knows? I might have some important missing factors."

"I hope so."

"Speaking of. . ." He opened the drawstring of his bag and brought out a plain manila envelope. "Look inside. She signed it to him."

Heart racing, Dini opened the envelope and took out a photograph. It was roughly four inches by six and featured Hedda as a young woman, obviously sitting for a portrait with a professional photographer. She was looking over one shoulder, boldly into the camera's lens. The giddy anticipation Dini had felt in sliding it out of the envelope was short-lived, however. She'd seen this photo a million times, for it served as the frontispiece of the book.

"This was in the box?"

"It's yours now."

"Thank you." She held it closer. "The photographer's studio dated it in the corner—1914. She didn't write her memoir until the late 1960s. Published in 1971. I always knew she used an old photo of herself, but this was taken before she even arrived in San Antonio. *Years* before. If your great-great-grandfather had a copy, she must have had two prints of it."

"And the writing on the back?" Quin reached over to flip the photograph. "It matches what she has written at the front of her book."

Truth and love must bind themselves to the same stone.

"Yes," Dini said. "That's part of it. In the book she writes, 'When truth and love wrap themselves around the same stone, together they can propel it to fly, or drag it to the lowest sand.' "

" 'In truth is beauty and beauty is truth. That is all ye need to know.' "

Dini looked and said, "Hey, math teacher quoting Yeats," before returning to the image on the flimsy cardboard. For the first time in a long time, Dini saw something new. Not a new face, but a new *time*. No wonder Hedda Krause looked so elegant in this photograph—her chin up with pride. She was a woman of prosperity at the time, a wife to a man of substance. This was who Hedda had been before the story started, before being relegated to the shadows. In this photo, she and Dini were the same age. Seeing this Hedda put a bit of salt in the sea of sweet familiarity. Dini had a new light in her brain, blinking in anticipation for the next one to make a new path. A whole new thread to the story she knew so well.

"I have to see more," she said, and when Quin didn't reply, she dragged her eyes away from Hedda's image to find him tapping on his phone keyboard again.

"What's that?"

"I said"—and then she stopped until he looked up at her—"I have to see more. Everything you brought. Let's go, just promise you won't make me run." She held out her foot, showcasing the heel of her boot. "I'll never make it."

"I—" He glanced at his phone, then back at her, his expression dampening Dini's enthusiasm. "I can't. I have—something's come up." He rummaged in his bag, produced a leather money clip, and peeled off a twenty. "Breakfast is on me, of course. Thank you for making me change my order."

His words and demeanor didn't match the morning. He sounded like this was over when, really, it hadn't quite started.

The battered book still sat in the middle of the table, more to his side than hers. He picked it up with the reverence it deserved. "I'm not *leaving*. I've just had something come up now. Something I have to. . .deal with. So—we can meet up again? Later?" He brought out his phone again and handed it to her. "Text yourself so I'll have your contact, and I'll text you when I'm free later today. Fair?"

The phone showed a blank message screen to an empty number. This she filled in, then tapped down to the waiting box and typed: DINI, I KNOW ABOUT THE CHRISTMAS PICTURE. MEET ME IN THE LOBBY BY THE COWBOY PAINTING. Q

She handed the phone back, leaving the message as a draft. "Don't send this until it's true."

He read it, smiled, and tapped the screen. Within seconds, Dini's phone buzzed in her bag. She nearly bounced in her booth. "You know about it?"

"I've seen it. I have it."

"Is it—wait. Don't tell me. Why didn't you tell me?"

He shook his head at the rapid redirection of her response. "You never asked."

"Aha," she said, triumphant that he still had so much more to learn. "Give me your phone."

Without question, he did, and as she prepared to write a new message, it vibrated, and a ribbon of text unfurled across the top. YOLANDA: WHAT'S YOUR ETA? DYING OVER HERE.

The heart-eyed emoji made it clear that the sender of the text, Yolanda, wasn't literally dying. Wasn't lying somewhere, pulse dangerously low, world going dark. Yolanda was dying the way Dini had, during those moments when she didn't think Quin was going to show. Or like the way her heart stopped when he stood to leave with such finality.

She closed the message app and handed the phone back. "Just text me whenever."

"Might be this evening."

Dini worked to keep her face neutral. Should she mention what she'd seen? Something flippant like, *Are you sure Yolanda will survive?* But she had no right, no reason—when all she cared about was the Christmas picture. Well, maybe not *all*. . .

"Evening's fine," she said, hoping to hide her disappointment in a cool-girl shrug. "I have stuff to do too. So anytime after six?"

"Sounds perfect." He wrapped *My Spectral Accuser* back in its towel and stashed it in his bag before standing. "Can we call it? Six o'clock."

"With the Christmas picture?"

"It's a date."

"No, it's not," she said, picturing Yolanda's name and the kissy face emoji. "It's the next part of the story."

Chapter 7

Excerpt from

My Spectral Accuser: The Haunted Life of Hedda Krause

Published by the Author Herself

The first traces of Christmas brought a lift to my spirits. My late husband was a man of great sentiment, and during the three Christmases we spent together, I joined him in crafting elaborate celebrations. We hosted evenings of wassail and caroling. Our cook worked for days on the meal; we spent hours in church. I secretly studied the hymns so I could join in the singing both in the pew and on his arm as we caroled with friends and neighbors. I learned that I was never so beautiful as when surrounded by evergreen and candlelight. The first time I ever read Scripture aloud was by a roaring Yule log, the house clouded with its scent, after my husband placed a Bible in my lap and claimed he hadn't the sight or strength to do so.

So, when the tree was erected in the middle of the lobby—one tall enough to reach through the encircling balcony of the second floor—I saw it as an escape from Sallie's grip. I read Dickens's classic *A Christmas Carol*, sipping tea while a dozen employees bustled about with steps and ladders, hanging baubles and draping tinsel. Surely, I thought, while filling my mind with the Spirits of Christmas, no wandering soul would materialize during such a holy season.

Bert took to concocting punch bowls of mulled wine for the guests, and I imbibed convivially, listening to their stories and feeling the warm spices lull me into an almost unbearable melancholy. Even the children (I've never much cared for them) tugged at an unexcavated sentimentality. I sang carols around the piano, standing shoulder to shoulder with strangers, and thanked Mr. Sylvan for the small box of chocolates (and Bert for the large bottle of brandy) and signed my name to a lovely card, which I addressed to the stepsons but did not send.

As I hoped, the spirit of the season kept my pernicious spirit at bay. For as long as the tree was in the lobby, I slept with the soundness of a saint. Silver, gold, and evergreen proved to be the secret to breaking the spell. Light returned to my eyes, color to my cheeks. I wore my finest gowns, my most elegant jewels.

On Christmas Day I walked the perimeter of the second floor, the treetop level with my eye, and looked down upon my fellow guests, imagining myself mistress of this place. After all, many of the faces were familiar to me—local people who enjoyed the fine dining and attended events in the ballroom, as well as visitors from out of town here for a festive holiday. Sometime in the early hours of the morning, a decorative screen had been erected beside the tree, with an upholstered chair stationed in front of it. I watched a well-dressed couple—not quite comfortable in their finery—step up, he sitting on the chair, she posed beside him, one hand on his shoulder. Such a familiar tableau. Then a familiar figure stepped into view: the photographer who had taken my picture at the Empire Theater all those weeks ago.

J. P. Haley looked slightly more professional than he had the night at the theater—his long hair combed back and secured, his suit less rumpled, his face shaved clean. Today he had an assistant working with him, a slender young man wearing a knitted vest under his jacket and a driving cap pulled low—almost to the point of touching his heavy brows. It was his job to corral the subjects and group them attractively, deciding who should sit, who should stand, and which pretty child should sit on Papa's lap. When I approached to add my name to the list, he looked at me, and my breath caught at the color of his eyes. They were truly gold, unlike any I have seen before. Beautiful, I might have called him, if not for the perfectly trimmed moustache and beard that framed his thin, unsmiling lips.

"I'd like a portrait," I told him. "Hedda Krause." I spelled the name, having none of the reservations I'd had when Haley took my picture at the theater. Who would see this but me? True, it might be worthy of being hung in the window of his studio—assuming he *had* a studio—but such a display would not reach outside the streets of this city.

When my turn came, Haley said, "I think I'd rather capture you standing," and bade his assistant whisk the ornate chair away. There was much positioning after that to capture the fullness of the tree, the right collection of ornaments, the right amount of light. I was wearing a choker of red beads with a silver-backed jade clasp resting on my collarbone, matching red beads dangling from my ears. Neither the necklace nor the earrings were particularly valuable, save for the jade in the clasp. We'd purchased it from a Native shop and paid a high price for it, along with the cuff I wore. I took pains in my stance to keep my hands clasped loosely in front of me, the largest stone of my bracelet on full display. I meant to keep my face frozen against the light and heat of the flash, but Haley spoke some direction.

"A softer expression, maybe? Sweeter? Imagine you're one of the angels smiling down on the holy infant."

I tried to comply, thinking of women I'd seen in magazine advertisements gazing softly at the babe in their arms. I had no aspirations of experiencing such a thing, but I tried my best, and soon the air was full of the familiar smell of exploded light, and my eyes burned as the spark faded.

"It might be a week or more before I'll have it printed," Haley told me as he slid the plate from his camera and handed it gingerly to his assistant. "If you don't mind, I'd like to add some tint."

I didn't mind. My late husband and I had delayed too long getting a proper portrait painted, so my image had never been captured in color.

And so I waited, lifting champagne toasts to the New Year, biding my time as the needles fell from the tree until it was finally stripped and hauled away the day after Epiphany. I was watching the entire process from the second-floor balcony and noticed the top of Haley's head the moment he stepped in from the street. With a squeal befitting a child receiving a gift, I raced down the stairs and met him at the desk. Only later would I mark how he watched my approach with both sadness and trepidation.

"Oh!" I exclaimed, dragging up some vestige of coquettishness. "A late Christmas present for me?"

"Yes," he said, refusing to meet my eye. "Take it as such. I won't be charging you. Truth be told, I don't know if I should give it to you at all."

And then he was gone, disappeared like a puff of dark dust. Upon closer inspection, I saw the package had been wrapped, sealed, and tied with the string circled three times around. Unable to open it with my own power, I walked to the desk and asked Mr. Sylvan to lend me his letter opener. Silver and sharp, it weighed heavy in my hand as I sliced through the string and along the sealed edges.

"It's my Christmas portrait," I said as much to myself as to Mr. Sylvan. I unwrapped the layers and uncovered the image printed on heavy paper. I felt myself frown at first. Haley had promised a tint, but I saw nothing but ordinary black and white.

Then the image blurred in my trembling hand.

"Mrs. Krause?" Mr. Sylvan's voice lurked beyond the roaring of the rush of blood in my ears.

I dropped the image to the desktop and braced my hands beside it. A sob caught in my throat, perfectly timed to Mr. Sylvan's un-Sylvan-like gasp.

The Christmas tree, it seemed, had failed in its spell to protect me from the ghost of Sallie White. For there she was, in the photograph. Right behind me. Her hand resting on my shoulder.

Chapter 8

Dini scanned the crowd. Families gathered with blankets and lawn chairs, leaving a nonlinear, narrowly winding path. Her phone buzzed in her hand, Arya's face on the screen. Dini swiped. "Where are you?"

"Look toward the raspa truck. We're in front of it."

Dini imagined a grid and made a purposeful search, finally seeing Arya distinctly. She and Bill had staked out a prime spot near the stage where three guys in ratty jeans and T-shirts rambled around plugging in cords and rolling amps. Dini picked her way through, dodging children and muttering apologies to adults who came to inexplicable dead stops in front of her.

"There she is," Arya crooned, setting Bea free to run and collide with Dini's legs.

"Hey there." Dini touched the top of Bea's head. "You just saw me yesterday, remember?"

"I told her we could go get a treat as soon as you got here." Arya had been lounging on the blanket in front of Bill but now stood with the agility that comes with a daily yoga discipline. "So, it's not so much about you as it is the shaved ice and sugar."

"Completely understandable." Dini offered a distant high five to Bill, who stood to greet her. He wore baggy cargo shorts, frayed at the hem, and a Jazz Ramblers T-shirt that was probably once a vibrant yellow but had now faded into something soft and undefinable. He brought out his wallet, extracted a few bills, and handed them over to Arya.

"What flavor do you want?" Arya asked, taking the money.

"Are you kidding?" Bill crouched, made his hands into grasping claws, and growled, "Tiger blood."

Bea screamed and ran the circumference of the blanket while he chased her, roaring.

"Every time," Arya said, grabbing Bea's hand on the next lap. "He doesn't even like it. Just gets it to make her scream."

"It's a safe scream," Dini said, falling into step beside her friend.

"So." Arya nudged her arm. "Tell me about breakfast."

"It was . . . good."

"He showed up?"

Dini had forgotten her one, panicked text to her friend. "He did."

"And?" Arya let Bea run ahead a few steps with the warning to stay where she could be seen.

"He gave me a picture."

"His picture? Strange for a first date, but let me see—"

"Not *his* picture, obviously. Hedda's. The same from the front of her book. Only now I know that picture has been cropped, because the original is dated—October 1914. Three years before coming to San Antonio. And the inscription written in the front of the book? It's handwritten on the back of the photograph. But it's not written in Hedda's hand."

"Do you ever stop to think how sad it is that you can recognize the handwriting of a woman who's been dead for a hundred years?"

"She hasn't been dead for a *hundred* years," Dini said, long past being defensive about Hedda. "This is something new. I always thought the quote was about her jewels and her love for her late husband and the truth about what—what happened. But now? They might not even be her own words."

They had arrived at the raspa truck. A hand-lettered sign written on poster board listed all the flavors of shaved ice available, with index cards of additional choices tacked along the edge.

"Read them to me!" Bea whined, tugging on Arya's long linen skirt.

"I'm not going to read them all to you," Arya said with a sigh, intimating she'd tangled with this request before. "Tell me what you want, and I'll bet they have it."

Dini scanned the list. "Why write 'blueberry' and 'raspberry' and 'blueberry-raspberry'? We all know we can combine flavors. Without the combinations, they'd knock this list down to"—she calculated—"twelve flavors. Tops."

"You do this every time," Arya said with the same edge of maternal impatience.

"And I'm right every time." She pointed at a decorative card. "Bea? Do you want to try a unicorn raspa? It's every flavor of the rainbow. And unicorns fly. So tigers can't eat them."

Arya shot her a familiar look that said, *Don't fill my girl's head with nonsense*, but acquiesced to Bea's enthusiasm. She folded her arms and took on a mock-serious tone. "And do you have money, young lady?"

Dini took her cue, fetching the silver dollar she had ever-ready in her pocket. Palming it, she reached down and behind Bea's ear, dropped it into her fingers, and touched the metal to the girl's little lobe. "Here. You can use this."

Bea's eyes grew wide, then suspicious. "Is this real money?"

"It's unicorn money," Dini said, making a mental note to get more from the bank this week.

"Can I keep it, then? Daddy already gave Mom money to pay for the snow cones."

"Put it in your pocket and say, 'Thank you,' " Arya said. "Go wait with your dad. You can come back when we're at the front of the line."

Bea complied with the smallest protest, and both Arya and Dini kept their eyes trained on her until she was safely at Bill's side. As they watched, Dini told Arya everything—how Quin showed up in running gear, how he carefully transported her book, how he'd read what she told him to read, and that she could keep the picture. As they inched forward in the raspa line, she told her friend too about the text she saw, seeing it clearly even as she dug her toe into the grass.

"Relax," Arya said, soothingly, "maybe she's his sister."

"*Dying?* With a heart-eyes emoji?"

"Okay. Maybe not a sister. But come on, Dini, I know you like the guy, but he is here for just a week, right? There was going to be heartbreak sooner or later."

"My heart isn't broken."

"It's okay if it is."

"It isn't. But why not just tell me he had a date or a girlfriend or whatever Yolanda is."

"Because right now it's not your business," Arya said, never one to placate. "Who knows why men do what they do? Better to find out now rather than later, though, right? There's a guy in our church group—"

"I'm not done," Dini said. "*We*—he and I—are not done. He has the Christmas picture." Arya stared, blinking behind her pale aviator sunglasses. "The *Christmas* picture, Arya. I'm meeting him later this evening. I'm going to get to see it."

"Mm-hmm." Arya didn't sound convinced. "So you're fine with him spending the afternoon with another woman and just being the girl sitting and waiting for a text?"

"I'm waiting to see the Christmas picture."

Arya put up her hands, causing a cascade of bangles to fall to her elbows. "I'm very happy you found someone to feed into this little obsession of yours, but don't throw your self-esteem out the window for the sake of some old picture."

Dini thought about laying out the whole story—reminding Arya again of a tale she had shared many times—but try as she might, Dini had never been able to bring her friend to share her enthusiasm. "It's not just an old picture," she said, checking herself for petulance. "It's my holy grail. It's a treasure I thought was gone forever."

The man behind them cleared his throat, and they moved up in line.

"Be honest," Arya said, leaning in. "Do you want to see this photo? Or do you want to see him?"

"He has more than the photo."

"That didn't answer my question. Why don't you text him right now, tell him to leave everything at the front desk. You can pick it up next week and mail it to him when you're done."

"He has my book."

"He can leave the book."

"We have the rest of each other's stories."

"And he has a girl who texts him love emojis. Look, I just don't want you to get hurt. This is the first I've ever seen you excited about a guy. Ever. At least a real live human guy. I'd get it if he came with the ghost, but there's a very good chance that he won't. So, I say take your ghost and run."

As Arya spoke, Dini's phone was ringing, the screen lit up with only "Q" and the 571 area code.

"It's him."

"Calling you? How old-fashioned and gallant."

"What should I do?"

"Answer it," Arya said, with a tone that could register anywhere between indulgent and annoyed.

Dini swiped the screen and said, "Hello?" while taking a step away from the line.

"Dini? It's Quin."

"I know. Your—my phone told me." She slapped her palm to her forehead as Arya snickered.

"Yeah, well. . .things here, um, wrapped up quicker than I thought they would and, well, I was wondering if you'd be able to get together a little earlier than we talked about."

"How much earlier?"

"Like now earlier?"

"Now? I'm a little busy right now."

"What are you doing?"

Before she could think to tell him that if his afternoon activities were none of her business, hers were none of his, she said, "I'm getting a raspa at an outdoor jazz festival."

"That is oddly specific. Is it close? Are you downtown?"

"Where are you right now?" She heard him ask who she presumed to be the Lyft driver, and he named an intersection. "Oh," she said, "you're just a block away. See if he'll bring you to Travis Park. We're close to the raspa truck. Speaking of, do you want one?"

"I don't know what that is."

"It's like a snow cone. Shaved ice and syrup. There's a million flavors." She turned to the board and started reading. "Cherry, blueberry, banana, strawberry, raspberry, coconut. . ."

"Coconut lime?"

Her eyes made a grid of the poster. "Yes. Sure. I'll get you one. My treat. You should be here in about five minutes." She closed the call and wilted under Arya's mocking glare. "What? Don't you want to meet him?"

"I'm just saying you could have left him to wiggle on the line a little bit. He cheats on you, and I'm buying him a raspa."

"He's not *cheating*." Dini slipped her cell phone into her back pocket and found the neatly folded five-dollar bill—the emergency cash she'd carried since she was twelve years old. She tucked it between her fingers and brought her hands through an elaborate display, front and back, and front again, making it magically appear in her palm. "I'll pay for Quin's."

By the time they arrived back to Bill and Bea, Dini could see Quin getting out of a car at the edge of the park. "That's him." Her hands were full, as she was carrying three drinks, so she used her elbow to distinguish him from the other people in the park. It wasn't difficult. He'd changed clothes since breakfast and was wearing a pair of tapered chinos and an untucked shirt that seemed to be made of some sort of calico.

"You're kidding," Arya said, and as she did, the first notes of the Dink Maxwell Quintet started up, much to Bill's delight. He took his raspa from Arya, kissed her cheek, and said, "I love these guys" loud enough that Dini was sure the saxophonist heard him.

"Why kidding?" Dini shouted, bending to give the bouncing Bea her treat.

"He doesn't seem your type."

Because her voice would never get his attention across the expanse of the crowd and the blaring music, she gestured broadly, waving the cups like someone directing a plane. The moment he caught her eye, raising his hand in recognition and directing his steps with new determination, she brought the cups close to her, fearing she'd lose her grip. "Why wouldn't he be my type?" She didn't think the question would carry over to Arya's ears, but all of her friend's senses tended to be sharper than the average woman's.

"He looks kinda like a square."

"A *square*? Do people still say *square*?"

"Sorry. I just never pictured you with Mr. Tight Pants and Laura Ingalls Shirt."

"I think technically that makes him a hipster," Bill contributed, jabbing the spoon into his ice in rhythm with the band.

"Hipster. Square. Nerd, whatever." Arya spoke through a smile as frozen as the ice in her Styrofoam cup. "Let's not forget that this Kevin spent the afternoon with another woman and probably has no intentions of being honest with you about it."

"His name is Quin."

"Like I said, whatever." This she tossed over her shoulder while stepping directly into Quin's path, hand outstretched. She introduced him to Bill and to Bea as if he had walked into her parlor or a major acquisitions merger meeting and not simply up to the edge of her checkered blanket. By the time he was face-to-face with Dini, he looked relieved.

"This is for you," she said, handing him his cup. "Coconut lime." She took a small envelope and sprinkled some of the contents onto her own watermelon ice then held the packet out to him. "This is chamoy. It's like a spicy red pepper. Gives it a kick."

"I think I had enough of a kick at breakfast." When he spoke, he leaned in close, his words cutting through every note and measure of the music, finding and fitting her ear.

"Fair enough." She handed the packet to Arya, who in turn held it out of Bea's reach.

They sat, a silent arrangement that put Bill and Quin in the chairs, Arya and Dini on the blanket, and Bea floating between and around them.

"These guys"—Bill gestured with his spoon—"it's their first time playing here. I've been following them for a while, though. We saw them just a few weeks ago, didn't we, babe? At that place at the Blue Star? Anyway, they're amazing."

He continued talking, something about the challenging polyrhythms and off-the-wall guest musicians. Dini listened in, her lips wrapped around a plastic spoon that delivered ice and heat and sweet in a single bite, as incongruous as the music coming from the stage. From her vantage point, she could keep her eyes fixed on Quin, proud of him, somehow, for how he leaned forward in his canvas chair, intent on Bill's monologue, breaking his gaze away only to look appreciatively at the band and nod in agreement.

She felt a touch on her knee and wrested her attention away.

You should go, Arya mouthed, pointing *away* lest Dini not understand. She sent a look over that said, *Are you sure?* And Arya gave a silent command for Dini to save herself and Quin from Bill's musical discourse.

"Well, then." Dini attempted to rise gracefully to her feet the way Arya had earlier, but the combination of the heels on her boots and the fact that she, in fact, did not practice yoga every day meant the necessity of a steadying hand on Quin's arm. "I suppose we should go."

Quin looked up. "You sure?"

"What?" Bill sounded disappointed. "You'll miss Argyle Avenue."

"What time do they come on?" Dini asked.

"Seven."

Dini didn't have to look at a watch to know that was more than two hours away. "We, um—"

"We have"—Quin stood—"I have some documents and pictures and things to go over with Dini. I'm sure she's told you. About the Menger ghost?"

Bea twirled to the center. "What ghost?"

Dini jabbed Quin's arm. He couldn't have known the level of Arya's protectiveness. "He said we have to go. To the Menger."

Bea's unicorn sticky face looked unconvinced, but she said nothing more.

"Let me know how it goes," Arya said, emphasizing *goes*. "Okay? Promise?"

"Promise," Dini said. She leaned in to kiss her friend's cheek. "I'm fine. It's all fine."

Quin and Dini said their goodbyes and made their way across the park, neither speaking until they'd made a comfortable space between themselves and the din of the music.

"Your friends are nice," Quin said, making the breach into conversation.

"They are. Arya was my first real friend. They take good care of me."

"And, boy, does he love jazz."

"Yes. Yes he does." Dini tipped her cup, allowing for a drink of the melted ice and thick, spicy syrup. "How about you? Do you love jazz?"

"Promise not to tell?" He was looking deep into his cup.

"I promise."

They came to a mutual stop, and he looked straight into her eyes as if delivering devastating news. "I hate it. I hate everything about it."

Dini matched his serious tone. "It is the absolute worst."

"I am so glad we got that out of the way. I consider the air totally cleared."

"Totally," she said, trying not to picture the emoji on his phone.

They stopped at a trash can next to an imposing, four-story red-brick building with windows advertising MAGIC on the top floor, RIVER SWEETS CANDY next to it on the ground.

"I work here sometimes," Dini said before tapping the last of her raspa from the bottom of the cup.

"The candy store?"

"No, the theater." She led him the few steps around the corner, where a green awning bloomed over a doorway advertising the Magician's Company Theater. "I do shows. Cards mostly and close-up stuff."

"Rabbits in hats?"

She laughed. "I'm not good with animals. Or maybe they're not good with me. I tried a bit with a mouse up the sleeve, and let's just say that we were both relieved to be rid of each other." She took him closer to the door beneath the awning, its glass surface packed with show bills and posters. "There I am." She pointed to an eight-by-ten flyer featuring her name, Dini Blackstone, in a dominating font that called to mind the four suits in a deck of cards. The *D* a spade, the *B* a club, and hearts and diamonds interspersing the rest. She herself was dressed in a form-fitting leather halter dress, short enough to reveal a generous amount of leg in torn fishnet stockings and spike-heeled ankle boots. Her hair was all one color then—something like a sunset pink—and she leaned on a green felt-covered table, a spread of cards fanned behind her.

Dini didn't spend any time looking at the poster—she'd seen it a million times. Had it framed in her hallway. Used it on her business cards. *Not* the ones she put in children's birthday party goodie bags. Rather, she watched *him* look at it. How his eyes fixated and his neck, between his ear and his collar, flushed the same shade of sunset pink.

Tearing his eyes away at last, he said, "It's not exactly sexy penguin."

Dini laughed, spell broken. "I'm glad you're not writing my Yelp reviews."

"I can't review what I haven't seen. Do you have any shows this week while I'm in town?"

"Not here." She took the first step leading them back to Alamo Street. "But if you'd really like to see me? See a show, I mean, I have one Wednesday."

"That could work."

"It's an afternoon matinee. Out of town, so we'd probably need to leave here by noon."

They came to a light just as the WALK signal lit, and blended in with the throng crossing the street.

"Perfect," he said when they got to the other side. "I should be all wrapped up Tuesday evening."

"Wrapped?" Now they were engulfed in the crowd gathered in front of the Alamo. They stopped again, this time at his behest, and stared at the monument tucked back behind the trees and ropes.

"You know? I didn't want to say anything on the tour, but I thought it would be. . ."

"Bigger?"

"Yeah. Like more. . ."

"Imposing? That's what people say, tourists, when they have this huge John Wayne icon in their minds and it's, well, not quite that."

"Still, I want to go see it. Be a *tourist*." He nudged her playfully with his elbow and started walking.

"You should have time before you go. You say you'll be wrapped up on Tuesday? Wrapped up with what, exactly? I thought you were here to learn about Hedda. And Sallie."

"*Sallie!*" He slapped his forehead as if just remembering a long-lost thought. "What a—I mean, you told part of the story on the tour. I knew she died—"

"Was killed."

"Yes, killed—"

"Murdered by her husband."

"But that bit about it taking her three days to die. *Three days?* Why do you leave that out of your tour talk?"

Dini shrugged. "Some of the hosts include it, but I don't. I don't like to think about her suffering. It's horrible enough, isn't it? How we can be so entertained by other people's pain? If I can give her a little bit of dignity, I want to do that."

"And it was right down there?" They stood at the corner of Crockett and Alamo Plaza, one Häagen-Dazs shop and a tourist center away from the entrance to the Menger Bar.

"No, actually it was on the other side. Back then the hotel also had a brewery, and the bar was a part of it. The bar as it is now didn't come until sometime after Prohibition."

"Well, Prohibition's over. Do you want to go in? Have a drink? Play a round of Hedda and Bert?"

Is he flirting with me? Dini thought about their kiss—Hedda and Bert's—and wondered if he was thinking about it too. After all, he'd only read half the book. He didn't know how it ended. She knew her lips were raspa stained, but he didn't know how they tingled with the lingering spice. And hadn't she been flirting too? Taking him over to see her picture, knowing—because the photographer told her endlessly—how good she looked, how her curves filled everything out just right. "*Queen of hearts*," he'd said, clicking away. *Queen of broken hearts, more like it.*

"No," she said and charged on, not letting herself surmise whether or not he was disappointed. "We came here—I came here—to see the Christmas picture."

"Right. The Christmas picture. Let's go."

They turned toward the front entrance and were soon within steps of a man dressed in the bedraggled layers of the homeless. He was weaving in an irregular pattern on the sidewalk, and as he approached, Dini felt Quin's hand on the small of her back, tugging her closer. Her first instinct was to pull away. First, because the man approaching was a regular on the plaza and—as far as she knew—harmless. Second, because her body wasn't used to touch of any kind. She'd made herself available to Bea's physical affections and even granted Arya the opportunity for a true, long hug when the occasion allowed. But she'd never been one to allow random physical confrontation. Not with strangers. Not with men.

Except Quin.

In just those seconds, she calculated every touch. The touch of their hands at Mi Tierra. The brush of his hip against hers as they walked in the crowded street. The nudge of his elbow. Now this. It bothered her mind but not her body, and she missed it immediately when he drew away to open the lobby door.

They passed a sea of furniture positioned in front of a massive black stone fireplace and headed, by some unspoken instinct, across the threshold to the Victorian lobby. "Do you want to wait here?" He indicated a grouping of sofas around a glass-topped table. Spanning the area, a painting depicted a classic cowboy in pursuit of roping down a stray. It was the very place she'd mentioned in her playful text before she saw the name and the emojis. "Or do you just want to come up to my room? That would be easier."

"I—I don't know—"

"Look"—he held up his hands in a gesture of surrender—"I know you don't know me well, but you can trust me. I'm a nice guy. A good guy. Not a serial killer or anything like that."

"Most serial killers don't introduce themselves as serial killers."

He laughed. "Point. *But*—we can leave the door open. I know, I know—that's what I would say *here* in order to get you *there* and—"

"It's fine," she said, suddenly consumed with nothing other than seeing the prize she sought. "Let's go."

Chapter 9

Excerpt from
My Spectral Accuser: The Haunted Life of Hedda Krause
Published by the Author Herself

I did not immediately shred the photograph. To do so in Mr. Sylvan's presence would have piqued his curiosity, and I was in no frame of mind to share my personal horror with him. Instead, I answered his curious gaze at my response by saying, "My goodness. We never appear to be quite ourselves in a photograph, do we?"

Then I took the photograph and the packaging straight to my room and locked the door behind me. There was a heavy crystal bowl on my writing desk, something the staff always kept full of sweet bits of wrapped toffee. These I dumped to the table before—*Zzzip*—I ripped off the top of the tree. *Zzzip,* and my skirt was gone. I tore and tore until I held between my finger and thumb nothing but our two faces: Sallie's and mine. Hers a blur, mine not. Despite what I'd said to Mr. Sylvan, I thought myself quite beautiful. My gown was new, purchased on a whim only days before, its neckline broad and sleeves capped. I stared at the dark hand outlined on my white skin. How could I not have felt that? How did I not sense her behind me? Had there been the slightest rustle of the tree? I closed my eyes and tried to recall some jostling of the ornaments, a whisper of blown-glass baubles brushing against each other. Now, many years later, as I commit my memories to the page, I feel it. The rough brush of her cotton uniform against my back. The cold touch of her flesh on mine. Her broken breath as she rushes through the boughs.

Finally, I said, "Goodbye, Sallie. May the devil take your soul," and dropped the last scrap of the photograph on the pile of shreds and set a match. The fire burned within the crystal, reducing the lot of it to curled, black ash.

I sat at the desk and took a page of stationery, prepared to write a letter equally as fiery to J. P. Haley, Photographer, but the pen hovered above the page. What could I say? I saw his face; he was as terrified as I. Perhaps Bert would have had some words of comfort or wisdom, but I couldn't bring myself to tell him either. Tears pricked my eyes, brought on only partially by the acrid stream of smoke rising from the crystal. Now that I no longer had the image to ignite my fear, my heart had time to seize its sense of shame for being hunted by such evil. Certainly a ghost could haunt my hallway, scratch at my door, say my name. I never asked any of my fellow guests if they heard her, for fear my own sanity would come into question. I assumed that is why they never asked me either. And if, on occasion, I would overhear a delighted whisper about a moving shadow, or a sudden chill, or the unexplained swaying of a hanging lamp, I said nothing. Let them keep their ghost their way, and I, mine.

But to see her in that photograph? Profane. Dozens of families stood in the same spot as I, their smiles frozen in the spirit of the holiday, yet they were spared the same ghoulish apparition. Or, I assumed they were spared. No, I didn't assume. I *knew*. The deepest part of me lived with certain assurance that I alone shared my photo with Sallie White. Her hand touched my shoulder only. The dream I had of reconstructing the good, respectable life I enjoyed with my late husband shattered beneath her skin. Her first touch burned my flesh, but this one broke my spirit.

At this, you might be thinking, why did I not leave? I could have packed my trunk, paid my bill, and moved myself to another establishment. The Crockett Hotel was just across the street. The Gibbs only a block away. Either would be a perfectly acceptable home, however temporary. Those of you who have enjoyed the luxuries of the Menger, however, well understand my choice. There is no equal to its elegance.

It is where my late husband would have insisted we stay, had he lived long enough to realize our adventurous dreams.

There is another reason, though, for my stubborn refusal to vacate. I may present myself as a lady of fine breeding, but I've never been one to back down from a fight. I was raised in streets and alleyways and courtyards of darkness. I've had more than one occasion to fight for my life. Rest assured, if I had been Sally White, this hotel would be haunted by the ghost of Henry Wheeler. I had two rivals for the affections of my late husband, one of whom was an heiress to a company known in every household in the nation. Yet I prevailed. Not by methods of which I am terribly proud, but if a fleshly woman with millions of dollars could not thwart my path to happiness, then neither would the remaining spirit of a long-dead maid. The quest for love compels risks.

Thus, I took on the role of the offense in our fight.

"How can I summon her to me?" I asked Bert this question in the dead of a bitter January night. By then we'd given up any sort of pretense that we were anything other than friends. Nights when the bar was empty, knowing the night clerk was dozing behind a magazine, I'd creep in, whereupon Bert would lock the doors, pull the shade, and join me at my table.

"What do you mean, *summon*?" he asked, filling my glass with a special brandy kept under the bar just for me. "You don't mean anything like one of those séances, do you? Witches talking to the dead? Because not only is that pure evil, but Mr. Sylvan would never allow such a thing on his property."

"Of course not. I mean Sallie herself. If she can be bothered to show up in. . .unexpected places whenever she wishes, how can I get her to come speak to me when *I* wish?"

"You know you sound crazy."

"Ah, but *you* know I'm not."

"I did until just this minute. Now I'm not entirely sure." He grinned at me over his cup. Coffee, straight, as he always drank. And though I could sense the levity in his comment, there was a hint of sincerity behind it. *I should have told him about the photograph*, I chastised myself. *More, I should have shown it to him, so he would know.*

"You believe me, don't you, Bert?"

"It's like what I told you at the beginning. You got to be careful about plantin' ideas in a mind, because they can take root, whether they have a life to them or not. It's like thinkin' to yourself, *I'd like to have me a little dog. A little black-and-white dog with spots.* And then, next you know, you're seein' little black-and-white spotted dogs everywhere. Places you've never seen them before. But maybe they was always there—you just hadn't brung them up to the top of your mind yet."

"You think Sallie is just something I have brought to the top of my mind?"

"No." He poured me another. "What you heard that first night was probably real enough. It's a different story than what most tell, but. . ." He left the thought unfinished.

"I have heard her since."

"I know you have."

"On multiple occasions. And in multiple. . .ways." He cocked his head, inviting me to elaborate, but I did not.

"I think," he said, his voice as gentle as I ever heard it, "that's maybe because you have stayed here for—well, longer than most do. Most people, they're here a night. Maybe two or three. Then they go. So if they see or hear somethin', they can put it out of mind because they don't have another night comin'."

I steeled myself. "Are you saying I should leave?"

"No." He shook his head for emphasis. "No, I am not sayin' that at all. What I *do* say, is that maybe just by bein' here, in a way, you're summoning her already. Maybe she thinks, when people leave, she's scarin' them off. And she just hasn't scared you off yet."

I let his words sink in with the brandy. "She won't."

"That's my girl." He offered his smile, which, along with the sentiment, managed to warm every bit of me that the drink left cold.

That night I left the bar in a manner quite the opposite of how

I left the nights before. Rather than keeping my head down, eyes focused on my feet, I kept my gaze employed in a constant sweep of the shadows, scanning left and right as I imagined a soldier on patrol might do. With every step I whispered, "Come out here, Sally White," just under my breath, keeping my teeth gritted closed behind my lips. I kept up my challenge in the hall, hearing the blood rush in my ears, knowing she and I would be trapped in the long, narrow passage.

I went into my room and shut my door as usual but stopped short of sliding the chain. No, I would no longer hide behind any forged protection. I would *see* her. At the slightest sound, I would throw it open to reveal her in whatever form she took.

Days passed then weeks. The bills in my wallet dwindled. By my calculations, I had enough cash on hand to maintain my residence through the end of February, with rations. Toast and coffee in the mornings, dinner *or* supper each day, preferably at the invitation of another. I took inventory of my jewelry, recording it in two lines of value: those pieces that would bring in the most money and those pieces that would bring the most pain in parting. Most valuable by far, the ring my late husband gave me to ensure our engagement. Emerald, surrounded by diamonds. Dainty and elegant but substantial. It might fetch the highest price, but at what cost? He gave it to me one night at supper, taking his knee in front of his sons, proclaiming a love that would last to the end of our lives. This ring branded me as a woman of quality. It gave me worth and respectability. Everything else—the pearls, the lapis, the gold, the amethysts—they were baubles in comparison. Rocks set in paste. Valuable rocks, nonetheless, set in a paste that would fetch a price.

One afternoon, in what had become a ritual of civil exchange, I asked Mr. Sylvan if he could recommend a reputable broker to whom I might sell a piece or two.

"I hardly live the life that calls for such adornment," I said. "Life really is simpler here in the West."

"Maybe California would be more exciting?"

I smiled, refusing to take his bait. "But that really is just farther west, isn't it? Not necessarily more exciting."

By the end of our conversation, he recommended a shop on Houston Street. It was a fine winter day for walking. Temperate, as they say, and I congratulated myself for not wasting precious trunk space with furs. My wool coat would more than suffice, and on a day like this one, with the afternoon sun streaming down, it proved to be too warm. At least that was the reason I gave for the trickle of sweat at the nape of my neck and the glistening of my brow when I walked into Paragon Treasures.

Despite Mr. Sylvan's reassurance that the store was not a typical pawn shop, it had all the vestiges of being exactly that. Small, with an attempt at elegance in its etched glass door and clean carpet runner, it was full of items that were obviously given over for cash. A line of silver teapots on one shelf, clocks of every shape and size imaginable produced a solid, soothing wall of sound. Books stuffed indiscriminately in a case were for sale—according to a faded card—at the tempting price of three for a quarter. A certain novel caught my eye, *Little Dorrit* by Charles Dickens, and something called *Tempest and Sunshine*, which looked like a story of pure escape. I wasted no time finding a third. I should have taken my books, left my quarter on the counter, and returned to pursue a quiet life of reading. Such had always been my escape, even during long evenings in luxury, reading aloud to my ailing husband in his final, quiet nights. But secondhand literature was not the nature of my errand.

The proprietor had offered a friendly enough greeting upon my arrival and was only mildly interested that I seemed poised to leave with twenty-five cents' worth of books. His white hair tufted around a bald pate, and he gave out an old man's groan as he rose from his comfortable stool to serve me.

"No other treasures I can interest you in?" His accent indicated that San Antonio was not his native home. "Nothing is better with a good book than a nice cup of tea. Mostly so on a cold winter night.

And I have some lovely sets here."

"No, thank you." I wondered if he would have attempted to sell me a tarnished teapot if I had been wearing my emerald ring, which I'd left at home lest I be tempted to sell it. "I would like to purchase these, but I also—" Words caught curiously in my throat. Curious, I say, because I had pawned things before. Shoes, dishes, silver spoons, and golden snuff boxes, all without a second thought as to how they came into my possession. A glance at the assembly of trinkets in the glass case in front of me gave assurance that such transactions were common here.

The proprietor looked at my bag and then into my eyes. "Something to sell?"

"Yes. Perhaps."

He took a square of black felt from behind the counter and smoothed it on the glass. "Show me."

I was wearing a simple ring, set with a cluster of seed pearls, which I removed easily from my left pinkie and placed on the square. Then I reached into my little bag and took out the cuff I'd worn in the Christmas photo and a brooch set with mother-of-pearl. He moved each to a corner of the cloth and looked up again.

"Not the earrings?"

My amethyst, given to me by my husband in a box lined with white fur. "No." *Not yet.*

"Does your husband approve of the sale of these pieces?"

"They are my own," I said, which, with the exception of the brooch, was true. I recognized the proprietor's steely heart of business. Still, there was a heart, so I added, "I am a widow."

He touched an age-spotted hand to his chest and said, "My condolences," before taking a well-diminished pad of paper from his breast pocket. He licked the tip of a stubby pencil and began scribbling figures, finally making a large, dark circle around a final sum.

"This is what I can do."

I stared at the figure and did my own calculations. The number was ridiculously low, even my untrained eye knew that. The pieces I offered exceeded the quality of anything in his case. But it was enough to see me through spring, with careful stewardship, and my acceptance might give me leverage in future transactions.

"Does this include a twenty-five cent deduction for my books?"

He offered a wry smile. "Indeed. And I will even throw in a teapot if you like."

"I've no need." What could I tell him? That I didn't have a home, let alone a kitchen or a stove?

"Then we are in agreement. Shall I write you a check? Or would cash be preferred?"

"Cash, please."

"Then I shall return. In the meantime. . ." He took a small card from the front of a tabletop file and placed the pencil next to it. "If you would fill this out."

On the card was a place for my name and address. Underneath, a small space with the heading ITEMS SURRENDERED FOR SALE OR PAWN. I hadn't touched the card by the time he returned.

"Why do you need this information?"

"For when you come back, in better times, to reclaim your property."

"I do not foresee better times."

"But you'll be back?" He slid a white envelope across the counter even as his gaze shifted greedily to my ear.

"I might. You have a wonderful selection of books."

"Well, then." He spun the card around, picked up the pencil, and licked the tip again before circling the word *SALE* in a single, definitive stroke. "Perhaps I shall save you the trouble and fill this out on your behalf?"

"You don't know my name," I said, thinking I may have met my first match.

"Sometimes," he said, without looking up, "that is for the best, isn't it?"

I opened the envelope and made quick work of thumbing through and counting the amount. "It is indeed."

Chapter 10

"I wasn't expecting it to be so girly," Quin said, standing aside to usher Dini in. "I feel like I'm hanging out in my sisters' bedroom."

Dini stepped in, understanding immediately his appraisal. The walls were painted a muted shade of rose, the drapes an antique floral pattern that matched—perfectly—the cover folded at the foot of the four-poster bed. The lamp could best be described as delicate, the desk obviously better suited as a vanity than a place for a sturdy laptop and haphazard stacks of paper. The dresser was heavy and ornate, with drawer space beyond what a weekend traveler would need; the mirror above it was tarnished at the corners. How many men and women had gazed into it, dressed for whatever festivities awaited in the ballroom? It was exactly the kind of room she dreamed of having as a girl—intentional and permanent.

She walked slowly, trailing her step along the patterned carpet. "You have a sister?"

"Three, actually. Two older, one younger. Classic middle-ish child."

She'd never bothered with family dynamics before. Instead, she fixated on the idea that a man who had sisters knew how to be kind to a woman, and she instantly relaxed.

"So, anyway," he said, taking his bag from over his shoulder and dropping it on the floor by the desk, "Here's what you came for."

In the brief moment the closet door was open, Dini noticed a heather-gray suit—the jacket sharing a hanger with a pale blue shirt and tie—a pair of soft leather dress shoes, two other shirts, and a hard-sided carry-on suitcase, a metallic-looking copper color. Quin reached to the upper shelf from which, next to the extra pillow, blanket, and iron, he took down a nondescript-looking black duffel bag.

"I've got the original box in here." He set the bag on top of the small table in front of the window. "I thought if I found anybody to show it to, they might want to see how everything's been kept." He unzipped the bag and gingerly lifted out an ancient, fragile-looking cardboard box. A shoebox, most likely its original purpose, tied with a length of loosely knotted string. "And I had to kind of stretch the string off, because that knot wasn't budging."

Dini's fingers itched in anticipation. "I think I should wash my hands. They're. . .sticky?" She winced at the immaturity of the word. "And really, before handling anything. . ."

"Sure. Of course, right through there." He pointed to the open door to the bathroom. "Watch your step." He indicated a six-inch difference in the bathroom's floor level. "It's a doozy."

Dini shrugged out of her backpack and dropped it next to his bag on the floor. Once inside the bathroom, she shut the door. The idea of sharing the moment of handwashing seemed far too intimate for strangers. The bathroom was kind of like a time machine in its own décor—sea-green tile, chipped sink, separate handles for the hot and cold water. She unwrapped the tiny bar of hotel soap and started the tap. Quin's open shaving kit was on the sink. No razor, obviously, as he wore a beard, but a small electric trimmer. A blue toothbrush stood, sharing a glass with a small tube of Crest. She picked up a black tube of Neutrogena for Men, flipped open the top, and inhaled.

That's him. She locked the scent into her memory.

Finally, she held her hands under the warm running water and lathered them with the soap, softly singing the chorus to "Mandy," turning off the water at the third repetition of the name.

"Manilow fan?" Quin was sitting on the edge of the bed, not jumping up immediately when she opened the door.

"You know how they say to sing 'Happy Birthday' to time twenty seconds for handwashing? I hate that song."

Quin stood and crossed past her. At the sink, he turned the water to its highest pressure and, not bothering to shut the door, launched into the opening verse of "Copacabana." He turned off the water and dried his hands on the same towel she'd used, saying, "See? If you tried that with jazz, you'd be washing all day."

Dini's laugh was somewhat obligatory, as the box and its mysterious contents occupied the best of her mind. Without waiting another second, she sat down and pulled it toward her, rewarded immediately by the scent of *old*. Although the string could have easily been pulled from around the cardboard corners, she went to work on the knot, spying its pattern straightaway. It wasn't anything complicated, just a basic square tying, but years had solidified the strength. She picked at it with her short, sparkly nails, thinking, *He tied this. My fingers are touching what he touched.* Not Quin's, of course, but his great-great-grandfather's. What secrets did he bind with this cord?

The knot finally loosed.

"Shall we?" Quin placed two fingers gingerly along one side of the lid, inviting her to join in the endeavor. She took a deep breath and complied, lifting it—weightlessly—off the box.

Inside were an assortment of papers, photos, and magazines. She almost wished Quin would go away. Maybe she should send him on an errand to fetch up an ice cream or coffee so she could sort and absorb at her own leisure. But then, wasn't it something to share this with another person?

"Where should we start?" That pronoun again. *We.*

"The Christmas picture," she said, eager to see the one thing she *knew* to be inside.

Quin pulled the box closer to him and rummaged gently through the contents, finally pulling out a piece of card stock, roughly five inches by seven. He held it gingerly by its edge, the image facing him. "Are you ready?"

Dini nodded.

"Close your eyes."

She did, and felt him shift slightly.

"Open them."

She hadn't bowed her head, so the first thing she saw was his eyes fixed on hers, his expression one of studied anticipation. He gave a slight inclination, and she followed.

Never could she explain the small, strangled noise that seeped from the back of her throat, but she immediately brought her hand to her mouth to catch it. There, in the beautiful pastels of antique tinted photography, stood Hedda. It was just as she described in her book. The tree, the dress. She held her hands in front of her as if clutching an invisible bouquet. Even without the future advantage of digital detail, the emerald of her wedding band shone. Her expression was one of peace—maybe not happiness, but a settled contentment, as if all was well in her chosen home. The tree, one of those so fashionable in the day, with its sparse, tinsel-draped branches, stood resplendent behind her.

And, really, a passing glance—if this were displayed on a mantel shelf, perhaps—might have yielded no reaction whatsoever. That is, if you could ignore that niggling feeling that something was *off*. Something was *wrong*.

Dini didn't need a second glance. She'd held this picture in her mind since the first time she'd read of its existence. She'd spent years filling in the details Hedda left out. The drape of the garland on the tree; the drape of the beads around Hedda's neck. And then, just behind her, over Hedda's shoulder in a gap between the branches, a pale, transparent presence. Not *transparent* per se, but translucent, because Dini could see the tree behind it. Behind *her*. A shank of dark hair covered her face, leaving the shadow of a single eye to stare from the softly blurred flesh. A cap. A coarse shoulder poking out from behind Hedda's soft, creamy arm.

And, on the back, a detail she had no reason to anticipate. A note, probably written in pencil given it was so faded as to be nearly missed:

This night began my ruin.

"There's something wrong," Dini said, holding the photograph closer to her face.

"I don't know. Looks like someone did a pretty good job—"

"This isn't how Hedda described it. She said Sallie's hand was on her shoulder. Like *touching* her. Here it isn't. And this one is tinted."

Quin got up from his chair, came around, and touched Dini's shoulder as he leaned in for a closer look. Though she was aware of the movement, the touch took her by surprise, and she jumped, knocking his chin with the top of her head. Not hard, though, because they both laughed and let out a perfectly simultaneous apology.

"I didn't think," he said. "I really wasn't trying to scare you."

"It's all right." She put the photograph on the table, and he returned to his seat, scooting it closer to hers. "But that's weird, isn't it? That she would add that detail when—" She stopped, got up, and began pacing the room, suddenly reminded of something even more disturbing. "How does this even exist? She says—you'll see in a few pages—that she destroyed the picture. Tore it up."

"The photographer obviously made two prints."

Dini went on as if he hadn't spoken. "I've always thought that was wrong of her—it could have helped later. Helped prove—"

"Prove what? This isn't real. It's a simple double exposure. Two images printed onto the same glass. Surely you can see that. I mean, it's pretty well done by 1920s standards, but looking at it now. . ."

"But why would she lie?" She began pacing again. "Because she's either lying about seeing Sallie's hand on her shoulder, or she's lying about destroying the photograph, because clearly, here it is." She reached the end of the room, turned, and walked right into Quin, who stood in her path.

"Why do you care so much about this, Dini?"

If she couldn't settle one incongruity, she'd attack another. "Why are you here?"

He shook his head, as if struck by the sudden shift in topic.

"I know you're not just playing history mystery tourist. You have a suit. And a beard trimmer."

"What are you, now? Spying on me, Nancy Drew?"

Dini pointed. "You have a suit hanging in your closet, and your beard trimmer is poking out of your kit bag." She stepped back because he was so close she had to tilt her head to look up at him. Also because he was so close she almost touched him when she pointed to his suit. Also simply because he was so close.

His posture deflated somewhat. "Okay. Here's the deal. I'm not just a high school math teacher."

She allowed herself that split second to entertain the next possible sentence. Private investigator, research historian, museum curator. . .

"I also teach a few classes at a community college, and I developed a program that would seek out nontraditional students within a connected community and group them nonhomogeneously into study and support groups."

"You—what?"

"See, nontraditional students, meaning those students who aren't enrolling straight from high school, sometimes struggle. Especially with math. There can be a gap in skills, or—if they've dropped out of high school entirely and are enrolled with a GED—or. . ." Now *he* was pacing, and Dini stood rock-still as he cut a path around her. "Even older students, because let's face it, we don't teach math the way we used to. Like maybe not the way they learned it back then. So this program lets them—or their academic counselor—plug in some info and help them meet other students to form study groups that fit with their schedule and ability. They don't always know how to seek help."

"Stop." He was speaking like one of those voices at the end of a pharmaceutical commercial. Dini held out a hand that would have caught his arm if she'd let it. "Why did you make me think that you were here just for. . ." She made a vague gesture around the room. "This."

He put his hands in his pockets, instantly transforming into something like an awkward teenager in front of her. "Because I followed you around for two hours listening to your ghost talk, and I thought you were so"—he looked away and back—"pretty. And then you were so cool with your hair and your card magic, and I thought if I told you I was here to pitch my software for creating algorithms to create nonhomogenous groupings of nontraditional community college students, you'd think I was some kind of tech nerd."

She looked meaningfully at his shoes. "Aren't you?"

He laughed, a literal *ha-ha*. "I suppose I am. Some people from Alamo Community Colleges reached out to me. I met today with one of the counselors who's helping me with the pitch. Look, this picture creeped me out, but I never considered actually coming here until this opportunity."

Truthfully, Dini hadn't heard much since Quin said she was *pretty*, but her ears locked this in. A business meeting. Not a date, not a girlfriend. Probably not. Most likely not. Not that it mattered, because Quin wasn't here to search out his roots or finish an old family story. Still. . . She kept her reaction hidden under the face she'd perfected. Already she'd been caught snooping in his closet, no need to add phone spying to her crimes.

"Some coincidence, getting a call from the same city where your great-great-grandfather lived."

"I don't believe in coincidence."

"Fate, then?"

He shook his head. "I believe that God has a plan, and that He brought me here. Put me in your ghost tour group."

"Isn't that the same thing?"

"Not at all. Coincidence and fate are random. I'm a math person. I don't do random. God is purposeful. We live in an equation of His design."

"Like an algorithm that brings nonhomogenous people together in a study group."

Quin looked pleased—no other word for it—like Bea whenever Dini could correctly identify the elements of one of her crayon-scrawled pictures. "I'd never thought of it like that before, but sure."

"Or like a card trick."

"Maybe?" He looked a bit more skeptical.

"The mark thinks I've magically made his card appear, when it was counted and hidden from the beginning."

"Exactly."

She wanted to answer back that her life had been nothing but chaos for as long as she could remember. Living on buses and trains, falling asleep in theaters and waking up in motel rooms. Her caregivers an unreliable parade of performers—singers, jugglers, dancers, dog trainers. Orphaned at sixteen, never having been a child. Having a foster mother for a best friend. Only friend, really, over the last five years spent springing between seasons of sleeplessness and scraping gigs. If her life was an equation, it was one of those crazy wall-sized ones. But she said none of this. Mostly because that very moment—isolated in time—seemed so settled. Balanced.

"What if they hadn't?" She wandered back over to the table and ran a thoughtful finger around the soft edges of the box. "If ACC hadn't called you. What was your plan for all of this?"

"I don't know, really. I didn't have a lot of time to think about it. I got pretty busy finishing the details on the software, meeting with coders, and working out glitches. All of it didn't click together until I was booking my flight and choosing a hotel."

"If all this fell in my lap, I'd cancel my life for a week and just stare at it." She reached in and gingerly lifted a large envelope. It was addressed to Irvin Carmichael, care of the San Antonio Police Station, but that address had been forwarded to an address in Virginia. A memory clicked. "You said this was a good photography trick for the 1920s."

"I didn't mean any offense."

"She didn't take this picture in the 1920s. It was Christmas 1916."

Quin raised his eyebrows. "Really? That's even more impressive."

Dini showed him the envelope. "This was mailed to Irvin Carmichael in 1925. Years later. Years after. . ." She studied the envelope again. "No return address."

"She mailed it to him?"

"She didn't mail it to him."

"How can you be so certain?"

"She said she destroyed it." Dini felt her skin flush, her throat growing tight as her voice turned reed thin. "She said there was a hand. On her shoulder."

"Hey—" He was stepping toward her, and she put her arms out like an invisible force field. It worked. He stopped. But then, perhaps sensing a weak spot, he reached for her hand and held it, his thumb pressing into her palm with just enough pressure to keep them connected.

"You have to understand." Her voice was controlled now. "I love this woman. I love her legend. My mother met her once, when *she* was a little girl, and she told me how she was like something out of a history lesson. I've read her book a thousand times. I can quote it to you." Dini closed her eyes and felt only the floor beneath her feet, the envelope in her hand, and Quin's pulse in her palm. The page appeared in her darkness. *"I thought myself quite beautiful. My gown was new, purchased on a whim only days before, its neckline broad and sleeves capped. I stared at the dark hand outlined on my white skin. How could I not have felt that? How did I not sense her behind me?"*

"Dini."

She felt the envelope slip from her fingers. Both of her hands were gripped now, and she was being led. She sat, as directed, on the bed, and opened her eyes only when she felt a weight beside her. His face was close—closer than it needed to be. He'd taken his glasses off and was looking into her eyes in a way that was far more clinical than romantic. Also, he was no longer holding her hand. Not really. He was taking her pulse. "Are you all right?"

"I'm fine." She bristled away. "I'm just feeling a little, I don't know. Angry right now. Betrayed."

His brow wrinkled in compassion where she'd feared mocking. "Hedda can't betray you, Dini. She doesn't know you. She's dead."

"But she lied."

"Maybe." The bed emitted an antique squeak as he stood. He walked over to the table, picked up the photograph, and brought it back. This time sitting a meaningful distance away. "But maybe she didn't. Do you know what this photo says to me?"

Dini held it, looked at it, looked at him, and shook her head. "What?"

"It means someone went to an awful lot of work to put the fear of Sallie White into Hedda Krause."

Chapter 11

Excerpt from

My Spectral Accuser: The Haunted Life of Hedda Krause

Published by the Author Herself

As I waged a private war against Sallie White in the dark confines of my room, the world, it seemed, stood on the threshold of a much larger conflict. Daily the newspaper told of battles fought in foreign trenches and German submarines attacking whom they wished at sea. More and more, as I introduced myself, my name would draw a leery look. *Krause.* German? And I was always quick to say that *Krause* was my late husband's name, hoping sympathy would overrule suspicion.

If I were to claim a sprig of hope, it came from the fact that I received no fewer than three Valentine cards from gentlemen I'd met over the course of my stay: two from local suitors, and one from a state senator addressed to Hedda Krause, in Residence of the Menger Hotel, with hopes that he would have the opportunity to take me to supper in the spring.

The previous year, before the first signs of his lingering illness, my late husband had lavished me with three dozen red roses (one dozen for each of our years of happiness), a box of French chocolates, and the amethyst earrings that the proprietor of Paragon Treasures most certainly had appraised on sight. This year I was content with my small tokens of admiration.

Despite being midweek, Wednesday, the bar was a bustling place, so after an early supper (alone), I took a slice of chocolate cake and a carafe of tea to my room and prepared for an evening with my novel

Tempest and Sunshine. The first sentence, "It was the afternoon of a bright October day," transported me back to the October day when I boarded a train bound for Texas.

The novel proved to be a perfect companion for the evening. I'd lived a long life without love, a short life with it, and faced an uncertain future with only one constant: myself. I curled up in bed, heedless of the crumbs. Outside the night was biting cold, but I'd cocooned myself in warmth, wearing my nightgown and robe beneath my pile of soft quilts.

This sense of contentment and satisfaction lulled me as much as did the tea and cake, and I fell into the sweetest sleep. Heavy and deep—*aware* of being overtaken, and quite happy to have been so.

Not so deep, though, that I didn't hear it. Hear *her*.

Faint and familiar. The scratching. Like whispers on wood, inviting me to wakefulness.

Tendrils of sleep tied me to my bed. Fear ripped my warmth away, even as I lay beneath the weight of comfort.

Scraaaaatch. Scraaaaatch. Scraaaaatch.

All of my bravado, my boldness, my challenge, lodged at the base of my throat like ice. But then I opened my eyes.

Most often, Sallie would come to me in darkness. Midnight hours and after when it was too dark for shadows. This night, though the hour was late, my room was fully lit, and while the scratching on the other side of my door held its same menacing quality, on *my* side, I saw home. My empty teacup in the folds of my bedding. My washstand with its collection of perfumes and creams and scented soap. My desk with its modest collection of books. Dresses draped across the furniture, stockings drying over the grate. My trunk with its lid gaping open, all of my worldly possessions within.

This was my room. My home. My territory to defend. Courage my only weapon.

I flung off the covers, sending a clattering of plate and fork and cup to the floor. In less than a breath, I was at the door, my hands steady as, in one fluid motion, I removed the chain and twisted the knob. I felt a *whoosh* of air as I opened it, heard my voice screaming curses to the wretched phantom, damning her to a hell of my choosing.

But again I was too late, moved too slowly. Hesitated too long. As before—as always—the hallway was dark and empty.

"No, no, no, no, no. . ." My protests grew in volume with each repetition. My mind swirled with madness, and I cursed her again in a stream of vulgarities I'd thought long buried. Strips of light appeared beneath two of the doors across the hall, and I clamped my hand over my mouth to bid silence.

And in that silence, my name.

"Hedda Krause. Hedda Krause."

The same broken-throated cry coming from the end of the passageway. The darkest corner, where it turned.

"Hedda Krause." Spoken from a deep, black place. The place where I'd cursed her spirit. Was she there? Calling out to me?

"Hedda Krause."

I stepped out of my room completely. The chill of the hall iced the back of my neck despite the weight of my loosely braided hair.

"Sallie." The whisper barely more than a hiss against my clenched teeth. Then again. "Sallie."

And there she was. Gruesome and gray, her work dress lank on a thin frame. I saw her first in profile, head bent down, towel draped over her arm as if ready to knock on a door in delivery. I might have thought it merely a maid, summoned by one of my fellow residents, but for the fact that I could see the darkness through her. Subtract her flickering transparency; I simply *knew*. How long had I called her name? How long had she called mine? And here we were, face-to-face. Almost.

Then, she turned.

We think we scream in our nightmares, and I suppose some do. Things I've suffered in my waking life pale in comparison to the most terrifying of gothic novels, and too often those memories roar to life in sleep. My late husband would often wake me, roused to find me shaking, my mouth open in a silent scream. Real screams, those loud shrieks women are supposed to emit, come out at the most nonsensical times. A mouse in the corner, a slip of a knife leaving blood droplets on the bread. True terror grabs at the throat, crushes it from within. And when Sallie White turned to me, I felt myself paralyzed in Henry's grip.

Slowly, how slowly she revealed herself, like a spinning dancer in a music box at the moment the tune disintegrates into elongated, discordant notes. Her cap askew, a shank of dark hair obscuring her face, revealing one staring eye and a mouth gone slack. But it was the angle—Lord help me, I can see it now—the unnatural way she held her head. Her neck twisted, so that even turned toward me, her face turned away as if weighted by one shoulder held lower than the other where the arm hung useless at her side. Now I could see the bundle of towels she held were pressed to her stomach, the corners stained dark. The center of her dress a translucent, amorphous shadow. Her feet, bare and pale, hovered above the floor.

"Hedda Krause." My name projected from the dangling phantom, but her lips did not move. Instead, there was a twitch to her shoulder before, as if with great effort, she raised her hand and presented it to me, fingers bent to a claw. Her listless legs bent into a crouch, and with an unholy sound like the call of death itself, she lunged. Her mouth stretched wide, but it was my scream that filled the hall. I'd found my voice at last, and it emitted a sound I'd never made before or since.

I'd felt her touch before and bore the remnants of it for days. I would not suffer it again. I know it seems, in the reading of these pages, as if our encounter lasted long enough for me to get my bearings and formulate a plan, but understand that it took place in less than a second. Stop now, in the midst of this page, and bring your hand before your eyes. Snap your fingers. In just that short amount of time, I saw her, heard her, turned away, and ran.

Incoherent babbles poured from my lips, leaving a trail of sound behind my steps. Heedless that I was in my dressing robe, hair loose, feet bare, I tore down the hallway and fled headlong down the stairs, my shoulder slamming against the wall at the turn. I didn't care. Blind memory guided me, fear of falling kept my balance. The shining bare floor was like ice to the soles of my feet, but I could not slip. I've learned since that the blurry forms at the edge of my vision were, indeed, fellow guests, but I had no notion of how they stared, snickered, and gossiped both that night and long after. One sharp corner, then another, and I threw myself against the heavy wooden doors.

Breathless, I panted his name. "Bert," and the man himself came out from behind the bar. In the moment, I cared nothing for decorum, propriety—whether of age or station or race. I too lunged—just as *she* had, but my target did not flinch. I ran into Bert's arms the way a child is said to run into its father's. I felt them wrap around me like strong cords, holding me against him. My face, now wet with unchecked tears, pressed into his clean white shirt. He smelled of soap and the linseed oil he used to clean the bar. His body was a solid mass, his voice low and smooth. Comforting. Lulling.

"Hush there, Miss Hedda." *Miss Hedda.* He'd never called me such a thing before, and I know it was in deference to those patrons scattered about. Had we been alone, he would have kissed the top of my head rather than simply cup his hand around it. "It's all right, people." He spoke over me, assuming a self-granted authority. "I think she's had a fright is all."

I clawed my hands to his collar, brought his head low until my lips nearly touched his ear. "She came to me."

He pushed me to arm's length. My arms, not his. "Perhaps a brandy to soothe your nerves?"

"No." I kept my eyes fixed on his face so there was nothing beyond it. "Do you understand? I saw her. I saw—" And he looked away, behind me.

"Sir. I'm sorry. She just—"

I gave myself over to Bert's grip and allowed him to turn me, slowly—just as *she* turned—to see a scowling Mr. Sylvan.

"What is the meaning of this?" He directed his question to Bert, not me. "I heard her screaming from my office. The guests are horrified."

"She had a fright is all," Bert said, dropping his touch. "Heard one too many stories about Sallie, I suppose."

"Nonsense." Mr. Sylvan turned to address the room in general. "My apologies, ladies and gentlemen. The lady is unwell, but let's not allow her to spoil your evening. Please, Bert here would love for you each to have a glass of champagne. On the house." His small hand surreptitiously gripped my upper arm, and he gave me the slightest yank as he hissed into my ear, "I will see you up to your room."

"No." I hated the whimper of that word. "I can't. I won't go up there."

"To the street then." His voice too soft to be heard beyond my shoulder. "Because in this state, there is no other place for you."

"I can't—" As if to prove my unwilling spirit, my body gave way, my legs liquefying beneath me, causing Mr. Sylvan to hold me up—a task for which he was ill-equipped.

"Please," Bert interrupted, having made no move to distribute the free champagne. "Let me take her."

"Take her?" Mr. Sylvan said, trying not to struggle beneath my weight.

"To her room. With you. She looks faint, sir."

At that, accompanied by a gasp from the crowd, I felt the entirety of my weight fall against Mr. Sylvan, who grunted as if handed a log.

"Here." In a moment unprecedented in my life, I was swept off my feet, Bert cradling me against himself as if I weighed no more than the phantom who chased me here. There were women in the bar that night sharing a Valentine's Day drink with their beaux, and I could hear the falsetto of their approval of the gesture. Bert's voice rumbled against me as he instructed one of the waiters, off duty after a long night, to get behind the bar and pour the drinks. Then it rumbled again, saying, "Just this one time, and never again," before assuming final authority to bid Mr. Sylvan to follow him upstairs.

I kept my eyes closed, my face pressed into his neck. My body recognized every step. I knew when we were in the lobby, passing the desk, the clock. I felt the lift of his legs as he took one stairstep after another. My corridor and, finally, my door, where I felt a hitch in Bert's breath and his whispered, "God above, what happened here?"

Mr. Sylvan uttered the same words, but with a distinctly different tone, and I lifted my head.

"Can you stand?" Bert asked.

I nodded, and he lowered me but stayed close enough to catch me if I were to fall. The three of us crowded in the doorway, surveying what had been my sweet, cozy room. All that I loved was obscured by a swath of disaster, as if a wind had blown through to destroy my peace. My plate and cup were broken on the ground, the carafe knocked over on my bedside table. The curtains were half tugged from their rings, the bedclothes tossed into a pile. My books—my precious little library—had been knocked from their stack, torn pages strewn around the room. I realized the scent of my perfume was so strong because the bottle had been opened and left on its side, the pricey amber contents dripping on the carpet.

"Oh, Hedda," Bert said, forgetting decorum. Even Mr. Sylvan cleared his throat in sympathy.

I took it all in with a single, sweeping glance. Strength restored, I carefully picked my steps across the room, mindful of the broken dishes, and crept up to my trunk. Lid open, as I'd left it, but the contents pulled and tossed with frantic abandon. Gowns, undergarments, hats. I dug through layers of silk and cotton, my mind fixated on a single target: the little brown box kept safely at the bottom, my entire past and future within. A great relief washed over me when I saw the intricately carved piece, but when I lifted it, I knew.

"No." Again, that word. As if it could reverse the events of the evening.

I set the box upon the bed and said something close to a prayer before lifting its lid. The sweet smell of cedar, the tufting of velvet, and nothing else. All of my treasure, every gift and token, every bit of gold, every gem, anything that would adorn my neck, my wrist, my breast, my hand—gone. Only the ring on my left hand spoke of the woman I'd been, the man I'd married.

"She took everything," I said, clutching my bedsheets, imagining her throat in my hands.

Chapter 12

Shrine seemed too strong a word. Dini preferred to think of it as a *display*. Her Hedda memorabilia—clippings and photographs, even a few personal items found on eBay fan sites. A rhinestone brooch, a monogrammed handkerchief, and most treasured, a fading snapshot of Dini's own mother, all strawberry blond and freckled, standing beside the elegant old woman. Dini knew exactly the spot where the picture had been taken, and sometimes when a long, empty afternoon stretched ahead, she'd go into the Menger lobby and plant herself for a few hours with a book, imagining what it would be like if she never had to leave.

She kept her treasures in a glass-topped table; adding the items from Quin's tattered box seemed presumptuous. He hadn't explicitly said she could *keep* everything she brought home, so they were laid out carefully on the glass. Besides the Christmas picture, there were articles from the *San Antonio Express* about the theft, sensationalizing Hedda's widowhood and calling on the scoundrels to turn themselves in to face justice. Dini had seen these articles before, but to hold the paper in her hand rather than squint at it on a screen was almost intoxicating. Odd how the newspaper accounts never mentioned the role of Sallie White's ghost. Notably, the only quoted sources were Mr. Sylvan, the property desk manager, and Irvin Carmichael, the detective investigating the case. This had always bothered Dini, the idea of the victim herself being silenced in the story, but she supposed the journalist's objective was to minimize the sensationalism of the crime. Too much focus on the ghost and nobody would try to look for the thieves. She chalked it up to the integrity of the paper, as most would have relished a good ghost story. Later, of course, when Hedda herself became somewhat of a specter on the property, articles would surface about the woman who came to the Menger Hotel and never, ever left. She even turned up in the occasional Reddit thread about little-known persons of the Alamo City or as a feature on MrsHavisham.com, a blog devoted to the true stories of eccentric women, alongside the Teddy Bear Lady at the Grand Floridian Resort. But those stories were about *after*, when Hedda became the "lady in residence" at the Menger Hotel.

It wasn't until Quin's treasure trove that she saw the ghost and Hedda linked in print in a June 1932 issue of *Spicy Detective Stories* magazine. The events were highly fictionalized, including a lurid illustration featuring a curvaceous Hedda, obviously nude but for the bedsheet barely clinging to decency, draped in the arms of a man who was a conglomeration of Bert and Mr. Sylvan—a white barkeep with a trim, dark moustache.

She read the story that Sunday night when she got home from her—*visit? Date? Encounter?*—with Quin. By the time she'd left, evening was falling, turning the room into shadows and prompting a decision: turn on lights and stay or let darkness fall.

"The Haunting of Helen Kroft," as Hedda's story was titled, started on page thirteen of the magazine and continued for five pages with columns interrupted by ads for dental paste and other men's grooming products. The sight of them called to mind Quin's shaving kit, the lingering clean man smell of his bathroom. Dini read while eating a supper of banana oatmeal, the bowl stationed a good six inches away from the antique pages. Not exactly a faithful retelling—this story took place in an unidentified city where the "Merchants" Hotel was haunted by the ghost of a murdered debutante—but there were too many details for it to have been authored by anyone other than someone with firsthand knowledge of the events. A Google search of the author's name, Herb Trellis, proved that "The Haunting of Helen Kroft" was either his only, or most successful, literary enterprise. It was published fifteen years after the event, thirty years before Hedda would pen her autobiography.

She texted Quin the minute she read the last line, just before 10:30 p.m.

D: Maybe HT was one of the guests? At the bar?
Q: HT?????
D: Spicy Detective author
Q: Are you calling my gggrandfather a spicy detective?

Dini smiled at the phone screen, picturing exactly what he would look like if he were speaking straight to her. Of course, he hadn't read the detective magazine.

Or the old *Photoplay* magazine, either, though she wasn't sure why it was included with the other pieces at all. She spent Monday morning poring through it, looking for any article or sidebar that might relate back to Hedda, but found nothing. It was dated 1918, so maybe Carmichael was just a fan? But why hide it?

D: When did Ggg Carmichael get married?
Q: Waiting to do presentation.
D: Will one of your sisters know?
Q: I'll ask.
D: Thnx.

Because maybe this was just something old Irvin Carmichael stashed away from his wife, along with all that old business about Hedda. All those old feelings.

D: Have you met Ggg Carmichael yet?

Q: He died before I was born.

D: I meant in the book.

Q: No.

D: No???

Q: Been busy but I will. I promise.

Thirty minutes later, Quin forwarded a picture of the front page of what was obviously a family Bible. The first name listed was Irvin Carmichael, followed by the date of his marriage, the birth of his children, the date of his wife's death, and—shortly after the marriage of his oldest son—his own death, followed years later by the birth of a grandson, etc. Dini zoomed in, looking at all of the careful detail, feeling a pang of longing. No such record existed of her own family, only boxes stuffed with old show bills and reviews. She zoomed back out to see Quin's birthday—October 15, snapping perfectly into place with his license. Something else, though, nagged at her, and she went back to the top. She looked at the first entry on the Bible page then took out the photograph of Hedda that Quin had given her over empty breakfast dishes at Mi Tierra.

The handwriting was a perfect match.

Detective Carmichael wrote the verse on the back of the photo. It was a sentiment he and Hedda shared.

She picked up her ghost tour costume at the dry cleaners, cleaned out her car for Wednesday's drive, treated herself to a fresh manicure, and packed her smaller case for the gig. This was no children's birthday party, so no balloons, rings, scarves, or flash paper were needed. This was all cards, so nothing but a green felt table topper and a few fresh decks.

Through it all, she was tethered to her phone. As busy as Quin must have been with his meetings and pitches and presentations, he found time to send her message after message. Monday evening he texted twenty times, practically offering a play-by-play of his reading.

Q: Hey! Just read the part you were quoting.

Q: There's the hand.

Q: Hedda Krause. Ghost summoner.

Q: A Poltergeist GIF.

Q: Bert's a good guy.

Q: Now I want a spotted dog.

Q: GIF of spotted dog.

Dini's responses were brief. One form or another of Keep reading, until he texted nothing but a full box of ghost emojis.

Then his name and number appeared. She answered the call, and his face filled the screen, exactly as she'd been seeing in her mind's eye behind each text. He wasn't wearing his glasses, and for the first time she noticed that his lashes were a dense fringe, two ginger shades darker than his brows. It occurred to her that she would never be able to look at him so comfortably and for so long if he were here in the flesh beside her. The device turned him into an artifact. She could let her gaze linger on the dark freckle above the peak of his brow, wonder if the narrowness of his nose came from his maternal line, and note how certain vowel sounds (particularly the long *a*) brought his lips to open more widely on one side of his mouth than another. And somehow, it didn't bother her in the least that he might be doing the same thing. In fact, she *hoped* he was. Seeing her image in the corner, she angled her face, having learned from Arya that nothing is less flattering than looking at a camera head-on.

"This is nuts." That's how he started the conversation. No "Hello" or "How's it going?" or any of the acceptable small talk that Dini despised.

"Some people thought so."

"Can you imagine? Being there that night, and this woman comes screaming into the bar?" He rolled his eyes upward in silent laughter. "Hey, are those *stars* behind you?"

"Twinkle lights." Dini was in her bedroom, all dark save for the pattern of small white lights tacked in a webbing along one wall. She panned the phone, giving him a better view of the design, then returned. "I'm not a huge fan of the dark. Too much time folded up in a box waiting for my dad to cut me into pieces."

"You sleep with those on?"

"I fall asleep, yeah. They're on a timer."

"I could not sleep with those on. I need one hundred percent blackout darkness."

"Then it's a good thing we don't sleep together." The minute the words were out of her mouth, she heard their implication and held the phone away while she buried her face in her pillow.

Quin's laughter came through. "That, and the fact that we don't know each other."

At least it was dark enough that he couldn't see her blushing when she faced the screen again. "Back to Hedda. Do you believe her?"

His angle shifted, and she heard every creak of the antique bed. "Honestly? I don't know. Do I believe something frightened her? Absolutely."

"But you don't think it was the ghost of Sallie White."

He closed his eyes. Tightly. "No."

"Because you don't believe in ghosts."

"Right." He opened his eyes. "And c'mon, Dini. You don't either."

Dini stretched out on her bed, propping the phone on the pillow beside her. "Why do you say that?"

"Because of what you said on the tour. That a haunting is just something that stays with you. So, a ghost is just a memory. A person you can't leave behind."

"Hedda was haunted by Sallie. Her story and her tragedy. That could have been Hedda's life too."

Quin said nothing, allowing Dini to trail out her reasoning. She remembered the passage in the book when Hedda tore the picture until there was nothing left but her face and Sallie's. In the darkness now, despite the twinkle lights, that was all that existed of Dini and

Quin. His face filling the screen, hers tucked in the corner above it. She knew in that moment she would be haunted by him forever.

"So," she said, welcoming him back to the conversation. "What's your reason?"

"My reason?"

"Why don't you believe? Is it a religious thing?"

"Kind of? I really did give this some thought after you left last night and. . . Hold on." He was shifting as he spoke. She heard a rustling of turning pages, and when his image was clear and still again, he was wearing his glasses and reading from a Bible. Not a hotel Bible, but something small and soft with gilded pages. His own. "So, I had to do some googling, because I knew there was something like this in here, but I couldn't remember exactly where. So I marked it. It says here about the dead"—he began reading—" 'When they breathe their last, they return to the earth, and all their plans die with them.' "

"And that's it?"

He took off his glasses again and looked straight at her. Straight *into* her. "For their plans, their consciousness, their spirit, yes. But we have memories and stories. Sallie's story keeps her alive. I know I'll never forget her. I'll never forget Hedda."

"You haven't even finished the book."

"I don't need to. But I will. It's late, though. And I have an eight o'clock meeting tomorrow morning in Universal City? Is it far?"

"Not really. About fifteen minutes."

"They're sending a car at seven fifteen. Then I'm meeting with teachers at a dual-credit high school housed on the campus. Then dinner with reps from all the colleges."

"Okay, okay. . .I get it. I won't bug you with Hedda updates."

"No! Please do. I mean, you don't bug me. I love this all, really. Being a part of this story—"

"You haven't even gotten to your part yet."

"I will. By the time I see you again." Then something happened—a nanosecond of a change in his face, like a hot bit of realization flitting across his features. Had they been just talking on the phone, if Dini had nothing but the stars on the walls in her eyes, she might have missed it. She would have heard the catch in his voice, maybe, or wondered about the deeper, huskier tone of the words that followed, but she *saw* it. That unguarded moment before he said, "I actually can't wait to see you again."

Those were the words, and that was the face that drifted through Dini's stars long after her phone screen went black. The silence of her room settled around her, and where she might have turned on some music or a podcast to help her busy mind settle as well, tonight she didn't want any kind of barrier between her memory and his voice. She was just plugging the phone into its charger for the night when it buzzed—another text from Quin.

Q: Are you sitting down?

Dini ignored the absurdity of the question and watched the dots on the screen as Quin was typing.

Q: So I've been messaging with my sister and. . .

Below it, a photograph, and she sat straight up, heart thudding, hands shaking, her entire body in such a tremble that she didn't trust her ability to successfully send a reply.

Q: Dini??? I'm calling you.

Her phone buzzed and she took the call, not knowing if her power of speech would be any better than her power to type.

"Dini?" Everything about him exhibited concern. "Are you okay? You look. . ."

"Is that what I think it is?"

"Yes."

"That is Detective Irvin Carmichael's notebook?"

"It is."

"Why didn't you bring it?"

"Honestly—it wasn't with the rest of the stuff I took. My sister has it. She has a thing for notebooks, journals. This was in the top drawer of his bureau—up in the attic along with more personal things, I think.

I called her a while ago to catch her up on. . .everything. Anyway, long story short, she's Fed-Ex-ing this to me tomorrow. You'll be reading it Wednesday evening."

"You could just ask her to send pics of the pages." Even as she said it, she prayed he wouldn't.

"Are you kidding? And miss a chance to see it with you? No way."

"Now you have to finish reading so you'll know the guy before it gets here. I've had a crush on him forever, you know."

"So, I'm in competition with my great-great-grandfather? That's not creepy at all."

"Not so much competition as—"

"Fulfillment?" He waggled his eyebrows.

Dini laughed, letting them both off the hook. "Tell your sister thank you."

Chapter 13

Excerpt from
My Spectral Accuser: The Haunted Life of Hedda Krause
Published by the Author Herself

Had it only been a robbery of all my worldly goods, I don't know that Mr. Sylvan would have brought the police in so quickly or given them full authority to assemble and question every guest on the property. But there had been some destruction in the room—at the very least, a mess created—and that sort of disrespect for the Menger in all of her majesty would not be tolerated. Doors were knocked upon, robes and slippers donned, and erstwhile sleeping (or otherwise engaged) room occupants were herded to the lobby to be gathered among the settees and questioned by a fleet of uniformed officers.

What did you hear?

What did you see?

What do you know?

I deemed the entire operation ridiculous, for why would a skilled thief hide within the scene of the crime when a dark city and a myriad of escape routes waited right outside the door? I voiced as much to Mr. Sylvan, who countered with an argument that sometimes the best place to hide is within plain sight.

The entire evening's activities were helmed by Detective Irvin Carmichael. I knew he was in charge long before our introduction. He stood at the apex of the second-floor balcony, stoic and still. *Still*, rather, with the exception of the almost imperceptible movement of his head and the constant scribbling in his notebook.

I was the last person Detective Carmichael—hereby known as

Carmichael, as his title always made me uncomfortable, and his Christian name a least favorite—to be interviewed. He told me he wanted a "clean" view of the scene and circumstances, not one tainted by what I, the victim, would want him to find. He told me too later, in private conversations that will remain so, that I appeared quite fetching with my hair tumbled loose around my shoulders and eyes a-sparkle with agitation.

I insisted we not conduct our interview in the middle of the lobby where, whether from the landing or through the windows, the thieves themselves might be watching. Instead, we went into the Menger bar, to one of the booths along the back wall, with Bert given charge to keep away any prying eyes.

We sat on the same side of the booth, his body shielding mine like a wall. He was not a particularly tall man, but he was solidly built. Stripped of his overcoat, it was clear he didn't have a soft bit of flesh to him. Everything about him reminded me of a bulldog—his build, his stance, the set of his jaw, his fixed attention. His hair was a coppery red, worn straight and short, brushed dry without a hint of cream, and every exposed bit of his flesh riddled with freckles. Face, brow, hands—up past his wrists. I'd never known a grown man to be so featured, and it served to tamper what might otherwise have been a severe persona.

After one small brandy to settle my nerves, Bert kept us warm with tea (for me) and coffee (for him) while we talked. As Carmichael was left-handed, I could not see all that he wrote in his little notebook. His massive freckled hand shielded the words, but I assumed he was merely recording my responses.

"You saw no one?" he asked, his moss-green eyes focused steadily on mine.

"I saw Sallie White," I replied calmly.

"Sally White has been dead nearly forty years."

"I can only tell you what I saw, Mr. Carmichael."

Then, after an exhalation that carried evidence of a cigarette habit, he scratched a line in his notebook. If he objected to my calling him *Mister* as opposed to *Detective* he gave no indication, only telling me later that it was the first sign of my indelibly stubborn spirit.

"And you heard nothing, Mrs. Krause?"

"I heard my name."

"Can you describe the voice?"

"Like that of a woman who had her throat crushed by a jealous husband."

More notes.

"And I can tell you," I continued, "this was not an isolated incident."

"You've seen her before?"

"This is the first I've seen her. But I've heard her many times. She's made it a habit to call to me. To say my name out in the darkness."

The tip of his pen scratched against the paper, reminding me of the *scratch, scratch* on my door. Without looking up, he asked, "Does this interrupt your sleep?"

"It sometimes prevents my sleep."

He made an affirmative noise, turned the page, and wrote something worthy of three bold underscores. "Do you find a glass of brandy to be helpful on most occasions?"

His question pinned me as much as his body and the booth. "No more than any other person. No more than is healthy or acceptable."

He held up a hand in defense. He had two freckles on his palm, and in that moment I wanted very much to kiss them. I told him as much one night, as we sat in the dark, his notebook between us, and he laughed, saying that any woman who took on the task of kissing all of his freckles would be lipless in the end.

"Easy, Mrs. Krause. I'm just trying to determine your habits. Your pattern, because the thief might have been doing the same thing. For example, are you a frequent visitor here in the bar?"

I glanced at Bert, who was on his way with a fresh pot of coffee. "I am not."

"Do you often drink in your room?"

"I do not. And furthermore, I'd had just one glass of wine with my dinner this evening, so if you want to pursue a theory that my visit from Sallie White was nothing more than an apparition brought on by alcohol, you are pursuing logic's folly."

He grinned. Not so much with his lips, which remained thin and set, but a spray of fine wrinkles unfurled from the corners of his green eyes.

"Logic's folly. I've never heard that before."

"I think you will find with me, Mr. Carmichael, quite a few things you have never heard before."

"Then let's take it a bit further." He gave a twist of his thick neck, assuring Bert was out of earshot, I presume, and turned his body, laying one arm across the back of the booth like a fallen branch. "Why don't you try telling me something no person here has heard before?"

I held myself straight, keeping my breath even. "What do you mean?"

"Tell me three things, Mrs. Krause. Three truthful things that nobody here knows."

"I assure you, Mr. Carmichael, everybody here knows exactly what I intend for them to know."

"And I assure *you*, Mrs. Krause, that unless necessary, I will keep your information known only to myself. First, how much cash would you estimate was stolen from you?"

I named a figure with such immediacy, his brows (freckled between the fine ginger hair), shot up in surprise before he wrote it down. "That took very little calculation, Mrs. Krause. Are you always so good with figures?"

"When one envelope contains all the money a person has in the world, that person knows the total to the dime, Mr. Carmichael."

"And so you are destitute?"

"Quite."

"No family?"

"None."

He leaned back a bit and somehow became more imposing. "Mr. Sylvan said you were a widow."

"I am."

"Then you have family?"

"My husband had family. I do not."

Carmichael later told of wanting both to throttle and embrace me after that remark. Throttle, because my evasiveness was not helpful. Embrace, because he thought in the moment that I was the loneliest woman he had ever met. He turned to yet another clean page in his notebook, wrote a bit, and slid it over to me.

"Answer these three questions, Mrs. Krause. And to make it easier for you, I'll only require one to be truthful."

"Why do I feel as if I am a suspect rather than a victim of a heinous crime?"

He said nothing, only held my gaze and pushed the notebook nearer to me. His handwriting was that of an educated man, neat and even, with a uniformly sharp angle to the left. I could detect a slight smearing of the ink and registered a light stain along the side of his smallest finger.

He'd written:

What is your name?
In which city is your husband's death certificate filed?
In what state were you married?

I read the first question aloud. "You know my name."

"If so, then I have your truthful answer. I'm going to step outside."

He left, taking a silver cigarette holder from his breast pocket and a match from the shot glass on the bar. He had the cigarette lit and between his lips before opening the door, leaving me to worry that he didn't take his heavy overcoat with him. I could hear sleet hitting the window.

He'd left his pen, still warm from his grip, and I held it over the page. Such questions. Such easy questions for any other woman. One truthful answer seemed a fair request. I wrote, my hand trembling equally with both the fact and the fiction.

The door opened, and Carmichael came back in, his face flushed between its freckles. At the same moment, Mr. Sylvan walked in through the hotel entrance and Bert stepped out from behind the bar. Carmichael acknowledged both men with a nod of his head, then made his way straight toward me. I could smell the cigarette and damp of the night. He didn't wear a wedding ring—few men did in those days—and I wondered if there was a woman in his house who would press her face into his broad shoulder and breathe him in. I had to grip the table to keep from doing so.

He reached down for the notebook. "Are we done here?"

"We are." Though, even then, I knew we weren't.

He thanked me, touching the notebook to his temple in an odd salute, and held out his arm. "Then I shall walk you down to Mr. Sylvan, who will, I am sure, escort you to your room. I understand he has set his staff of brownies to put it right for you."

Brownies. A nod to his Scottish origins.

I took his arm and brought myself out of the booth—an action that has yet to be easy for a lady to accomplish. He gave my arm a reassuring pat once I was standing next to Mr. Sylvan. "You'll see to it that our Mrs. Krause passes the night safely?"

"As I have these past three months, sir." His moustache twitched with the effort of containing a sneer.

"Good, then. I'll be in touch."

Carmichael left by the street entrance, wishing a good night to Bert, who returned the same. The moment the door closed behind him, I felt the same ball of fear that I had when I ran into this bar hours before.

"I don't know if I can go back there."

"Very well," Mr. Sylvan said without a hint of humor. "I'll have my *brownies* pack your things. I'll even have Bert here escort you across the street to the Emily Morgan."

"She took all of my money. You know I can't go anywhere else. Please—" I touched his sleeve, pleading, "Let me have another room?"

"I wouldn't give you another room if we had one. Since you've no problem putting yourself on display, I'll allow you to spend the night in the lobby. Prop yourself up on one of the sofas. That or the sidewalk. As you're so far a paying guest, I'll see to it you get a blanket. Those are your options. I've other guests to attend to. Please do let me know your preference."

And he left, in direct defiance of Carmichael's orders.

I looked to Bert, my arms folded tightly against myself for warmth. For strength. "Walk with me?"

"You know I can't." He stepped closer, touching a single finger to my elbow. All of the patrons had been chased from the bar for my interview with Carmichael, but the door was not locked. Someone could come in at any moment. "Last thing you need is more scandal. Now, you've had a fright, but you haven't done nothing wrong. I can't walk with you, but I can walk behind you, sure as anything. And just see if any of them in the lobby will have something to say."

"Thank you," I said, knowing I was speaking to the only friend I had in the world.

His eyes held me, his steps filled the wake of fear mine left behind. Out of the bar, down the hall, and through the lobby still dotted with guests—curious and festive. Hushes fell as I passed, and I left a trail of silence like a field of grass trampled behind me. I could only guess as to the expression on Bert's face, the size to which he'd puffed himself, the implied threat in his posture and gait. He walked with me to the bottom of the stairs. Once there, I turned and whispered, "Thank you," and he tipped an invisible hat.

Carmichael was correct. My room had been put to rights. Were it not for the thudding in my chest, I might never suspect that a crime of such supernatural horror had occurred only hours ago. My bed was turned down, everything neatly arranged on my desk and vanity. My trunk was closed. Every garment that had been draped about the room had been put away, including the stockings that had been drying over the grate. I noticed a teapot and cup on the bedside table, and a touch revealed it to be warm. I poured a cup, sloshing a bit with my shaking hand, and sat on the edge of my bed to drink it.

The night stretched before me, and I knew I would not sleep. I had no desire to try, to even lie upon the bed. I took my teapot and my cup, my grip now resolved, over to my desk. Once settled, I drew a fresh page of hotel stationery and penned the now familiar salutation to my husband's sons. Ink poured forth as I explained my plight, pleading for mercy—and what was owed to me.

Then, glancing aside for thought, a glimmer caught my eye. A wink from the corner of the room. Not a reflection; the light was not strong or bright enough for that. Nonetheless, an existence made itself known. I put down the pen and went to my knees, my hand finding the attention-seeker immediately. My earring, the amethyst. I clutched it like a promise, brought it to my lips, and kissed the stone. As I was in a position of prayer, I offered one of thanks to the God who always seemed to rescue me. One earring would be useless for adornment, but the gem held value. It wasn't much, but it was *here*. And it was *mine*.

Without leaving the floor, I reached up and grabbed the unfinished letter. I balled it within my other fist before crumpling my body in imitation. *Those brats*, I thought, picturing their names on the page. *Fat, drooling monsters.* It was just a matter of time now before they found me. Before they took the last of any good thing I'd ever have in my life. I knew this as well as I knew the pattern of the carpet on the floor beneath my face. I knew this because I was a fool. It had taken only one glimpse into a moss-green eye, one moment seduced by the scent of cigarettes, and one question that I'd answered with the truth.

Chapter 14

Excerpt from

My Spectral Accuser: The Haunted Life of Hedda Krause

Published by the Author Herself

I brewed for days, fearful to leave my room. In fact, I didn't, choosing instead to order up pots of tea and simple meals of toast and cheese and fruit. Even of that, I ate little. Twice Mr. Sylvan tried to summon me by sending a note, and I responded to each by saying I felt too ill to speak to anyone. The poor messengers were sent away without even a nickel for a tip.

Midmorning on the third day, I answered a knock at my door to reveal Mr. Sylvan himself, shadows under his eyes and an overall weary expression on his face.

"Mrs. Krause, there's someone to see you—"

"I've no wish to see anyone, Mr. Sylvan."

I attempted to close my door, but he stepped forward just enough to ensure that I would crush his small foot if I did so. "It is Detective Carmichael. He's requested an interview with you, and when I told him of the unlikelihood that you would come down, he informed me that he would carry you down himself, and I am inclined to believe him." He spoke the entire sentence in a single breath. "Now, please, Mrs. Krause, you have caused me enough embarrassment for an entire career. Just put yourself together and come downstairs. Fifteen minutes."

I did not take issue with his final statement, being in no shape to meet or visit with anyone. My hair was ratted and loose, my skin dry, my dressing gown stained with jam and dusted with crumbs. I looked every bit a madwoman deserving to be locked away, and the survival instinct that had guided me since I was a small girl kicked in. My hair was given the most attention, brushed until it crackled, then braided and pinned. A shoddy hairstyle is the first giveaway of class; the truly destitute don't have the time or resources for such grooming. Anyone can wash a face or put on a clean, serviceable dress, but unkempt hair will remain unkempt without the proper ministration. A few precious dollops of my face cream brought a healthy sheen to my skin, and my best day dress had been returned from the cleaners the week before.

"Oh, Hedda," I said to my reflection, satisfied, "with three minutes to spare."

Carmichael was waiting for me by one of the large green fronds in the lobby. He stood as I approached, and I wondered if he realized how pleased he looked to see me. Later, in one of our cozy evening chats on that very same sofa, he would confess that he preferred my look on the first night we met, because he imagined that was what I would look like first thing in the morning, and I'd turned to liquid under his words. But *this* morning we were still all business. I extended my hand. He took it and asked if I was feeling any better.

"What I'm feeling," I said, "is hungry. I haven't had breakfast this morning. Shall we talk in the dining room over some eggs?"

He gestured with his hat, and I led the way, feeling the tips of his fingers on the back of my arm, just above my elbow. Guiding me? Guarding me? Ready to grip me if I ran away?

I ordered a fried egg and two pancakes, urging Carmichael to order too as it would be Mr. Sylvan's treat. He kept to a cup of coffee, however, and took his detestable notebook out of his coat pocket and dropped it on the table.

"I looked over every officer's interview notes," he said, flipping it open. "They talked to all of the guests. Nobody heard or saw anything unusual until you came down the stairs."

"And you believe them?" I looked at him over the rim of my cup. "All?"

"Yes. Right now I've no reason not to."

"But you have reason not to believe me?"

"You're claiming to have been robbed by a ghost, Mrs. Krause."

"No." I extended a finger of correction. "I *saw* a ghost, and when I was running in fear for my life, my room was robbed."

"A coincidence of occurrence?"

"We often taunted each other."

"Taunted?"

"She'd scratch at my door or howl my name, and I would sometimes call to her, daring her to show her face."

He wrote. My food arrived, and without a momentary care, I dove in and took quick, successive bites, like a farm boy brought in from the fields. Carmichael chuckled.

"Hungry?"

"I've not been allowed to leave my room." It was an exaggeration but one designed to inspire pity. I learned later that it did not. "Anyway, as I said, she teases and mocks me endlessly."

"But this is the first you've seen her?"

"Yes." I shoveled a bit of pancake, remembered, and said, "No." I took the time to chew and swallow, pondering the better or worse of my telling. But then, what could be worse? "I saw her once before in a photograph."

"A photograph of Sallie White?"

"Of her ghost, yes. I posed for a photograph, and when the print was delivered, an apparition appeared behind me. It was her."

"How could you tell if you'd never seen her?"

"I know. A woman knows. A woman recognizes an enemy for what she is."

"And you think Sallie White is your enemy?"

"Not the poor woman herself, God rest her soul." He repeated my words and made a brief sign of the cross. A good Catholic boy.

"Her ghost."

"Yes. But you sound like you don't believe me."

"I'd believe you more if you showed me the photograph." He turned a page in his notebook, preparing.

"I burned it." I speared a mouthful of egg and took a deep breath before shoving it into my mouth.

Carmichael sighed, knowingly. "Of course you did."

"You don't believe me?" It had become a refrain in our conversation.

He was sitting in the chair opposite me and committed his first break in etiquette by propping his elbows on the table, doing so with enough force to make the cups jump in their saucers. I, however, remained perfectly calm. At least a dozen men have treated me with violence, and I could see in his eyes that he didn't have a heart to hurt me. Later he asked, "A dozen?" And when I nodded yes, he took me in his arms and said he'd find and kill them all if I only gave him their names. I laughed against his sleeve because, of course, I couldn't name them. I'd been a child.

Now, though, he stared me down and said through gritted teeth, "I don't believe you saw a bloody ghost."

Bloody. "You don't believe there *was* a ghost? Or you don't believe I *saw* a ghost?"

"Both."

"Then what is your theory, Detective?"

"Mr. Sylvan said you are always"—he flipped through his notebook and found the page—"*spotty* with your payment. He says he never knows from one week to the next if he is going to get even a dollar from you."

"That's not true. I—"

"Says you ingratiate yourself with other guests, getting them to buy you supper or invite you to join their party. Says you spend a good bit of time with our friend Bert in the bar."

"Bert has been a friend to me when no one else has."

"Mr. Sylvan says you have a lot of friends."

Oh, how I hated the way he said the word, dragging it through every bit of mud and filth I'd worked so hard to rid from my skirts.

"Mr. Sylvan hates me."

"That doesn't make him a liar."

"And what makes me a liar?"

Instead of answering, he ran the pages of his notebook across his thumb before opening it to rest on the page where I'd answered his questions.

I set down my fork, finally sated.

"You want my theory?" he said. "I think you ran out of money, then chose a night when this place was packed with people and ran screaming from your room, saying you were robbed."

"I wasn't robbed when I went *screaming from my room.*" I matched the timbre of my voice to his in near-perfect mimicry. "I was robbed *after* I ran from my room."

"So you say."

"So I say."

"How do we know you didn't hide your money and your jewels to make it look like a robbery?"

"Did your uniformed elves or hotel staff find anything when they were putting my room to right?" I thought of the single amethyst earring I had stashed in my pocket. Had it been overlooked? Or left to taunt me?

"They did not. But then, there's a chance such a fortune never existed at all."

At this, I laughed aloud, taking no measures to temper my outburst into something ladylike and demure. "I wear—rather, *wore*—my jewels every day. Every evening. Scarcely did a day go by that I didn't receive a comment on one of my pieces, which I admit I found odd, given that it is quite rude to speak of one's wealth in such an open, curious manner."

"Did you have any record of an appraisal for their value?"

This question riled me, and I felt the survival instinct of my premarriage days kicking in. "Are you suggesting my jewels were fake?"

"I'm not suggesting anything."

"I have proof." How rewarding it was to see him sit back in surprise. "A few weeks ago, I took some of my pieces to a—"

"Pawn shop?"

"*Dealer* in fine jewelry. At least, that is how he was described to me by Mr. Sylvan." I dripped the man's name with contempt before describing in detail the items sold, and—with disgust—the price paid. "I will go with you right now to him."

"What day was this?"

I furrowed my brow, thinking, and he produced a little calendar from within the pages of his notebook. The card was embossed with vines and roses in the corners, with six months of the year printed on each side.

"Well," I said, holding it first close then far away, attempting to focus on the tiny boxes, "isn't this nice? A little something from your wife to help you remember your anniversary?" I kept my eyes trained on the calendar to give the illusion that I didn't care how he would answer.

"I'm not married."

"Sweetheart, then?" I zeroed in on February. "Is there a birthday somewhere on here circled with a heart?"

I heard him tapping his pen. "What's the name of the shop, and when did you go?"

I told him and set down the calendar while he made a note. "Just give me five minutes to pop up to my room and freshen up, then—"

"You're not going with me."

"But he'll remember me."

"I don't need him to remember you. I need to see proof of the transaction."

"Then, here." I took the earring out of my pocket and pressed it into his hand. "Show him this. He'll remember. He wanted very much to buy them."

"Them?"

"It's an earring, silly. They come in twos." For measure, I tapped at my empty earlobes, remembering how they had often been complimented for their dainty beauty.

"Where is the other?"

I pursed my lips. "Sallie White has it. This is all I have left."

He considered it, rolling it across his palm with his thumb. "Then I'll ask if anyone has tried to pawn a single earring." He dropped it in his pocket as if it were nothing more than a matchbook. "Wait in the lobby for me."

"Afraid I'll run off?'"

"Maybe. I get a feeling you've been a runner before."

Back within the hour, Carmichael found me in a favorite spot, sitting next to the fireplace, the morning's fire burned down, reading a copy of the newspaper thoughtfully left behind by a guest. The story of the robbery had not made the front page but had been given a single column in the section with other tales of petty larceny and minor violence.

"Reading about yourself, I see?" He took off his hat and asked to sit in the chair opposite, making me wish I'd opted to sit on the little sofa instead.

"Hardly." I folded the paper and set it on the small table between us. "I see very little detail that would apply to my account."

"Well, you can thank me for that." He'd walked in with a cigarette and tossed the remains into the fire. "I talked to the editor and said he was going to hear a lot of crazy details but to ignore them. If we can act like this was just an ordinary small crime, our thief might get comfortable. Lazy, maybe even try to hock some of his ill-gotten goods at a shop like the lovely one I just visited."

I leaned forward and cooed, "So you *do* believe me?"

"Your story about going to Paragon Treasures, I'm afraid, isn't going to do your case any good." He opened his notebook and proceeded to read off a list of names, looking up as he finished. "No record of you, Mrs. Krause."

"Read them again," I said, listening harder. "There!" I stopped him. "Mrs. Dorrit. That's me. I didn't actually give him my name, but I bought a copy of the novel *Little Dorrit* by Charles Dickens. He has quite a nice collection of books. Did you notice that, Mr. Carmichael? Do you read?"

He marked the page with his finger and closed his notebook. "Why didn't you give him your name?"

I sat back. "It's embarrassing, I suppose. Being reduced to such circumstances. Did you show him the earring? Did he recognize it?"

"I did, and he did. So someone out there knew you had a tidy sum of cash, and valuables besides."

I lowered my voice. "Do you think it was Mr. Sylvan? I've never trusted him."

"Did you know this guy was putting down a false name? Because, you see, a transaction like this, conducted with a false identity, makes you both look bad. Do you know who gives a fake name to a pawn broker? A thief trying to unload stolen goods. And if the broker *knows* he's dealing with a thief? Makes him a fence from one criminal to the next."

He reached out, the amethyst pinched between his fingers, but I kept my hands clasped in my lap. "Keep it. What use have I for one earring?"

"You could sell it. Get yourself started someplace else."

"And who would buy a single earring?"

"I think that fellow would buy just about anything that sparkles."

A new hopelessness washed over me, and tears came—unbidden and profuse. I covered my face, and when I heard him say, "Hedda," I could feel his breath on the back of my hands. He was on his knees beside my chair, his face level to mine, and so close that I could see dots of tinier freckles interspersed within the larger ones. We did not touch each other, not in any physical way, but we each gave off an anticipatory tremor that bound us as strongly as any embrace. Slowly, I lowered my hands, resting them at the edge of my knees. Had I unfurled a finger, it would have touched the button on his coat.

"I am not a thief," I said, keeping my words barely above a whisper, making no more noise than the hiss of our dying fire. "I have been many things in my life, but I've stolen nothing."

"What have you been, Hedda?"

"I have no doubt you'll know soon enough, Mr. Carmichael. You needn't hear it from me."

He stood, a small *click* emitting from his knee, though he didn't acknowledge it. Notebook once again nestled in his pocket, he donned his hat and turned halfway to leave before looking back, as if suddenly remembering something. "One more thing. That photographer you mentioned? With the studio?"

I cleared my throat. "Yes. J. P. Haley. What did he have to say for himself?"

"Nothing. Turns out he doesn't exist."

Chapter 15

Dini woke Wednesday morning moments before the chorus of Barry Manilow's "Daybreak" served its programmed purpose of being her alarm. She unplugged her phone and rolled back into her pillows, scrolling through the stream of messages that flowed between her fingers and Quin's throughout the previous day and long into the night. Bits of his day, his purpose—funny details about the sincere hearts of Community College academia, questions about the ever-present streamers and eggs and paper flags.

D: It's Fiesta. You wouldn't understand.

He sent her a picture of two ducks flapping happily in a campus fountain, then a second with his mock-frightened face in the corner—a selfie with the ducks banished to the background.

D: don't tell me you're afraid of ducks.

Q: ducks in the picture appear smaller than they are in real life.

They made plans for lunch (burgers), and she coached him through the menu at Alamo Café (green chile chicken enchiladas), and sometime around eight in the evening he texted that he was in his room, and he'd ordered up chocolate cake and tea in Hedda's honor and was reading.

Q: Detective Carmichael just came on the page.

D: Handsome guy, isn't he?

Q: Hedda seems to think so.

D: Keep reading.

He interspersed their conversation with reaction GIFs that she perfectly placed to moments in the book, along with a screen shot of the exact location of Carmichael's notebook en route at that moment.

D: Cannot wait!!!!!

Q: Why do I feel you only want me for my memorabilia?

D: Because you are a very smart guy. lol.

Flirting was so much easier in text messages, though she found she had just as little control over her fingers as she did her tongue, with quippy responses flying out so fast she imagined tiny jolts of lightning beneath her fingers. Still, she appreciated the invisible communication, given that she had a semipermanent color cream on her hair and a charcoal mask to get rid of what she lovingly called the famous Blackstone blackheads. She'd set Quin's number to notify with the first warbling notes of Bread's "If" and was rinsing her face when the song summoned her.

Q: The end.

D: Of the book, not Hedda.

Q: You didn't tell me it was a romance.

D: Every story is a romance.

That was the last text of the night, and as she read it in the pale morning, she found herself smiling through the entire chain. Laughing just where she'd laughed yesterday.

When they set eleven as the time she'd pick Quin up at the hotel, it seemed perfectly reasonable. Now, after lazing in bed reading text messages, the hours had been swallowed up. She'd done some reconsideration on her outfit for this show, now wanting something that Quin would appreciate as well as her audience. This was new, this idea of dressing for a man. Audiences, yes. Slinky black for the magician's theater, kooky cool for children's parties, jeans and T-shirts for school functions, silk jacket and slacks for private parties. She chose a black, sleeveless turtleneck sheath dress. Its modest length came to her knees, but the fabric hugged her figure. Arya had been with her when she tried it on, declaring Dini looked like a hot cartoon character bad girl. With a nod to spring, she added a wide belt embossed with floral stitching and slipped her feet into a pair of pale yellow stilettos. She didn't wear heels often, but she wore them well. A twisting look in the mirror revealed tattoos he hadn't seen yet—a trail of tiny card suits—hearts, clubs, diamonds, spades—which, from a distance, mimicked the look of old-fashioned seams on a stocking stretching from just above her ankle to a midpoint on her thigh. Were the dress any shorter, it would also reveal the deep, ragged scar from her surgery following the accident that killed her parents. That she wasn't quite ready to reveal.

She took special time with her makeup too, creating a perfect wing tip with her black eyeliner, a pale shadow behind it. She'd darken her lips after lunch; now she dabbed on a concoction to plump them up a bit and enhance their natural color. She stepped back, looking at herself in the freestanding vintage gilded mirror, overall pleased with every angle. The only lingering question: her hair.

Yesterday she had decided to ditch the confetti for something. . *.pretty*. She'd come out with something. . .lavender, though not solidly so, just hints, like sprigs of lilac. Wide rollers softened her curls, and she knew without a doubt someone today would tell her she looked like Marilyn Monroe.

She wore a single pair of simple silver hoops in her ears, leaving the other piercings empty, save for the ever-present chip in her cartilage. For her first-finger, right-hand ring—the one she'd wear as a distraction from her trickster hands—she chose the one handed down to her by her mother, from *her* grandfather: a collection of seed pearls encrusted around a citrine stone, shaped into a heart, with a crown of tiny diamonds sitting atop. It was her favorite piece, and her most valuable—sentimentally anyway. When she'd taken it to a jeweler to have it fashioned from a brooch to a ring, she learned that its monetary value had been greatly exaggerated through the years.

Quin was waiting for her at the Menger valet parking, as they'd agreed, wearing a light sport coat with his jeans and T-shirt. He was studying his phone, and rather than honking for his attention, she opened the passenger window and called, "Hey, Professor!"

He grinned even before he looked up and closed out his phone while making an easy lope to her car. He filled the space with presence and scent, bringing an anxious frisson along her skin. The only other person ever to occupy that seat was Arya, and then only on the rare circumstance that she couldn't drive them to their girls' day escape.

"I'm warning you now," she said once he'd clicked himself in, "I am an unconfident driver. I did online training and all my practice driving with Arya. So I'm going to have to ask you not to talk to me while I'm driving us to Burger Boy."

"Burger Boy?"

She eased onto the street, holding a hand up to hush him. "Yes. A San Antonio icon. I hope you skipped breakfast."

"Can I at least say that your hair looks cool?"

"Yes." She popped on her blinker and held her breath as she eased into the next lane. "But nothing else starting now."

As always after maneuvering through city traffic, Dini felt an adrenaline drop as soon as she put the car safely in PARK. She turned to give a sheepish grin. "Sorry. Driving is a necessary evil, but I hate it."

"I'm too hungry to talk anyway."

"Good." She punched the ignition switch and spoke as they were exiting the car. "I know it's an awkward time—too late for breakfast, too early for lunch, but I don't want to eat at the event."

Quin didn't reply. Instead, he stood, fingers raked in his hair, staring. "You look amazing."

She ran a hand over her hip, smoothing the skirt, adjusting the belt, and said, "Thank you," before donning a light denim jacket. The dining room was tiny, so they'd be eating outside.

"Like a space-age Marilyn Monroe."

"Exactly what I was going for."

He held the glass door open and touched the small of her back as she walked in, a gesture now almost familiar. Still, the imprint of it stayed while she ordered for them at the counter, insisting on paying despite his protest. Then the same process as they walked outside to wait for their food. His glasses transitioned to dark lenses, and she fished her sunglasses out of her bag.

"Now," he said, taking a seat on the bench opposite, "can you tell me exactly where we're going?"

"It's a Red Hat club. Literally a group of older women who get together as a social club. They wear purple shirts and red hats. I visited their group about a year ago to give a talk about Hedda. They liked me. Asked me back."

"And they won't mind me crashing?"

"I called and asked. It's fine." It hadn't, in fact, been *fine* at first, but Dini had insisted. "So, is your business all wrapped up?"

"It is."

"No distractions?"

"You. You are a distraction."

Right then, their number was called and Quin got up to bring their food: burgers and fries, a tall glass of water for him, and for Dini, Burger Boy's proprietary orange drink.

"You know, you don't really look like a burger girl right now."

She dabbed a corner of her mouth with a napkin. "There's no such thing as a dress code for burgers."

"You just look fancy." He touched her ring.

She picked up a fry and extended her hand, admiring both. "It's an heirloom, handed down. See how the stone is cut? Like a heart? Kind of drifted off to the side? The design is called witch's heart. In ancient times, it was the ubiquitous protection against the evil eye. But later a woman would wear it to summon a lover. Kind of like the gemstone equivalent of drawing a guy's name in a heart in your notebook."

She regaled him with neighborhood lore while they ate, and as their food dwindled, the thought of getting back behind the wheel churned in her stomach.

"We're going to hit lunchtime traffic," she said, folding up their empty food wrappers.

Quin took their tray inside, and when he came out he said, "Why don't you let me drive? Really, I'm a good driver, and I hate the idea of a long ride not talking to you."

"You don't know where we're going."

"You do."

"To be honest, I'm almost as bad at navigating as I am at driving."

Quin took his phone out of his back pocket and steered her to the passenger side. "Then I shall take care of both."

Dini wallowed in her passenger status as Quin drove expertly, guided by the chipper voice speaking directions from his phone, as if he'd been driving in this city all his life. She offered a few tidbits of trivia about their surroundings as they passed, but for the most part they stayed quiet until the Waze app proclaimed, "Thirty-five miles then exit right."

"So," Quin said, relaxing his posture and dropping one hand into his lap, "let's talk about that ghost."

Dini laughed. "Did you become a believer since last night?"

"No, but it was creepy."

"I didn't want to say anything before you read her account, but there's an old theater trick called Pepper's Ghost. Pretty simple, really. It's been around since the late nineteenth century. You just need a camera, darkness, a plate of glass—"

"And susceptibility?"

"I suppose. I figured out ages ago how it would work. Of course, I don't know *exactly* which room was Hedda's. . ."

"She never says, does she?"

"No. But I can imagine why. I can show you when we get back, if you want. Walk you through it."

"Tell me now." He made a smooth move into the left lane. The fast late. The lane she never used. He'd taken his jacket off before getting into the car, and she noticed how the sunlight brought out not only the red in the hair on his arms, but the underlying carpet of faint freckles as well. He didn't grip the steering wheel, despite the hundreds of cars hurtling down the highway at seventy miles per hour, but rested one hand on the bottom of the wheel, moving it in infinitesimal increments to keep her little Soul from colliding into the semi on the right.

"It's not distracting?"

"Not at all."

"Okay, then. A bit of trivia on Pepper's Ghost. It's how they project the dancers in the Haunted Mansion. People think it's some sort of great big green screen special effect? But on the other side, it's just a bunch of mannequins on a spinning platform projected on the glass."

He made an appreciative sound and checked the mirror.

"I should have said, the Haunted Mansion at Disneyland. Have you ever been?"

"Not the one in California. But the one in Florida? Yes. I, uh"—he drummed his fingers on his leg, then brought them up to take the wheel in a perfect 10 and 2 position—"I went there on my honeymoon."

For a long moment, Dini heard nothing but the hum of all the cars around her and wondered, without merit, if she'd simply heard him wrong. Or if "honeymoon" had some other meaning in an alternate universe. The only way to know for sure was for him to repeat it, but he suddenly seemed engrossed in the road, staring straight ahead, lips set thin.

She would have to pursue clarification. "Your *honeymoon*?"

"Yeah." His eyes were hidden behind dark lenses, but from his profile, she could see the tensing at his temple.

"You're—" How was she going to ask this question without sounding like some kind of shrill, soap opera victim? "You're *married*?"

"Was. A long time ago."

"A long time ago?" *Was he ten? Or was he now somehow sixty years old?* "Is she. . ." Dini braced herself. "Did she pass away?"

Quin laughed, taking her completely off guard, bringing her into a joke she couldn't yet understand. "No. She didn't die. We were kids when we got married—literally. I was nineteen, and she'd just turned eighteen."

"So, high school sweethearts."

He slowed for traffic. "More than that. Youth group sweethearts. Not only did we go to school together and see each other every day, but we went to church together and saw each other every weekend. And everyone assumed we would get married, so *we* assumed we would get married." He dropped his hand again. "So, summer after high school graduation, we did."

"But you loved each other?"

He shrugged his nondriving shoulder. "I suppose. As much as teenagers do. I was this chubby kid, she was a beautiful girl, we were super familiar with each other, so. . ."

Dini didn't finish his thought.

"It's a reason that works for a lot of people," he continued. "But once we didn't have mission trips and Ping-Pong tables and Wednesday game nights, we found out we had absolutely nothing. We'd always been together, but never *alone*. Not for any significant time. And we ended up not really even liking each other."

"Doesn't every couple go through that?" She thought about all the times she had to "rescue" Arya from another Saturday afternoon with Bill.

"Yeah, but Pam and I didn't devolve. Our first fight was on the Small World ride. It only took a few months for us to figure out that we didn't love each other the way we needed to make a marriage work."

They'd come to the source of the slowed traffic: two cars crunched against the guardrail. Quin slowed and held up a hand, saying a prayer for those involved—the drivers, the passengers, and the responders. By some instinct, Dini closed her eyes and listened, not opening them until he'd spoken Jesus' name. It didn't seem the time to resume the conversation, especially not with any of the million questions zooming through her mind, so they drove in silence until he was once again in the right lane, zipping along in confidence.

"Anyway, so one night we were at dinner—Arby's, go figure—and we hadn't been speaking the whole time, and she just looks up and says, 'I think we need to release ourselves from this marriage.' And, I tell you, it was the first real breath I took probably since the day I proposed."

"How long were you married?"

"Seven months. I moved out that week, and it was awful at first because I'd never gone more than a few days without seeing her. But then, I'd never seen myself *without* her, so it was exciting too. Like getting a second chance at growing up."

"And since?"

"Nothing serious. I dated a lot in college." He turned to her and waggled his eyebrows above his glasses. "A. Lot. But I lost my way a bit too. Drinking. Parties. Put on another fifty pounds. I came back to God a few years ago, stripped away everything in my life that worked against me. Focused on my body and my mind. Brought everything together."

"And your—Pam?"

"Oh, she's good. Married a doctor and just had her second kid. They live in Dallas. I'm friends with her mom on Facebook."

"Is there a reason why you didn't tell me any of this earlier?" After all, she had shared some important, intimate details of her past.

"I guess it just didn't come up. I don't introduce myself as a 'divorced man.' It's part of my past, but it doesn't define who I am. If I'm dating a girl, I don't bring it up until the third or fourth date, and then only if I think there's something. . .you know. . .*there*."

Dini wondered if their time together constituted dates, and if he thought there was something. . .*here*. She was left to her wondering, however, because Quin's phone began to speak directions of upcoming exits and turns.

"What's this town?"

"New Braunfels," she said, pronouncing the name correctly, unlike his disembodied navigator. She filled the space with trivia about the German-founded Texas town.

They exited the highway and made their way up a long, twisting, eclectic road. Their "destination, on the left," was the historic Prince Solms Inn, a solid, two-story brick structure with a set of double front doors painted in an inviting shade of tomato red.

"Bed and breakfast?" Quin said, reading its large green sign.

"Yes, formerly a hotel. It's got a great space downstairs. Used to be a speakeasy. That's where the show is."

It took a bit of driving and luck to find a parking spot, leaving Dini and Quin with a half-block walk to the inn. He worried about her shoes, which she thought was sweet, but then she produced a pair of flats from the back seat. "Always prepared."

Her bag for this show was a favorite—vintage powder blue and round, probably part of some woman's honeymoon set. Dini opened it and stashed her heels into the shirred pocket that spanned the width of the inside of the lid. The case had a small, looped handle designed to be slipped over a dainty wrist, meaning Quin looked a little ridiculous carrying it.

The walk to the inn was rough and uneven, in places totally without a sidewalk, and with each step Dini was glad to have ditched her heels. "We're going to the Sidecar. There's an entrance around the corner, but let's go through the house."

They walked up the stairs, through the inviting red door, and into a narrow entryway. On the right, a white banister stretched to the second floor; a sharp hook of a turn revealed a door that opened to a steep, dark set of stairs.

"After you," Quin said, gesturing with his free hand.

"Nope," Dini said. "I have a thing about walking down stairs with someone behind me."

"Because if I fall, we both fall?"

"Exactly."

Stepping into the Sidecar at the Prince Solms Inn was like stepping out of a time machine. Exposed brick walls, dim light from electric bulbs. Tufted black leather seating ran the length of one wall, tables interspersed in front of it. At the back stood an impressive-looking bar with a mosaic of bottles on the shelf behind it.

"Well, hello, Miss Magic."

Dini turned her attention to the woman who'd snuck up from behind. "Hey, Miss Lorraine." She was heavyset, in a way that looked like a controlled, trim figure let loose with age.

"We weren't expecting you for another half hour or so." Lorraine's tone was more efficient than friendly, but Dini knew not to take offense. She hoped Quin did too, considering the mildly disapproving assessment Lorraine was giving him.

"This is my friend I told you about. Quin? Also known as Irvin Carmichael the Fifth. Can you imagine? Today is his last day in town, and he's never seen my show. Thank you for letting him crash."

"Someone's got to carry the bag," Quin said, grinning self-consciously.

"That's an American Tourister hat case. Nineteen sixty-four, sixty-five, maybe," Lorraine said with disdain. "It's a woman's bag."

Dini jumped in. "Lorraine was a flight attendant back in the day. She knows her stuff."

"Back when flying was a class act," Lorraine said. "That's a fine bag."

"Thank you," Quin said, not at all awkwardly.

"I've got this." Dini relieved Quin of the bag and shooed Lorraine back to her table of chattering women, but not before learning of the afternoon's signature drink—something called a Virgin Pink Flamingo—and instructions to wait in the Pipe Room until it was time for the show.

There was a small stage at the foot of the stairs, most of which was taken up with a baby grand piano lacquered to black silk. At Dini's request, a small table sat next to it. While setting up, she looked around to offer the occasional smiled greeting, noting the ladies had dressed for the venue: an illustrated flapper on their T-shirts, and red hats in 1920s styles. To think, some of them might have been born in the decade.

She held the suitcase closed without zipping the lid and stepped down from the platform, picking her way over to an alcove behind the stage. Open booth seating ran along all three walls, with a glass case parallel above it displaying hundreds of artfully arranged pipes.

"You think this is the Pipe Room?" Quin asked. He held two margarita-style glasses filled with a thick pink drink.

"I think the better name would be the Fox and Pipes Room," Dini said, pointing to the mounted fox posed above the case. She reached for a drink. "Strawberry?"

"Grapefruit," he said. "Frozen and delicious. I had a taste before he poured."

Dini took a drink and concurred. Tart with underlying sweetness. She sat in the booth, and Quin brought over a chair while she changed her shoes and retrieved an open deck of cards from the case. Leaving the Jokers in the box, she commenced to shuffling, the feel of the cards fanning through her fingers immediately comforting.

Not—for once—that she needed it.

"This is called The Lovers," Dini said as Quin sat down. She fanned the soft cards, cut them, and shuffled again. "Appropriate, because this place too is haunted by a tragic love story."

"Is it?"

"It is." She shuffled as she spoke. "It was just after the turn of the century, 1901, maybe '02. There was a wedding to be held here, and the bride and her family arrived a few days early to make preparations." Dini set the deck on the table. "Take the top half and shuffle the cards."

"I can't do fancy shuffling."

"Any shuffling will do." Dini did the same with her own half.

"Anyway, the morning of the wedding, the groom didn't show up. The bride waited and waited. All day and the next." Dini set down her half of the deck, signaling Quin to do the same. "Her father sent her brothers out to track him down. Drag him back if need be. They found a set of tracks leading out of town, but the trail ended, cold. Nobody had seen him, and as far as the family knew, nobody saw or heard from him again." She picked up her half of the deck. "Cut it"—she demonstrated—"and look at the card in the cut. Don't show me."

Quin did, bringing a familiar furrow of concentration to his brow.

"Remember it?"

"Yep."

"Okay. Now put it on top." She reached out, took Quin's half of the deck, laid hers on top, and began a series of swift cuts, moving small groups of cards throughout the deck. "The woman refused to leave the hotel, knowing that her lover would return. She stayed after her family left, and the owner let her work as a maid, and she eventually ran the place. She died sometime in 1930." She looked up, fully focused on Quin. "Do you remember your card?"

"Nine of spades."

"Nine of spades. Mine was the four of hearts." She began turning the cards over, one by one. "A few years later, the new owner is about to lock up for the night, when suddenly the door bursts open, and a man dressed like someone from the last century comes running through the door. And—get this—he runs *through* the owner. Like a chill. And right up the stairs. Those very stairs we saw when we walked in." She turned over his card. "Nine of spades."

"There it is," Quin said.

"There it is," Dini said. "And then, the guy turns, looks up at the top of the stairs, and what do you think he sees?"

"The bride."

"The four of hearts," she said before turning her card over. "Like the lovers, finding each other."

She liked to do this trick at wedding showers or bachelorette parties, having learned a few bits about the bride and groom's story. She'd even done it at birthday parties, turning the cards into a rescued princess, or even mortal enemies meeting for a final battle. It was the last part that made it a show, timing out the final telling so the revealing of the card fell in rhythm with the story. She'd done it hundreds of times, but today was the first time she'd sat across the table from someone she wanted very much to find again. To return to.

"Amazing," Quin said, leaning in, his elbows on the table.

She felt her cheeks flush and took a sip of her drink. "Not really. It's pretty simple."

"Not the trick, no offense. But *you*. You're mesmerizing. You're the magic."

"I love that story."

It was dark in the Pipe Room, the alcove lit by a single amber bulb. The women were nothing but a soft, far-off sound. Dini shuffled the cards. "Want to see another one?"

Before he could answer, Lorraine stuck her head around the corner. "Five minutes, sweetie. You might want to freshen your lipstick."

"I'm up!" Dini said, focusing. She took another sip of her drink. "There's no alcohol in this, is there?"

"The bartender assures me, no."

"Good to know."

For the next ninety minutes, she worked. The crowd was sweet, laughing at her jokes and offering a few back without heckling. She kept up the banter through all the illusions, snapping the cards and tapping the deck on the table with every punch line. The Triple Deal. The Swimmers. The Switcheroo. She brought volunteers up from the audience just as she would at any other party. She asked, "What's your name, sweetie?" and "How old are you?"—a question that bore no stigma in this room. The oldest, Betty Jean, had turned ninety-nine the previous week.

Dini saved The Lovers trick for the last of the show, bringing Lorraine up (on Quin's arm) as her participant. She walked through the story as she had with Quin, but didn't dare risk even a glance his way. It was hard enough to control her hands, remembering how he'd looked at her. How—according to the weight she felt on her skin—he looked at her now. At the final reveal, the ladies emitted their now-familiar gasp and applauded generously. Afterward Dini stood for photos, knowing her face was going to be posted on a dozen different Facebook profiles and Red Hat group pages.

"Just remember to hashtag Dini Blackstone," she said, handing out her card as a reminder.

When all had dwindled down to Lorraine settling up with the waitstaff, and Dini had packed up her case, Quin took her hand and led her to a secluded, dark corner saying, "I want to show you something. Look." It was a narrow phone booth, lit by a single, bare bulb. Inside, a green rotary dial phone, represented by the American Telephone and Telegraph Company, presided like something from a time machine. "Just think, kids wouldn't even know what to do with that."

"Okay, Grandpa Irvin," Dini said. "Maybe you spent a little too much time with the old girls today?"

"That Betty Jean, she kind of stole my heart."

"Want me to run outside and see if I can catch her?" Dini took a step.

"Nah," Quin said, reaching out to stop her with a touch to her forearm. "I think I might have something else going on. I don't want to break her heart."

"You're a good man, Quin Carmichael. Now, have we seen enough of the phone? Or is there a fax machine somewhere you want to show me?"

"Would you take my picture? In the booth? My sister collects phone booths. I mean, not *actual* phone booths, because that would be insane. But pictures of phone booths. She has a thing."

"Like with the notebooks?"

"Different sister."

"I don't know if you're supposed to go in there."

He held his finger to his lips and opened the door. "See? Not locked."

Dini took his phone and snapped a variety of poses—Quin looking serious, Quin holding the green handset and miming conversation, Quin taking off his glasses, gripping his shirt as if any second Superman would appear. Then he held out his hand. "Come here." She did, and he maneuvered her against him, the two of them pressed together as he held his phone out for a selfie. "We want to be sure to get the phone in," he said, working for a better angle.

"We want to get the squirrel in too," Dini said, referring to the head mounted on the wall above the phone. It wasn't easy to make the joke, given the closeness of him, the way his chest pressed against her spine, his beard close enough to tickle the exposed skin on her shoulder.

"Hey!" The intrusive voice came from around the corner, attached to the bartender. She was expecting some kind of chastisement, but he merely offered to take a picture of the two of them.

"Thanks, man," Quin said, stretching past Dini to hand him the phone. He was still behind her, but he put his hand on the curve of her waist and brought her somehow closer. Dini's mind raged at her body's pliability. She wasn't one to mold against another person and yet the rigidity that would grip her in the most accidental of brushes didn't reach past her lungs. They froze, their duty of breathing in and out temporarily halted.

Once the bartender said he'd gotten some "good ones," he returned to his duty while Quin scrolled through. "I'm sending these to you," he said before picking up her bag. "Ready to go?"

Dini, not having uttered a single word since pointing out the squirrel, nodded. Not until they got to the stairs did she say, "Wait there. Ten steps."

"So if you fall I have time to brace myself and stop you?"

"Exactly."

The late afternoon—nearly four o'clock—air was cool and gray. While Quin got the car, she leaned against the beveled newel and opened her phone to the camera. It took a bit to find the right angle for her face and the red door behind her, but once she got it, she posted to her Instagram, tagging the Inn and the Sidecar, thanking them both for an afternoon of history and haunted romance. Within seconds, the red heart beneath the post lit up, and she saw that @QCMichael liked it. Quin. Then his own post popped up, the picture of the two of them—one taken by the bartender—with a caption: *This girl is magic and amazing.* No hashtags (just because a guy develops an app doesn't mean he "gets" the marketing aspect of IG), but the picture. . . She'd posed with men before—the dads at birthday parties, guys from the audience after a show—and she always looked so *stiff.* So *uncomfortable.* Because most of the time she'd just taken a step from their proximity or shrugged off their touch or steeled herself against an unwelcome embrace.

But here, the two of them stuffed into a tiny room built for one, she could see the way their bodies formed to each other. Her lines intersected his lines. His fingers splayed against the stitching of her belt. Had his arm *encircled* her? And she hadn't noticed? Didn't twist herself away with a frozen smile?

No. In fact, there was no smile on either face, unless you counted the contented half lift of Dini's lips. Quin, however, wasn't even looking at the camera. He was looking at her, his glasses loosely held in his left hand, his face turned at an angle that betrayed his gaze. Even though she was *there*, even though it was *her*, Dini felt like she was peeping in on a private moment. Nobody would ever look at this picture and not think that Quin was in love. He couldn't have posed for this. Surely in the series of the bartender's snaps there was one where both of them wore cheesy friendship smiles. This was a moment unguarded and captured. This was a trap like the one the poor fox in the Pipe Room must have wandered into. And, like the fox, Quin had put it on full display for her and—she checked—all 117 followers.

Chapter 16

Excerpt from

My Spectral Accuser: The Haunted Life of Hedda Krause

Published by the Author Herself

One week passed. Then a second. And perhaps a third—measuring time became the least important of my priorities. I knew I should leave the Menger. Even more, I knew I should leave San Antonio, but I knew that if I left, I would never see my worldly goods again. Sallie White had gone from being a mischievous irritant to a force of destruction. I knew people thought me to be mad. I heard the sniggers of the staff as I passed them in the hall and the whispers of guests who somehow knew my tale. I may not have been robbed by Sallie White herself, but I'd been robbed by this place. My hands might be empty, but I would not walk away until they grasped some kind of justice.

One afternoon, after a stretch of mutual avoidance, I took it upon myself to step behind the front desk and knock on Mr. Sylvan's private office door. At his terse "Come in," I entered, holding myself tall, lest he think I came to grovel.

"Mrs. Krause."

"Mr. Sylvan." Then an uncomfortable minute before, "May I sit down?"

"I've never known you not to do exactly as you wish."

I took a seat in the chair opposite his desk, noting how absolutely tidy it was, not a stray paper in sight. Just a blotter, a telephone, pen, ink, and massive ledger. "I'm sure you realize why I am here."

"Has it something to do with the staggering amount of money you owe the hotel?"

"Surely *staggering* is an exaggeration."

He licked the tip of his fingers and flipped to a page at the back of his ledger. I did not see the specific figures, but even from this distance the amount of red ink appeared as damning as anything in Carmichael's notebook. "Would you like to hear the total?"

"I would not. Not right now, thank you."

"I'd be well within my rights to have the police come and toss you out on your bustle, you know."

I suppressed a smile at the way his moustache twitched at the word *bustle*. "I understand. And I am thankful for your generosity—"

"It is not *my* generosity, I assure you."

"Then, I suppose the owner?"

"The owner is away on extended business, not expected to return until summer, at which time I am certain to lose my job. No, Mrs. Krause, it is not so much a matter of generosity as practicality. Better to keep you here than to have you in jail where you might speak with the press and sully the name of this property."

"I would never—"

"Perhaps not, but I am unwilling to take that chance. Rest assured, if word of that ridiculous tale comes to life in print, you will have spent your last moments under our hospitality."

"I understand completely, Mr. Sylvan. I want the truth to come out, even if only to the two of us."

He lifted the left side of his moustache in response.

"And," I pursued, "I truly am grateful. I hope—I intend—to pay my debt one day."

"Again, it is not I you should thank. Had I any power in the situation, I would have had you taken down the street and jailed that very night. Such carryings on. Ghosts and shrieks."

"There is a ghost, Mr. Sylvan. Your own staff told me—"

"Nonsense. Superstitious babble. All the more reason to bid you farewell, but you can thank your friend Detective Carmichael for your current accommodations."

"Detective Carmichael?"

"He is nothing if not a persuasive man."

That persuasive man came to visit me that evening, the first I'd seen him since he knelt beside me by the fire. Though barely seven o'clock, it was dark. Two raps on my door, and I opened it to find one of the messenger boys with a note. I recognized the handwriting at once, inviting me to meet him in the Menger Bar and join him for supper. I say "invite," though the tone left no doubt it was a summons written on a scrap torn from his notebook. I recognized the paper, the color of a not-quite-ripe peach.

I was still dressed and respectable, but I lingered in my room a good fifteen minutes so he wouldn't think he could expect me at the drop of a hat. There were quite a few patrons in the bar, and Bert gave me a nod in the direction of the booth in the back corner, where we sat that first evening.

Carmichael stood as I approached. "Good evening, Mrs. Krause."

I returned his greeting and took a seat on the opposite bench. "This is a surprise."

"Not unwelcome?"

"Not yet." I noticed a train case on the seat next to him and a spot of coal dust on his collar. "You've come straight from the station?"

"I have. And I'm starving. Stopped in here for a drink, and Bert offered to make up something for me." He looked aside and began rubbing his hands together in anticipation. "And here it is."

Bert, looking for all the world like one of the dining room waiters with a towel draped over his forearm, approached with a steaming plate of chopped steak cooked with onions and peppers, and a stream of fried potatoes on the side.

"My man," Carmichael said. "You cooked this yourself?"

"Sometimes they let me fire up the stove in the back," he said with a modest smile.

I absorbed the scent and the steam of the food with such obvious desire that Carmichael asked if I wanted a bite, going so far as to offer me his fork.

"No, thank you," I demurred. "I've already had a light supper."

"I can make you a small plate of your own," Bert said. "Got some left on the stove."

My stomach guided my words. "Well, I wouldn't want it to go to waste. You can put it on Mr. Carmichael's tab, since he insists I join him here."

Carmichael politely left his food untouched while we waited for Bert to arrive with mine. We chatted about the train, the luxuries of such travel, and the drawbacks, though neither of us had ever traveled extensively any other way.

"I wouldn't have lasted five days on a wagon train," he said, digging into his food as soon as I'd taken my first, savoring bite. "I don't hunt, never built a fire without wasting a handful of matches, and I hate horses."

I laughed. "Nobody hates horses."

"I do. Big, stupid animals, and I cannot wait for the motorcar to run them all off the streets and back to the farms where they belong."

"You don't see the motorcar as a passing fancy? Some kind of giant toy?"

"Have you ever driven one?"

I clutched at my blouse as if offended. "Never. Why, just riding in one is terrifying enough."

He took a bite of his food and chewed thoughtfully. "Not even when you were in Tennessee?"

I stared at my plate, collecting my thoughts, my appetite not the least diminished. Still, I left my food untouched and looked straight into his eyes, meeting his challenge without response.

"There is no marriage certificate filed in your name in Tennessee."

"No." I held a forkful aloft. "I don't suppose there is." Then I filled my mouth with the savory taste of a small victory.

"Which means your name is false, you were never married in Tennessee, or you were never married at all. Which is it, Mrs. Krause?"

"How does any of this help solve the crime that was committed against me?"

"It helps me establish whether there was any crime at all."

"You know there was."

"Forgive me, but three days going through records in Nashville makes it difficult to believe you."

I pointed to my band. "I was married."

"That answers two of my three theories."

"Why should I make your job easier?"

"It's not my job."

"I beg your pardon?"

"I resigned from the force weeks ago. In fact, the night of your adventure? That was my last night on duty."

"So why are you pestering me?"

He laughed, a sound that began and ended with a great inhalation through his nose. "I was accepted to train with the Bureau of Investigation. I'm due in Washington at the first of May. So, now I'm just entertaining myself."

"Entertaining?"

"I find you highly entertaining, Mrs. Krause. And it's an interesting bit to investigate. I asked the police chief if I could keep at it until I left. Keep myself busy."

I could feel rage threatening to spoil my delicious supper and fought to express it through a superior disdain. "So, I am a *hobby*?"

"I suppose you could say that. My favorite one at the moment." Never would I have thought to describe Irvin Carmichael, a solid wall of a man, as boyish, yet there he was, with a grin that could only be described as playful. "I volunteered to work the case in an unofficial capacity. I have eyes on every local pawn shop, ready to answer back on anything matching your description of the missing pieces. Plus"—here his face settled into a more serious expression—"it gives me a reason to see you. To invite you to supper, to give you an update."

"You could do all of that without going to Tennessee."

"I'm working with two things, Hedda Krause. My heart and my head. My heart took me to have a conversation with every lowlife crook in this town and tell him to keep his eyes open. Because I want to help you. My head took me to Tennessee."

He spoke so simply, as if he hadn't just declared some sort of love for me. I felt the same battle—my heart and my head, though I'd learned well how to discipline both. I stabbed my last potato and ate in silence.

"I know there's something, Hedda. I don't have a single bit of authority right now. I'm just a man."

"And what do you want from me?"

"Answers."

"You won't get any. I don't talk about my past."

He moved his plate to the edge of the table, mine too, and stacked our forks on top of both. A good son, he was, raised in a family and expected to do his part. With the dishes cleared between us, he reached across the table and took my hands in his. My first instinct was to pull away, but he held them strong. I glanced over at Bert, who offered a small smile of approval before refilling a glass for a patron at the bar. So I gave myself over, and for a stretch of time I could never measure, he held my hands, softly, his thumb stroking the hollow between my thumb and my wrist. Neither of us spoke. It was the same touch I shared with Bert months ago, the first night I heard Sallie White's voice. Then it had soothed me. Lulled me. Carmichael ignited just the opposite.

"Do you talk about your future, Hedda?"

Any other man, the smattering of suitors and admirers I'd enjoyed since my widowhood, would have received a flirtatious challenge, but my tongue remained still. I could hear my heart beating, the rush of my pulse in my ears.

"All right then." He took his hands away, and I could have chased them across the table. "Before I go, I have a gift for you." He reached into the train case on the seat beside him and took out a book. "I realize I never answered your question about whether or not I read. I do, as a matter of fact. But I never cared for *Little Dorrit*. Too convoluted and sentimental. This is my favorite Dickens."

I read the title stamped into the cover. *"Great Expectations."*

"Have you read it?"

"I have not." The cover was a rich brown leather. A quality book, an expensive book. "I never went to school, Mr. Carmichael. I taught myself to read when I was twelve."

"It's a good story," he said, as if I hadn't spoken. "Lots of secrets and revenge."

My coquette returned. "Do you think I am a woman of secrets?"

"I do."

"And revenge?"

"I hope not."

Bert came to collect our dishes and the dollar Carmichael tucked under them.

"I kissed him once," I said as he walked away. "The first night Sallie came to me, and I was so frightened. He kissed me." I touched my lips. "Does that bother you?"

"No."

It was such a swift and solid answer that I believed him completely.

Days later, Carmichael kissed me. It was a moonless night after a long walk during which we talked about Billy the Kid (his boyhood hero) and whether justice is ever truly served without an arrest and a trial and a jury before an execution.

"Sallie White's murder saw no justice at all," I said. "She died right here, you know. Rather, she was killed here. It took days for her to die."

He took off his gloves, put them in his pocket, and laid his warm palms against my cold cheeks, his thumbs pressed against my temples.

"If I could work one bit of magic, my sweet Hedda, it would be to take the thoughts and the stories of that woman out of your mind.

She was a poor soul who died a wretched death. But here you are, with warm blood running through you and a full life stretched ahead."

His face was so close to mine and the light so dim that the freckles merged. I could smell his last cigarette on his breath, and then I was tasting it as his mouth found mine.

Make no mistake, I had kissed many men in my life, most of them little more than vile intrusions. Carmichael's kiss scattered them all and left me feeling much like a girl experiencing her first. I did not respond immediately, only allowed his lips to make the slightest movement against mine. His hold was tenuous, his hands little more than poised along my face. My own hung limp and heavy at my side. I don't believe I fully felt his touch, his kiss, until the moment came when he meant to take it away. His lips once more motionless against mine, the cold air on my skin where his strong, warm palm had been. And so I gripped his elbow, holding his arm in place, and went to my toes, chasing up his kiss, and in that tiniest of moments, everything broke between us. He caught me around my waist. I wrapped my arms around his neck. (Later he would laugh about the similarity of circumference in the two.) He lifted me off my feet and spun until I felt the Menger's wall at my back and the wall of himself crushed against me. For a morbid second I thought of Henry Wheeler and Sallie White. How he had held her in almost this same place. But where Henry held Sallie's throat, Carmichael held my heart. We breathed life into each other.

We were inseparable from that point, as inseparable as our situation would allow. Sometimes he squired me around the city, taking me into this restaurant or that, where we would be given a jovial greeting in lieu of a check. My favorite times were when we visited a humble home of one of the many people he had helped over time and were fed a meal straight from the stove: mashed beans wrapped in soft tortillas, or stews infused with magical spices. Here, to my surprise, this freckle-faced Scot would rattle off entire conversations in Spanish, reassuring me that most of it was a commentary on my beauty and style.

One day he rented an automobile, and we drove out east of the city. It was a sharp, cold day, far too cold for a drive, but we marshaled on, turning onto a property once Carmichael sighted a dilapidated barn not far off.

He brought the car to a stop in the untended field, and chilly as the day was, I got out of the automobile, if only for a chance to clear my head and stretch my legs, not wanting him to know about the fear that unnerved me despite his calm, capable hands. Once outside, he produced from his satchel one of those small Brownie box cameras and suggested we commemorate the day. I posed eagerly for him, leaning against the car for some silly pictures, and finally wheedled and whined enough for him to pose exactly once for me. When my cheeks were nearly numb with cold, I climbed inside the car again, this time behind the wheel, to pose as if I were driving, but finally had to admit I was chilled to the bone. He came to the open door; my teeth chattered against his kiss.

"There's a perfectly fine barn over there," he said against my ear. "We can go inside. Warm up a bit."

I mentioned the missing slats and damaged roof. "It won't be much warmer in there."

But he kissed me, and as the warmth of the sunlight did its job now that we were stopped and still, his intent became clear. I pushed back, planting my palms on his massive shoulders. "Mr. Carmichael, surely you don't think I'm the kind of lady you can toss down on a haystack, do you?"

He said nothing, only handed me down. No sooner had my boots touched the hard-packed earth, than he swept me up in his arms, carrying me the scant distance to an entrance around the side, where a door was partially open. He nudged it with his shoulder and carried me across the threshold.

Inside, the barn smelled surprisingly sweet, and as my eyes adjusted to the semi-darkness, an even sweeter tableau took shape. Rather than being covered with straw and debris and rusted tools, the floor was swept clean—as clean as a barn floor can get—and patterned with stripes of sunlight. Off in a corner, a quilt stretched on the floor along with two cushions, and a picnic hamper.

"When did you do this?" I giggled, yes—giggled, like a girl—and stepped in a wide, slow circle, taking in this ghost of a building as if it held the splendor of the Menger herself. "Is a farmer going to come in wielding a pitchfork to chase us off his land?"

"I will always protect you, Hedda." His voice filled the space, mending the walls and the roof and all the broken places. "You will always be safe with me."

Later, much later, the car returned to its garage, we walked the final blocks home, my arm tucked in his, something to which we had become very much accustomed. He asked me again if I liked—if I *truly* enjoyed—his famous beef paste sandwiches, and I assured him that of all the beef paste sandwiches I had ever eaten in my life, his were the most delicious.

When we arrived at the ornate door of the hotel, we stopped. Suddenly, to walk inside as I'd been doing all of these months felt like an act so unnatural as to be ludicrous. For Carmichael and I to part from each other after an entire day spent drifting between quiet and conversation, never having more than an arm's length of space between us, seemed like a new layer of cruelty.

He took my hand and brought it to his lips, a gesture that would appear quaint and subdued to any passerby. But his eyes burned into mine, and when he spoke, his words carried no such innocence.

"I live not a quarter of a mile from here, Hedda."

"I cannot, Irvin. You must understand that."

He dropped my hand, took a cigarette out of his pocket, and lit it with a match struck against the wall. His face glowed in the flame's light and the cigarette bobbed as he spoke. "I'm going to be gone for a few days."

Instantly, I was cold. Ice cold, the heat of the day forgotten. "You don't have to."

"Why? Because you'll tell me the truth here? Tonight? Introduce me to the woman I'm in love with?" At some point, he'd gripped my arm, dropping it the moment I winced at the pain. "God forgive me, Hedda. I'm sorry."

My throat burned with tears. "Don't say that."

"Don't say what? That I love you? Believe me, Hedda—if that's even your name—I wish I didn't. But God help me, I do."

Twice in a minute he'd called on God—for help and for forgiveness. How I hated that I'd brought him to that place.

"Then don't go." I felt the tears on my cheeks, and I gripped him, though he shrugged me off before my fingers could find their purchase.

He blew a puff of smoke over my head. "What am I going to find?"

I stood, anchored. "You've already made it a point of not believing me. Go and see what you'll learn for yourself."

Without another word, without waiting for him to open the door, I strode inside. The usually welcoming warmth of the lobby seemed stifling, its ornate beauty like an overeaten sweet. Even though the hour was late, Mr. Sylvan stood behind the desk, and given the straightforward stride he made in my direction, I knew he had been waiting for my return.

In just a few minutes hence, I would behold myself in the mirror above my bureau. My hair tousled, my cheeks and nose red from cold, my lips swollen from a thousand kisses, my dress wrinkled beyond decency. My eyes empty of hope. But before that, the two of us well out of earshot of the hotel's less pitiful guests, Mr. Sylvan leaned close.

"Had you delayed one half hour more, Mrs. Krause, you would have returned to find your belongings on the sidewalk waiting for you. I will not have you flaunt your affairs at the expense of this establishment. Our generosity to you is beyond compare, and I promise you this: I might not roust you out like the bum that you are, but walk out of these doors again, and I will bar you from coming back."

Throughout, his message never rose above a hiss, and had I turned to look at him, I am sure I would have seen a forked tongue darting from between his thin, shiny lips.

I went straight to bed without so much as washing my face or cleaning my teeth. When the sun rose, I willed myself to sleep until midmorning. Then I clutched my pillow and wept into it. Such plans I had here. Such hope I'd brought along with all I needed to begin life anew. I pictured Carmichael's face. "*An ugly mug*," he called it as I dotted it with kisses. "*God, help me*," he'd said, wishing he didn't love me. "*God, forgive me*," he'd said when he hurt me. Now I too wished I didn't love him. I wished I hadn't hurt him, but my soul was too empty to call on God to forgive me. Surely these were the least of my sins.

I took a long bath, punishingly hot, and spent the next several days in seclusion. Mr. Dickens's work was my sole companion, and I found true kinship with Mrs. Havisham, deserted by her lover and left to rot alone. Is that why Carmichael gave me this book? Because he knew my fate?

Nearly a week had passed when, willing myself invisible to the other guests, I crept down to the bar, relieved to find it empty except for Bert, as ever, in attendance.

"Mrs. Krause." He was shocked at my appearance. The secret to my beauty has always been a healthy confidence and constitution, and at the moment I had neither.

I took myself to what I had begun to consider *our* booth, and in a short time Bert was there with both a cup of tea and a whiskey, not knowing which would better suit my mood.

I drank both.

"She's ruined me, Bert. That cursed ghost. Do you know what I've a mind to do?"

He'd been standing in attendance at my table, then reluctantly sat at my invitation.

"I've a mind to have a séance. Right upstairs at the landing."

"Oh no, Mrs. Krause. You can't go dabblin' in that kind of nonsense."

"Nonsense? I haven't heard her or seen her since that night. And I need to know why she hates me. Why she would go to such pains to ruin my life."

"You can't blame the ruin of your life on some poor dead woman. What do you have that she needs? It's someone else that robbed you. Someone with flesh as warm as yours but with a darker heart."

"Who could hate me that much?"

"There's some people who don't know better than to grab on to hate and hold it. But it don't have to be someone who hates you. Could be just someone who wants what you have."

"But I *saw* her," I whispered, though we were still alone.

"I know."

"You believe me?"

He heaved a sigh from someplace deeper than I could fathom. "I been in this hotel longer than anybody else here. Nobody knows better what's lurkin'. Could be that your heart and your mind just conjured her better than any séance ever could. But that kind of conjurin' "—he pointed and waggled his finger, drawing an invisible bridge between those two forces of my body—"that's good and safe. You got a smart head and a good heart. They just got messed up with a little bit of fear. God Almighty can work with that. But that other? You start summoning from darkness? You invite in some forces that don't have no place here. And I'll stop you myself if I have to."

I felt small and thoroughly chastised. "Don't be angry with me, Bert. You're the only friend I've got."

I hadn't been serious about the séance, not really. My late husband and I attended one, a silly man wanting to summon his dead wife to reveal where she'd hidden his pipe. It was a sham and a show led by a con artist who had a fine wire threaded through a tambourine. Still, I felt every bit as unsettled as Sallie. Roaming and empty. Listless, bored. I knew she'd never visit again. We had wreaked havoc on each other, and I remained here to live with the consequences.

My sleep had been deep and dreamless from the first night

Carmichael kissed me. His kisses were the sheep I counted, reliving every one until the dark of the room and the weight of the quilts cocooned me for the night. Even with the memories turned bittersweet, they lulled me. I was on the edge of sleep, remembering a stolen kiss behind a particularly camouflaging corner in the lobby, when I heard it.

Not a knock.

Not a *scraaaatch*.

But something soft. Small. Like the tapping of a fingertip against my door. And then, "*Hedda.*" This too, soft. Like a purr.

I rose and pressed my ear to the door. Looking down, I saw his shoes—wide and sturdy—tied with the laces uniform and neat.

Tap. Tap. "Hedda, darling. It's me."

It took an hour for me to turn the knob, a lifetime to open the door, and there he was.

"Irv—" And he was inside, the door recklessly closed behind him, my body in his arms, his lips on mine. All the kisses from all the drifting darkness brought to life in that moment. He kissed me like a man chased by a demon. He kissed me as if he never had before and never would again. He buried his face in the soft warm space of my neck, and when I opened my eyes, I saw the faint bits of coal dust on his collar. My toe nudged the train case at our feet.

I pulled away and saw the tears pooled in his eyes. And I knew.

I stepped away, staggering back until my knees hit the bed, and I sat down upon it. He loomed over me, this mountain of a good man, his face twisted in pain.

"You've done it, haven't you," I said, staring at the carpet between my toes. "You've been to Denver."

Chapter 17

For most of the drive home, Dini explained her illusions.

"The Flighty Aces?" Quin asked.

"Trick deck."

"And the Reverso?"

"Palm the reveal card." Dini knew she was merely placating him, as the majority of the explanations came down to memorizing the bottom card and holding it in place, something he surely could figure out for himself. Some, though, required decks that were already sorted (hence the multiple themed decks to toss out as door prizes). She had her own machine that resealed them, strip and all.

"Isn't that cheating?" Quin asked, steering them deftly through I-35 traffic.

"It's illusion," Dini said. "When I open the first deck, I say, 'Now, this is a brand-new deck of cards, never opened until this moment in time.' But I don't say that again. The audience assumes that the next deck is brand-new too. And the next, just like they assume that shuffling the cards creates some random, chaotic disorder, when really, I know exactly where every pertinent card will land."

They were early enough to miss most of the evening traffic, only coming into true congestion when they edged into downtown, where the final stretch to the Menger was harrowing enough to make Dini wince as she gripped the edge of her seat. Quin grew quiet, more for her sake, she suspected, than for his. He pulled into a lot across the street and, before she could get herself out of the car, was swiping his credit card to pay for the parking.

To her surprise, he took her hand, and to her greater surprise, she let him keep it as they stepped off the curb and crossed the street. They entered through the bar and greeted Gil—Quin doing so in a way that made Dini think the two had banked hours of conversation since that first night.

"They delivered the package to my room," Quin said, leading her straight through. "Come up with me? Show me how that ghost thing would have worked."

"Pepper's Ghost," Gil said as they walked by. "That's still your theory, Dini?"

"Until I find another one."

It was a conversation the two had rehashed over and over. Gil was always quick to defend Hedda, calling her "the Old Girl" with unusual affection. He often took a Socratic tone, leading Dini through with questions. Was Hedda delusional? Or deceptive? Did she make the whole thing up for attention? Or, and this was always the late night talking, was that Sallie White herself floating in that dark hallway? Did she wreak her havoc and disappear?

This time when Dini and Quin walked through the lobby, it was more of a stroll, making comments on the décor, the statues, the pianos. When they got to the stairs, Dini surrendered to discomfort and took off her shoes before climbing them. Quin's room was to the left of the staircase, overlooking the second-floor balcony.

"Hedda's room was opposite," Dini said. "This way." Hand in hand, they looked down the empty hallway, which gave off an optical illusion of growing narrower toward the end. "Come on."

They walked, passing door after door after door. "It was either here," Dini said, indicating an offshoot hallway, "or here," she repeated when they came to the end. "All they would have to do is position a pane of glass—mirrored glass—and project the image onto it. So if Hedda's room was all the way at the end of the hall, given the low light, she wouldn't have seen it."

"And you really think that's it?" Quin asked.

"It's relatively simple technology. Totally available at the time—they used it in theaters regularly. Think ghost of Marley in early stage productions of *A Christmas Carol*. People in my neighborhood do this in their entryway for trick-or-treaters."

"She wouldn't have heard the projector?"

"There was a full orchestra in the ballroom, plus the sound of all the people downstairs. And the shock of the moment, the fear. Have you ever been really scared before? Your ears fill up."

"It's your blood pressure," he said. "Heart rate and pulse going nuts."

"Yep." Dini was experiencing that now somewhat, although she couldn't say if it was the fact that they were strolling toward Quin's room or the anticipation of seeing Carmichael's notebook waiting within.

"Tell you what," Quin said, taking the keycard from his pocket. "Why don't I run in, grab the notebook, and let's take it downstairs? We can sit in their booth and have a coffee."

"Sounds good." Something inside her had changed—something *between* them had changed—since the last time they were in this room together. Alone. True to his word, he was back in less than two minutes, carrying a FedEx envelope and assuring Dini that he'd washed his hands.

She washed hers too, stopping in the lobby's restroom while he went on to the bar, and by the time she got to the booth, Gil was setting down two heavy mugs of steaming coffee, her own the perfect shade of creamy brown. Quin stood, allowing her to slide in (never an easy task in a narrow skirt), then sat next to her. How different from that first night, when they studied and circled each other so warily from across the table. This was just as Hedda described the night she met Detective Carmichael, only Quin didn't smell of cigarettes.

"Guess what we have here?" Dini said as Quin handed Gil back a sharp knife he'd used to open the envelope.

"The notebook of Detective Irvin Carmichael?"

Dini frowned. "How did you know?"

"Quin told me about it the other night. Can I get y'all anything else?"

"Sit with us," Dini said, indicating the empty seat. "Aren't you dying to see it?"

"Well, I'm working right now, so I can't just *sit* with you, but I'll stay here for the grand opening."

Quin, taking his cue, opened the envelope and drew out a mass of Bubble Wrap. This he unfolded, revealing a narrow black book bound with a faded red elastic. "You do the honors, Dini," he said, handing it over.

She noted at once its cheap cardboard cover. This was not a high-quality journal. It was utilitarian, meant for lists and notes, not deep thoughts and musings. Age made it fragile, and she feared the elastic might snap as she stretched it around the edge of the pages. The cover made a cracking sound, and she gasped when a fluttering of photographs fell to the table.

Quin picked one up, scrutinized it, then passed it over. "Is that her?"

It was. Hedda, dressed in a dark skirt and close-fitting car coat. She was outside in a field, leaning against an antique automobile—though to her it wasn't antique at all. She looked relaxed, happy, her posture slack and her smile genuine. Wind had whipped her hair away from perfection; wisps of it blew across her brow and cheek. She looked at the camera—more specifically, at the man *behind* the camera—as if confirming this to be a perfect moment in time.

"Look." She handed the photograph to Gil. Rather, held it as he bent to inspect it.

"Ah, Hedda," he said with the affection of a longtime friend.

Tears pooled in Dini's eyes. "Can you believe it?"

"That's her," Gil said, standing straight again. "That's the real Hedda."

Quin studied the picture now, holding it at an angle as if that would explain their emotional reaction. "What do you mean the *real Hedda*?"

"Just how she was—how I'd picture her in real life," Gil said. "Not so formal."

"And here's your great-great-grandfather," Dini said, sharing a second picture over to Quin. In it Detective Carmichael struck a pose against the same car. He wore a plaid jacket, unbelted slacks and suspenders, his head bare, revealing the short-cropped hair Hedda described. The quality of the photo was pretty much what one would expect from a 1916 Brownie, but the image was clear enough to record his most prominent feature. Freckles. Hedda had not exaggerated their scope.

Gil gave a cursory look and said, "Yep, that's him," before leaving to tend to another patron.

"He's handsome," Dini said, then caught the implication. "He looks like Brian Keith."

Quin took the photo gingerly. "Who?"

"Uncle Bill, on that old TV show *Family Affair*." While Quin studied the picture, she googled an image on her phone. "We stayed a whole summer in Chicago once, and reruns of this show came on at six in the morning. I was obsessed. Begged my mother to let me wear my hair in little pigtails like Buffy's." Dini knew she was babbling, and she knew Quin wasn't hearing a word. So she stopped, scooted closer, and shifted her gaze from the photo to him and back, looking for a resemblance. "I can see him in you. Narrow nose. Not the freckles, though."

"I had them when I was a kid," he said, not taking his eyes off the image. "And I'm careful in the sun."

She recalled the Neutrogena in his hotel bathroom. SPF 20. "But surely you've seen pictures of him before? He's family."

"Nothing like this. I've only seen him as an old man. This guy—come on. Look at him." He turned toward her, holding the photograph next to his face. "Just a couple of lady-killers, am I right?"

Dini laughed because she knew he wanted her to. There were more. Hedda sitting in the car, head resting on her folded arms as she looked out the window. Hedda sitting on what looked like an overturned barrel, posed like a queen. Hedda, hands up to her mouth, her eyes betraying a laugh trapped behind them. Hedda leaning against the rough side of a barn, looking dreamily disheveled.

"None of the two of them together," Dini muttered. She'd laid them out in a grid on the table.

"They were alone," Quin said, stating the obvious. "And those cameras back then weren't great for close-ups. No selfies."

Dini's mind went to those moments earlier in the phone booth. "And no instant images."

"Nope."

"By the way," she said, not looking at him, "you didn't tag me in your Instagram post." There, he knew she'd seen it.

"Sorry, I always forget. Look at this." He picked up the photo of Detective Carmichael again. "You can tell he's not comfortable. It's the only picture of him in the entire lot."

"Maybe Hedda had the others?"

"No, I don't think so. Remember that movie, the Christmas one, in England, and that Mr. Darcy guy is writing a novel?"

"Love Actually."

"Yeah. And remember that scene when Natalie Portman—"

"—Keira Knightley—"

"—is watching the video footage of her wedding and realizes it's all just a bunch of close-ups of her, and that's when she realizes that the guy from *Walking Dead*—"

"—that he loves her."

Quin remained focused on the photos and adjusted his glasses in a manner she'd never seen before. It was a nervous gesture, a distraction. A tell. "He loved her."

"And look at this one." Dini picked up the image of Hedda standing beside the barn. Her clothes rumpled, her hair nearly tumbled down. There were, as far as Dini had ever been able to find, so few pictures of Hedda Krause. Her mind's eye conjured the image of Hedda in front of the Christmas tree, haughty and defiant in her finery. Or the photo portrait at the front of her book, the one she'd given to Irvin at some point. Or Hedda in a *San Antonio Express-News* special feature, aged, elegant, and wistful. In none of those did she look this beautiful. This natural and content, like she'd just exhaled and could easily do so again.

"She loved him too."

They sat next to each other, just breathing, the series of black-and-white photographs displayed like a timeline of romance. A man and a woman living a lifetime together, isolated, over the course of a single perfect day. Suddenly she felt the distinct guilt of a voyeur. She picked the photographs up one by one—gently, like she was gathering cards from a card trick.

"One thing," she said, jarring them both back into the moment, "these are in incredibly good shape, given they weren't preserved in an album or anything."

"They've been hidden in here all these years," Quin said, scooting the notebook across the table.

"Hidden?"

"Think about it. He married my great-great-grandmother just a few years after he arrived in Washington. He couldn't exactly have these framed and out on the bureau."

Dini set them aside and ventured a sip of her coffee. Bolstered, she took the notebook back from Quin and began its examination again with the first page.

"You don't want to start at the back?"

She ignored him. The pages were darkened around the edges but toward the center held what must have been the original hue—a light peach, with cadet-blue lines. The first three were blank, which she found puzzling, but then the workings of a detective's mind came out in full force. Lists, addresses, names. The handwriting was neat but occasionally blurred, evidence of his left-handedness. What she would give to spend an afternoon at the library, scrolling through the archived newspapers to find the crimes and cases annotated here. She read the detective's questions, written to himself, and his answers—some marked with stars, others obliterated with a heavy hand.

And then—

February 14, 1916, 22:30
Robbery/Menger Hotel
Ghost??? (~~Annie~~ Sally White)
Arnold Sylvan, mgr

Dini and Quin had chosen to sit on the same side of the booth so they could peruse the notebook together, but it was soon apparent that Quin had little interest in much before this date. She was aware—extremely, acutely aware—that he was studying her as intently as she was studying Carmichael's notes, offering a disinterested *hmm* between sips of coffee. But now he set down his mug and drew closer.

"Can you imagine what was in his mind when he had to write *ghost*?"

"He spelled Sallie wrong." Dini hovered her finger over the name. She turned the page and gasped.

"What is it?"

"The three questions." She pronounced it as if it were some notable historic document.

What is your name?
Hedda Krause
In what city is your husband's death certificate filed?
Denver
In what state were you married?
Tennessee

Dini marveled at it—his handwriting so prevalent and her responses neatly scripted within. And that single word. *Denver.* Two truths, one lie. For a moment, the heart pounding in her ears was Hedda's. The tips of her fingers tingling as she imagined the grip of the pen; her wrist involuntarily twisting in the act of writing. How could she choose what to confess and what to conceal? And did she want him to know, want to unburden herself?

Finally, Dini took the little notebook in both hands and brought it to her face. Careful not to touch her nose to the page, she closed her eyes and inhaled, deep enough to feel her shoulders rise with the effort. There it was, trapped in the living pores of the paper. Cigarettes. *His* cigarettes. His breath, his skin.

After a few such breaths, she lowered the book and opened her eyes to find Quin's face, closer than she remembered, looking amused.

"You are such a nerd," he said.

"I know."

And then he was closer still, one finger along her cheek, turning her toward him. At once the pulse was her own, the man beside her alive, and he was about to kiss her. Silently she pleaded with herself—*don't freeze. Relax. Breathe.* But the closer he came, the icier the chill down her neck, and when his lips touched hers—so lightly as to be fairy's feet—her hand broke free from its grip on the notebook and splayed itself on his chest, pushing him away.

"Don't," she said so softly the word was little more than a click behind her teeth.

"I'm sorry," he said, sitting back. "I thought we—"

"It's just that I—" She swallowed, buying time. "I've never. . ."

"Dini, we're here in a booth in the middle of a bar. And even if we weren't—I was only going to kiss you." He sat back, away. "But I'm sorry if I misread."

"You didn't misread." He hadn't really. "I've just never. . ." *Please don't make me say it out loud.* She watched, unwavering, as understanding dawned and he finished the statement.

"Been kissed."

She nodded, biting the inside of her cheek.

"How can that be?" His question held no shock, no incredulity, but a genuine, curious tone. "Because honestly? That's pretty much all I've been thinking about since the night we first talked."

It was the perfect thing to say and the perfect way to say it. She leaned in, resting her palm against his beard, and stayed very still. Not frozen, not locked. He touched her again too, expertly bringing her lips to meet his. She'd always been a singular person, and content to be so had anyone asked. The idea of being fitted together with someone, for any sort of physical contact to comprise itself of angles and connection, was more than she could imagine for herself. And yet, as soon as it began, this was no longer her first kiss. That designation would go to Quin's first attempt. This, she concluded, as he drew her ever closer, would be her truest.

Dini didn't know how or when to end, but Quin did, and inexperienced as she was, she felt his reluctance as he pulled away.

"I didn't go to high school," she said, using her mouth for some other purpose right away before following the temptation to fall into him again. "I didn't have a high school sweetheart or—anything. I couldn't have boyfriends. I couldn't date."

"Dini, you don't have to explain anything."

She plunged on. "And, understandably, my mother kept me away from—well, everybody. Because it's not the most honorable types who go on magic road shows, you know? And then my parents died, and everything was crazy, and I was hustling for shows myself. And, I'm sorry, but *dating* was just not a priority."

"I get it."

"You can't possibly get it because you are so *normal*. You know, except for my parents and Arya, I've never spent as much time—as many consecutive *hours*—with a person than I did with you today."

"It's been a great day."

"Can I keep this?" She clutched the notebook close. "For a while anyway. I want to read every word in it."

"Of course, but I want to see one more thing." He took the notebook and ran his thumb along the pages in the back, then held it out. "Here's the torn page when he sent the note up to her."

Dini took it and saw, right above the heedless tear, a series of abandoned starts, a line drawn through them, but still highly visible.

Dear Hedda,
Mrs. Krause—
I've just come back and I need
Some disturbing truth has come to

"In the end, he just invited her down to supper," Dini said.

"Speaking of. . . It's been a good day, but it's been a *long* day. I'm starving. Want to get something to eat? Here, or—choose someplace for my last San Antonio supper."

She didn't want to think about that. Didn't want to leave this moment. Technically, they wouldn't have to; the bar served nachos and such. They could stay in this booth and eat and talk. Laugh, kiss. But at some point, the time would come for them to part. She to her little bungalow and, tomorrow, he to his home in Virginia. Each hour only prolonged the inevitable. It was best, perhaps, to cut that short. To say goodbye with the feel of his kiss still pleasantly haunting her.

"I think," she said, not caring to hide her reluctance, "I should just go home."

"That's probably a good idea."

"What? Why?" His acquiescence felt like a sucker punch. Maybe part of her had been hoping that he would persuade her to stay.

He laughed. "It was *your* idea."

"I thought you'd try a little bit to stop me." She pouted, the kind of fake, flirty pout she would never have attempted a week ago.

He took her hand and studied it. "Look, if I had my way, you'd never leave. I wish you could stay here with me all night. Like literally, *here*, in this booth. Just to be with you, talk to you. Maybe kiss you again?" So he did, smaller and sweeter than the last.

"And then catch your plane? One of those crazy 4:00 a.m. drives to the airport? Which, by the way, I cannot drive you to the airport. I'm sure you understand that."

"Actually, while I was waiting here for you, I changed to a later flight. I'd stay through the weekend if I could, but Saturday is my niece's birthday and I promised to be at the party. She's turning eight. Apparently that's a big deal."

"Eight is a big deal. What's the theme?"

"Glitter ponies."

"Glitter ponies?"

"She made it up herself. Anyway, my point is, I doubled my airfare so I can spend more time with you tomorrow. Can I see you tomorrow?"

"Of course." Every bit of her filled with a feeling both new and familiar—a joyful anticipation. A next time. A tomorrow. Their last, but she wouldn't focus there. "Come to my house. Early. Or, early-ish. Until then, I am going to spend some quality time with your ancestor." She ran her thumb across the pages, fanning them like a deck of fragile cards, and almost missed the object that floated to the table.

"What is this?" Quin lifted it gently. Lying across his palm was a thin braid, half the width of the ribbon that marked another page. Dini looked closer, in awe of the perfection of the plaiting, tied at both ends with a bit of dark thread.

"It's hers." She ran her finger, the one wearing her signature witch's heart ring, along the length of it. Was this Hedda's handiwork? Or Carmichael's? There was no mention in the narrative about ever giving him such a gift, but then there had to be sweet, secret exchanges that lived on only in her heart. And his.

Gil showed up at the table ready to refill their long-cold coffee, even though there was an entire waitstaff he could dispatch for the duty. "Seems safe to come by." He gave Dini a wink, obviously signaling that he'd witnessed the more intimate moments of their conversation, but then took on a grave expression as Dini held out Quin's hand.

"Look," she said, overcome to share the artifact with the one person who truly knew, and truly understood, her passion. "It's hers. Hedda's."

"I always knew he loved her," Gil said, pouring. "Was a fool to leave her behind. She was never the same."

Dini noticed the questioning furrow on Quin's brow. "Gil's read the book almost as many times as I have. Right?"

"Right. And the staff talk too. People who remember."

He took one last look, the treasure now laid out on top of the journal, and hovered his hand above it. "Miss Hedda. Quite the beauty in her day."

Dini carefully placed the plait back within the pages of the notebook and noticed Quin browsing through the photos again. "Do you ever wonder if maybe he fell in love with her because he knew he was leaving?"

"How do you mean?"

"I never really knew him myself, but from family stories, he was. . .humorless. Typical, stereotypical, G-man. Exacting, high standards. Not exactly stern or mean, but not"—he held out the picture of Hedda, disheveled and lovely—"this guy. The guy who would take this picture. Or who would forgive. . ." He trailed the thought.

"You mean he felt safe to give in? Because he knew their relationship couldn't go anywhere?"

"Exactly."

"But maybe *this* is the real Irvin Carmichael. And he just became that stringent, exacting person after. . ."

"No. You saw those notes. Details. I'll bet in the whole book you don't find anything scratched over until you get to where he's trying to write a note to her. He didn't investigate her because he loved her. He investigated because that's what he was hardwired to do."

"But he loved her anyway."

"Yes. Because it was easy to do. He could let himself. Because he knew, at some point, he was going back to Virginia."

"He was going *to* Washington."

"That's what I said."

"No, you didn't."

And then it was really clear that neither of them were talking about Hedda and Carmichael anymore.

Chapter 18

Excerpt from

My Spectral Accuser: The Haunted Life of Hedda Krause

Published by the Author Herself

I always hated the winters in Colorado," I said, finally speaking into the vast expanse of silence between us. Carmichael had come to sit beside me. More like *perched*, on the edge of my bed, his head buried in his hands. "Was there snow?"

He looked at me, first only peeking through his fingers, and then dropping his hands to reveal an expression of disapproving curiosity. It was as if he couldn't quite conjure a response, torn as he was between irritation and amusement.

"I went to the county records office and saw the death certificate."

"God rest his soul," I said. Because I could call on God too.

"Then I went to the library and tracked down the newspaper carrying the obituary. You are named as his wife, Hedda."

"Of course I was. I wouldn't lie about my name. I was—am—proud to have his name."

"I took down the address." Here, like a reflex, he touched the pocket where I knew he carried his notebook. "And I went to your house."

My breath caught. I loved that house. I could picture it now, a drift of new snow on the shrubbery like icing on a cake. The walkway shoveled clean and covered with tiny rocks of salt. And inside, a roaring fire. There was a back room that faced the garden, an entire wall of windows. In the winter, when it was too cold to spend time outdoors, my husband ordered the garden swing to be brought inside so we could sit next to each other and watch the snow fall. It was the kind of indulgence a father would do for a child, and his own sons hated me for it. For other things too of course, but the swing was a particular sore spot. The scraping of our feet wore a pattern in the carpet, and we were making plans to have it replaced when he took ill. The day after the funeral, I awoke to find the carpet had been removed and the swing a pile of chopped wood in the yard.

"I loved that house."

"I can see why. And I can see why you'd want to keep it."

"I never thought I would keep it. He told me—my late husband—before he died that I would not. But there were. . .things. Things I purchased with my allowance, things I picked out for my own gifts. A darling little sofa at the end of our bed—I slept on that for the final months, you know. My tea set, lamps, works of art—all things that were *mine*. I only ever wanted what was mine to have. Nothing more."

My gaze fell on my trunk in the corner of the room. My husband had bought it to carry all the gifts, the trinkets and silks and furs, he bought me during our courtship. One night is all they gave me. One night to fill it with all I could, and that is what I was allowed to take. My mind ached at the memory of it, never doubting that I would be able to return again to lay claim to the rest. I could not have imagined the lengths they would go to in their selfishness.

"Did you see the boys, then?" My throat was dry, and the question came out more as a croak.

He huffed a laugh. "The *boys*?"

"He always called them that. Even though they were grown men. They are older than I, you know."

"I know."

"Did you meet them?"

"I saw them, but I did not make their acquaintance."

"Are they still fat?"

Carmichael threw his head back and laughed in earnest. "They are."

"Oh, how they hated me. From the moment I stepped across the threshold. The horrible things they said. They thought I wanted to steal their father."

"They think you wanted to kill their father. That maybe you did something to make him sick before you turned into a nurse trying to make him better."

And there it was. My secret. Carmichael's voice always reminded me of the sound that comes with a first bite into perfectly toasted bread. It always warmed me, made me want to hear one more sentence. One more word. It was no different now as he spoke my greatest fear. His tone held no condemnation, only a statement of quiet, unavoidable fact. We sat, no more than three inches between us, but a wall filled that narrow space. Impenetrable and towering. I had no experience of going to church before meeting my late husband, and even then, no experience with spoken confession. Yet my spirit took Carmichael as its confessor.

"I loved their father."

"I understand."

"I don't think you do. I don't think you could. He was the first person ever to be kind to me. I had no idea of the vastness of his wealth before I agreed to marry him. I thought he was only a good-hearted gentleman who doted on me much the same as a man would his daughter."

"But you were not his daughter."

"Of course not. Nor was I his mistress. I was his wife—in every sense—and the years I spent with him were the first of my life knowing without a doubt that I would wake up and lay my head down on the same pillow each morning and night. I never questioned if I would eat or if I would have to fight. Or run. Why"—I turned to him now and spoke to his stone-graven profile—"why would I give that up? Never mind that he held my heart's affection. Why would an animal turn on its master?"

His head snapped toward me at this. "Don't call yourself that."

"It's true. It fits. You wouldn't recognize me if you knew me then."

"I know you now, Hedda." In a single, swift movement, he grasped me by my upper arms and pulled me close, to where I was pressed up against him and had to tilt my head back to fully see the moss green of his eyes. "I can give you everything he did. Maybe not a mansion, yet. Or jewels, all those *things* you walked away from. But I give you my love. And I'll keep you safe."

"Safe from the boys?"

"Safe from the world."

He bent his head to kiss me, and slowly his grip softened, his fingers spreading across my back and gently laying me down upon the bed. His body covered mine and I thought—*why, yes. He will cover me.* If one of the boys came through the door at that moment, I would have been completely hidden beneath the breadth of this man. I could go through life with him as my shield. My protector.

His kisses grew more ardent. I sensed a defiance in his affections, as if he were overcoming his own doubts, ready to take me before I had a chance to become something monstrous. He knew I could claim no innocence with my body—in that we were equal. But he was a good man who saw the world divided and measured by the rule of law. And this, I feared, would always be a fission between us.

Carmichael sensed my cooling passion and disengaged our kiss, rolling off and propping himself up on one arm beside me. "I'm sorry, my darling. I shouldn't have intruded on you like this. And I didn't mean—" He sat up and inched over to the side, leaving a wide berth for me to straighten my dress and move myself to the safety beside my desk.

"Does this mean that you believe me?"

"This means that I love you."

"But when I tell you that I had nothing to do with my husband's death, other than to be his nurse until the end—"

"Meaning you gave him his medication?"

"Of course I did."

"According to the doctor's instructions? Precisely?"

I closed my eyes, remembering, and said, "He was in so much pain." There was nothing to be done, and from the moment I'd met him, he'd given me everything I ever wanted. Everything I asked for. How could I not do the same? I said none of this to Carmichael, though. I kept every drop to myself, to my thoughts. I opened my eyes again and poured forth truth. "I bathed him and fed him and"—I brought the back of my wrist to my mouth to stanch the memory—"*cleaned* him when he was too ashamed to allow anyone else. Those ungrateful buffoons wouldn't come near him." I pointed, as if they were lurking outside the door. "That was me, knowing full well I'd be turned out of the house he was dying in. Knowing my name wasn't in the will. So when you say that you love me, are you saying too that you believe me?"

While I was speaking, he took a cigarette from his pocket and rolled it nervously between his fingers. Now he stood and crossed the room in a single step to deposit it in the waste bin. He went to his knee, just like he had that night by the dying fire in the lobby, and took my hands in his. "What I'm saying, is that it doesn't matter. Who you were, and what you might have done before the night I laid eyes on you—I don't care. We can put it behind us. Come with me. Marry me tomorrow. Heck, it's after midnight. Marry me today. There's no impediment. We don't ever have to think about any of this again."

"You could marry me thinking I might be a murderess?"

"There's no evidence to say you are."

Nothing but the suspicions of two ungrateful, spoiled men. But Carmichael hadn't gone on a quest to investigate the peaceful, unavoidable death of my husband. He'd gone in search of my credibility. To that, there was no evidence other than my word.

I attempted to pull my hand away. "You could marry me thinking I'm a fraud?"

"I've told you before, it's a battle between my head and my heart. And tonight I'm telling you that you consume both. Whatever suspicions I might have—they've lost their power over me."

"Maybe so, but they would always hold a certain power over me." I stepped back and, as he loosened his grip, pulled my desk chair beneath me and sat on it, bringing our faces to perfect alignment, neither looking up nor down at the other. "I have no reason to doubt my innocence. I harbor no guilt. I am as sure of my late husband's promises as I am of his illness. I know I did nothing to hasten his death. I know I stole nothing from that house. I know I sold my own jewels in good faith, and I know a phantom drove me from my room so that all I had left could be taken. But even now, my darling—" I touched his face, glancing away. "You can't hold my eyes. I can't hold your trust completely, even in this moment. Don't you see? There would always be a part of you that wasn't ever truly, completely mine. I would always wonder if you were. . .*wondering*."

"I wouldn't."

"Ah, but that's not the point. *I* would. You are a good man, Detective Carmichael. You deserve a good woman."

He was still kneeling but now appeared coiled, his jaw clenched, his lips hardly moving as he spoke. "You are a good woman."

"You need one who won't require so much convincing."

I opened his hand and turned his palm up, spying the two errant freckles on its heel and kissing them.

"Come with me," he said, my head still bowed.

"No." I brushed my lips against his pulse and stood. He followed in a fluid motion, our fingers still entwined.

"I won't ask again."

"I know."

We stood, the weight of my decision suspended between us for what seemed an eternity before he bent to me and placed a kiss so gentle against my lips, I found no purchase to pull it deeper. Without another word, another touch, another breath, he was gone. The moment was so silent—not even the creak of a footfall or the finality of a closed door. I looked down through the slatted vent and saw the cuff of his pants and the sturdiness of his shoes as he stood, facing away. And then I watched his step. Of all the frightful things that happened on the other side of that door, this was by far the cruelest. I crumpled to the floor, my head resting on the mattress where I'd allowed myself to dream of a life with him. Long days and cozy nights, reading books and sharing stories, curled together on a different bed. Waking to the first frosty morning of fall, dozing in each other's arms on a Sunday afternoon. Our day together multiplied a thousand times over, endless in beauty and passion.

What had I done?

Heedless of my loose hair, my belted robe, my bare feet, I threw the door open and ran down the hall, down the stairs, my cries for him caught in my throat. This time no ghost of a dead woman chased me. Rather, I was running from the restless spirit I would become without him. I didn't so much run as hurl myself, guided by the instinct of following a path I could travel in my sleep. The night clerk was nothing more than a blur of a scathing look as my steps slapped against the polished floor.

I ran up to the front door and was about to open it to the night when the memory of Mr. Sylvan's voice came back. *"Step out, and the doors will be locked to you forever."* I stopped, balanced as if on a precipice, my toes on the strip meant to keep out the cold. Could I run barefoot into the street? I pressed my face against the glass, looking for his unmistakable silhouette in the darkness. Not to the left, nor to the right. I could run, yes. And hope for one more chance to see his face break into relief with new tears sprung in his eyes. Or I could wait for his resolve to soften, for him to plumb the depths of his heart and find no charge to hold against me.

My breath steamed against the glass, and when I lifted my sleeve to wipe it away, I was startled by a shimmering reflection behind me.

I spun. "Bert!"

He stood, a solitary, immobile figure steps away from the bar in the lobby. I held out my hand, beckoning him to me, ready to send him out into the street to find Carmichael and fetch him back, but something about the grim set to his face stopped me. Taking careful, measured steps, I approached him.

"That detective went out through the bar," Bert said when I was in earshot.

Through the bar? Of course. I'd turned the wrong way and lost him.

"He told me to give you this."

That's when I noticed the envelope in his hand. With a steadiness that surprised myself, I reached for it, saying, "Thank you."

"Are you all right, Mrs. Krause?" He asked as if he didn't know—didn't always know—the exact state of my mind and spirit.

"I will be, Bert," I said, laying a hand on his sleeve. "I always am."

Feet weighed with consequence, I climbed the steps, taking them as if a woman condemned. Once on my floor, I could not bring myself to go back into that room, not while the scent of him still lingered, not when I could imagine the dent and the warmth of him on my bed. Instead, I sat on one of the cushioned settees along the second-floor balcony. There was enough light to see my name typewritten on the envelope. My name and nothing more. Turning it over, I could see that it had been opened—partially, at least—and easily gave way for me to do so completely. Inside was a single, folded sheet with a letterhead so familiar I felt the punch of it in my core. Johnston and Thornhill Associates. The law firm that represented all of my late husband's business activity, as well as his death, burial, and final testament.

They're coming for me, I thought, before allowing my eyes to access the salutation. *Carmichael told them where I am.* No wonder I'd felt such weight at my last ascent. I *was* a woman condemned. This letter would be my invitation to the gallows. No doubt there were officers on their way to claim me.

My eyes grew so dense with tears that I could hardly focus on the words, so I allowed time for them to empty, then brought the paper close, focusing on my name—*Dear Mrs. Krause*.

I cannot, at this writing, reproduce the words in their exactness. I am not a trained legal mind, and the vocabulary escapes me. The letter itself became worn, read to shreds, though I kept it until the Denver newspaper (to which I treated myself a Sunday subscription) carried the obituaries of the boys, rendering it no longer necessary to defend myself should the need arise. In short, Mr. David Thornhill, Esq., wrote to inform me that unknown to those boys, my husband had provided for me in a will separate to the one connected to his estate. The terms here provided for my keep—the same allowance as he provided during our time together. No more, no less, to be paid to me on a monthly basis—as the account would allow—spanning from the day of his death to the day of my own. In my haste to escape the boys' accusations, I had no opportunity to be contacted, and until the day of Detective Irvin Carmichael's visit, my whereabouts were unknown. I was to rest assured of two promises: the sons had no claim or knowledge of this circumstance, that the back payments due to me had—as of the date on the letter—been wired to an account in my name at a prominent San Antonio bank, and I need only present this letter to activate the account and begin to withdraw funds as needed.

How to describe my feeling upon reading this? I have known the experience of drowning, my head plunged and held under with a villain's hand on my neck, and I knew the triumph of gathering my strength and throwing him off, rising again to sweet, life-giving breath. I have known what it is to fall, pushed into a street, the feeling of hooves and wheels across my skirts, but my life spared. Sometimes, in a way to prove to my husband how literally he had saved my life, I would tell him these stories from the safe warmth of our bed. He would listen and pat me and tell me that I was his greatest, sweetest joy. And that I would never have to fear for my life again.

I brought the letter to my mouth and kissed it, whispering my gratitude aloud. Whispering his name to echo softly in the vastness of this space that spanned three floors below the sky. The envelope fell from my lap, and as it did something else slipped from it. Even in the dim light, I recognized the distinctive shade of a paper torn from Carmichael's notebook. A new tremble came to my hands as I gingerly picked it up. The sheet had been carelessly ripped away, the note hastily written.

Please know I had no intentions of withholding this, no matter your choice. I wanted us to choose each other for the sake of love alone. ~~I. C.

I folded Carmichael's note into the letter and tucked both into the envelope. It was frightfully cold, and I had a warm bed waiting. I passed the stairs on my way and wondered for a moment if I should sneak down to inform Bert that all was well. All was settled. But there would be another time. I knew this as surely as I knew that I had finally found the home I searched all my life for, and I would share it only with those spirits who would come to visit in my dreams.

Chapter 19

It had been decided that Dini would take a Lyft home from the Menger, and Quin would deliver her car in the morning when he came over for breakfast and a final visit. Downtown was choked with the kind of traffic that always happens with a Spurs game, and while the normally fifteen-minute drive took nearly an hour, at least she could experience it in the back seat of a late-model sedan rather than white-knuckled behind the wheel of her Kia Soul.

She used the time to read through her battered copy of *My Spectral Accuser*, which Quin had returned to her with all the solemnity of exchanged custody. Illuminating the pages with her cell phone light as darkness fell, she read about the burning of the Christmas picture, knowing a copy of the picture was waiting for her at home. She read between the lines of Hedda and Carmichael's day together, filling them in with the photos of that day. She read and reread that final night, following her desperate chase, clinging to irrational hope that maybe she'd read it wrong all these years. Maybe Detective Carmichael would come back this time. Carry Hedda away into the winter night.

Once home (after a hefty tip to her driver, who remained blessedly silent for the entire ride), she put on a pot of tea and went straight back to her bedroom, stepping out of the high heels and peeling off the black dress en route. She washed her face and stared at her reflection as the water dripped down. She was a different girl than the one who'd stood here in the midmorning, expertly fanning her eyeliner. Her lips were full, soft, and naturally pink—and they'd been kissed.

Moments later, dressed in a Hamilton T-shirt and flannel pajama pants, she sat with her tea and a stack of buttered toast, Carmichael's notebook open before her. "What do you know?" she asked aloud, waiting for a miracle moment when a breeze would blow in and magically open the notebook to the right page, revealing all. But of course there was no breeze, and no miracle answer. His notebook didn't address anything beyond Hedda's account. Chewing, she brushed the crumbs off her hands and turned to the last page. The lawyer's name in Denver, his address, and a monetary amount. Underlined, and smeared—a victim of the detective's left hand. The next page was torn out, as she knew it would be. Not carelessly ripped like the page where he'd scribbled an invitation to dinner, but perfectly, as if he'd been biding his time.

Her phone vibrated with a text from Quin.

Q: You make it home ok?
D: Yes. Sorry. . .should have texted you.
Q: Do I need to bring anything tomorrow?
D: Just my car. . .safe and sound.
Q: Don't worry. She's in good hands.
D: 9:30 too early?
Q: Perfect. See you then.
Q: Good night, Dini.

Something about the last text, maybe the full minute that elapsed before he sent it, stirred a bit of excitement within her. She giggled, then clamped her hand over her mouth as if hiding it from—what? Her teapot? She read it over and over again, marveling at the punctuation. She pictured his thumb hovering over the keys and then, unbidden, heard the words in his voice. He'd said them as they waited on the curb for her Lyft, and she felt the breath of them on her cheek right before he'd placed a kiss on the corner of her mouth.

D: Good night, Quin.

For fun she added a GIF of a bunny snuggling down into bed. Immediately she wished she could take it back. It was the same GIF she sent to Arya all the time, but somehow, sending it to the man who had kissed her (and kissed her and kissed her), a new, suggestive angle took hold.

Then Quin replied with a GIF of two animated kittens sharing a sweet kitten kiss, and Dini giggled again, all of her fears of unleashing the sultry bunny forgotten.

She was about to put the phone away and take her dishes to the sink when Arya's face came on the screen. Dini took the call, settling back with her final piece of toast and tepid tea. After the usual rundown about Arya's day—drama with Bea's school butterfly project, Bill's inability to appreciate a good take-out dinner—her friend stopped midsentence and said, "Wait a minute. What's up with you?"

Dini wiped the corner of her mouth with her shirt sleeve. "What do you mean, *What's up?*"

"You look different."

"I know." She raked her fingers through her curls. "But it's not as bad as it looks in this light. Really, more of a lavender—"

"I'm not talking about your hair." Arya took on a look of extreme concentration and moved her face closer to her camera, filling Dini's screen with an exaggerated view of her friend's nose.

"Stop," Dini said, moving herself out of range.

"You just giggled."

"I did not."

She had.

"It's that nerd. Something happened with him." She was back to a safe distance, but the angle of her head demanded details.

"He went with me to a show." Dini tried—but failed—to control the invisible wires tugging at her lips as she spoke. Nothing escaped scrutiny on FaceTime.

"You two looked pretty cozy on Instagram."

"You saw that?"

"I did."

Dini felt an involuntary smile at the memory. "We spent a really nice day together."

"And?"

"And"—the smile quivered—"he's leaving tomorrow. So that's that. A nice day, a nice kiss, and tomorrow is goodbye."

"He kissed you?" Arya's big brown eyes glistened. "Aw, boo—your first kiss."

The two laughed and swiped ridiculous tears from their cheeks. This was a moment Dini would have shared with her mother—or maybe a sister if she'd had one. Arya was both. "I feel like I'm sixteen, making such a big deal out of it."

"That's okay. You were busy doing other things when you were sixteen. I kissed plenty of boys back in my youth. You're not missing out on anything." A long sigh and then, "You like this guy, don't you?"

"I don't really know how fair it is for me to say that, because I've never really dated, right? But yeah, I do."

"First love is a powerful thing."

"Who said anything about love?"

"Girl, your face is saying it all over."

Dini woke up a little before seven, immediately alert in anticipation. Her alarm wasn't set to go off for another thirty minutes, but the buzzing of her phone made her realize she hadn't woken naturally. She'd been summoned by her phone's vibration, and she reached for it, unplugging the charging cable in one fluid motion. A text from Quin. Actually, five texts from Quin.

Q: Are you awake yet?

Q: Text me when you're awake.

Q: I thought of something, but I don't want to text it.

Q: Seriously, I woke up with this thought.

Q: Realizing how stalker I sound, so I will see you at 9.

Dini read the one-sided conversation over again, hearing every word of it in his voice, picturing his thumbs racing around the keyboard. She replied with the big-eyes emoji.

D: See you at 9!!!

Having showered the night before, she immediately got dressed—if pulling on last night's flannel pants and T-shirt counted as getting dressed. Slipping her feet into her soft, worn pair of fleece-lined Crocs, she went into the bathroom, washed her face—noting the sheet creases still embedded in her cheeks. She squeezed a dollop of gel into her palm and worked it through her hair, defining the curls in their natural state. There was plenty of time to get back to the idea of makeup.

The coffee table in the living room had been transformed into an evidence area, of sorts, with all of Quin's offerings displayed. It reminded her of those investigation boards on crime movies, with the red yarn pinned between elements to show connections. There was something here. Something that would put to rest Hedda's haunting. Detective Carmichael had figured it out—Dini had her own revelation to share with Quin. Unfortunately, as far as she could tell, he didn't leave a final report.

In the kitchen, she measured double the amount of her home-ground coffee and put on a pot, loving the moment when the little house filled with the sound and smell of brewing. But there was one thing missing.

"Alexa," she spoke into the dawn-filled room, "play soft seventies." Within seconds, Neil Sedaka's "Laughter in the Rain" set the tone for the morning. She pulled flour and baking soda from her sparse but neat cupboards. Quin's face had been near rapturous with the flour tortillas at Mi Tierra, and he'd sent three texts describing the tortillas at Alamo Café. She almost told him how, really, they were super easy to make, but then the conversation had turned. . . . Measuring deftly, she combined the simple ingredients and set to singing as she kneaded the dough. Three songs—"Bluer Than Blue," "Summer Breeze," and "Midnight Train to Georgia."

While the dough balls rested beneath a wet paper towel, she made her bed and got dressed—for real this time. Her house was comfortably, but not overly, warm, and the forecast called for sunshine and cool temps, her favorite weather. Denim shorts, a black thin-strap cami, and a forest-green sweater. Little River Band's "Lady" came on, seeming to affirm her choice. She pulled on a pair of no-show footies and slipped her feet into the Ugg boots she'd bought with her first four-digit gig check. Even she, who never cared much about fashion outside of dressing for her audiences, knew they had out-lasted their popularity, but she loved them anyway. She looked at herself in the long mirror, twisting to see the strip of tattooed card suits stretching out of the boots. They weren't nearly as alluring with this ensemble as they were with the skirt and heels, but then this morning she dressed for an audience of one. Quin. If he was only going to see her for one more day, she wanted him to see the *real* her. All her favorites, carefully—if artfully—chosen and arranged, revealing her scar, jagged along the outer side of her right thigh. In the bathroom, she put on a minimum of makeup—CC cream, mascara, a touch of blush for color on her cheeks. Nobody needed to look *that* real.

"Just be. . .normal," she said to her reflection. "You're a girl who kissed a boy, and now you're going to make chorizo tacos and solve a century-old crime together before he ditches you and goes back to high school."

She repeated affirmations while working her fingers through the now-dry curls, softening them into something cloud-like. After two shampoos the night before, the color was fading (as it was designed to do), and if she had any regrets about anything this week, it was the fact that Quin never got to see her real hair. Eschewing any other accessories, she slid her spoon-handle silver ring on her finger and went back into the kitchen, stopping to open the front door to this glorious morning and let the sunshine pour through the glass one behind it.

The coffee was ready, and she fixed a cup, pouring it over the generous amount of powdered creamer Arya berated her for using. The cast iron comal was ready too, having been warmed in the oven. She took it out, placed it over a low flame, and rolled out the first tortilla. Try as she might, she could never achieve uniformity, and the first was always more amoebic than round, but it puffed nicely and made a perfect little *pouff* when she flipped it over to cook on the other side. She was singing with the Monkees—" 'Cheer up, sleepy Jean' "—when she heard his knock. A glance at the stove clock showed it to be not quite eight thirty. If it was Quin, he was early.

Her phone buzzed.

Q: I'M HERE. EARLY. SORRY.

Her house was small enough that a single step brought him into sight, and it hit her all at once that she'd been waiting for precisely this moment since he handed her into a Lyft the previous evening.

"Come in," she said, motioning with her hand in case he couldn't hear her. She waited long enough to see him step over the threshold then returned to the kitchen, pulling the tortilla off of the comal before it scorched.

"You don't lock your front door?"

She wanted to say that of course she locked her door except for those times when she was expecting company, but that made it seem like she had company often, which she didn't. So she ignored the comment and summoned him into the kitchen.

"What is happening in here?" He prefaced the question with an appreciative sound that she took at first to be a comment on her, but then he rubbed his hands together as if someone tied a napkin around his neck and presented him with a plate of ribs. "Coffee?"

"Right there." Though the kitchen was so small he couldn't miss it.

"I am so glad to see that you are a good old-fashioned Mr. Coffee girl. Keurigs are ruining the world."

"Right? It's my own blend, so I hope you like it. And I have other creamers in the fridge, I think."

"I'm good, thanks. Take it straight."

He filled the SeaWorld souvenir mug she handed him and took a sip, his eyes popping with appreciation before taking another.

"That is really, really good." He was talking at a rate that made him sound like he was already three cups in, but then Dini realized he might be nervous too, given. . .everything that happened the night before. As a kindness, and a chance to keep them *both* distracted, she instructed him to wash his hands and take up the task of rolling out the tortillas while she manned the stove.

"You've used a rolling pin before?"

"It's my job when we have biscuits for Saturday morning big family breakfast. So, yeah."

"Same principle. Pressure, but gentle. You want to spread them out but not flatten them." She watched, approving, before jumping in. "So, what's the big conclusion you hit upon last night?"

"Nope," he said, not looking up from his task. "No important talk before we eat, right?"

"You remember that?"

He paused in his rolling. "I remember everything." A beat or two fell between them, and if he was remembering the same moments, they might have chosen to stay embedded in that silence. "I never knew," he said, finally breaking the spell. "I mean, didn't really know anyone made their own tortillas."

Nudged into motion, she put the newly cooked tortilla on the stack of finished ones and dropped a fresh one on the pan. "I had a stretch of time between gigs last winter, so I took a two-week Mexican cooking class. It's perfect for someone like me who loves the food but hates to drive." She approved his work, and he set out to roll the next.

"So, tell me about this house. This kitchen? It looks like you should be wearing a little apron and pearls. Is everything original?"

"All but the fridge. Either original or replicas. It's been in the family for generations—like Carmichael's, I guess. I was only sixteen when my parents died, and I inherited it. It was still in good shape, but we didn't live here much of the time, you know? It was a stopover place. So, until I could take full possession—I was in the hospital for, like, six weeks, then Arya fostered me—we found a guy who was a professional handyman-slash-restorer who did all the work in exchange for living here rent-free. Labor of love—for the house, I mean. And it got Arya interested in real estate. Every year for my birthday she presents me with the tax assessment and offers to get me a million dollars so I can buy a condo downtown and hang out with the cool kids."

"This isn't a cool kid neighborhood?"

"Not really. More older people, like my parents would have been. But I don't want to sell anytime soon. I own this. The title was transferred to Arya while I was a minor, and we've kept it that way, but it's truly mine."

"It's a great investment."

"It's a *home*. When I was little, I never wanted to leave. I felt like I was on some old TV show when we were here."

He twisted his neck, looking around. "I can see that."

"I'll give you the grand tour after breakfast. Plot twist, you can do the whole tour from the living room."

They worked together for a while after that in a silence that was far more comfortable than the initial coffee conversation. Dini stole the occasional look at his forearms, thinking she'd never known that to be a sexy part of a man's body, but nearly jumped away when he caught her eye as if she'd been peeping at him through a window. For her part too she felt his eyes on her and was thankful for the heat of the stove to explain away the flush she felt. In no time, the comfortable silence squeezed them into an unspoken tension, intensified when the first strains of the Bee Gees' "How Deep Is Your Love" flowed through the Bluetooth speaker perched on the antique phone table by the kitchen door. Quin rolled, Dini flipped, while the smooth harmony sang of eyes in the morning sun, touching in the pouring rain, and coming to each other on a summer breeze. Under normal circumstances, this song would have stopped Dini short so she could devote the next four minutes to sinking into it, but now she stiffened, imagining the lyrics floating from her mind and wrapping around the two of them engaged in such kitchen synchronicity. Then Quin grasped the rolling pin like a mic and, in a pitch-perfect match to Barry Gibbs's falsetto, sang, " 'You may not think that I care for you when you know deep inside that I really do,' " then held the pin between them to invite her to sing the next few lines, which she did, with passable harmony.

The cheesy romance of the lyrics gave Dini an escape route for all of the feelings that built up to this moment. Did she want to be in those arms? Yes, but there was no way of knowing if he wanted the same thing. How could they, when they weren't the same people? Quin, divorced and dating; she, not even twenty-four hours past her first kiss. And yet maybe in some construct of time they were the same, both having missed out on the normalcy of being young and single. Both of them dropped in the path of a first, true love—at least first and true for her. But for him?

She watched him during the lyric-free verse, the two of them *la-da-da*-ing, the full commitment of his body to the song, and thought simultaneously that he was the biggest nerd she'd ever imagined and that she wanted to have this moment every day for the rest of her life. Was he the only light in the darkest night? No. But he was a source that illuminated the space around her. She'd never shared herself with another person. She loved her parents, but she spent much of her time alternating between being part of the act and being alone. She loved Arya but had come into her life as a legal responsibility—something that still underscored all they were to each other. She and Quin had fallen into each other's lives the same way they'd fallen into this duet. She didn't know if she loved him deeply, but she knew that she loved him in the way she'd always imagined love would feel—immediate and consuming.

Eventually the song faded into another soft gem from the seventies, and Quin resumed his rolling. "So, you have an old music soul too?"

"It's what I listened to with my mother," she said, remembering nights in a darkened dressing room, listening to the radio while her father finished his act. "I never bothered to develop my own taste, I guess."

"Yeah, I was born in 1990 and always felt like I brought a curse to the music world."

"Well, now I know who to blame."

"I mean, I haven't heard that song in years, and all the lyrics were still right here"—he tapped his temple—"and here." He tapped his heart.

There was an edge here, daring Dini to take him seriously, but she wasn't about to let an old disco song be the vehicle of her profession of love. "I've always thought the lyrics in disco music are inconsequential. Lots of repetition and cliché."

"Right," he agreed. "If you listen, the vocal is really more of a lead instrument, rather than a purveyor of great truth. Just a bunch of let's dance, then go to bed, then dance again."

Dini assumed an authoritative air. "You know, Quin, we're living in a world of fools."

"Breaking us down."

"When they all should let us be."

"We belong to you and me."

What she initiated with mock sincerity, though, took a turn. It was a rare moment in the breakfast chore when both the skillet and the rolling board were empty and they stood idle with the unfortunate background sound of "Baby, I'm-a want you" standing between them, until there was nothing between them, because he had pulled her close, and she could taste her special coffee blend on his breath, then on her lips. The rim of his glasses touched the top of her cheek, and she wanted to take them off, but that seemed presumptuous. She touched his face, and he changed his angle, which made room to draw her deeper in. Not trusting her strength, Dini gripped his bicep, her fingers dipped beneath the sleeve of his T-shirt, lest she fall back into the glowing blue flame. This other flame, the one burning red hot within her, deserved no caution. She would throw herself in—gladly—and alternate between burning and melting as she did in this moment.

Until Quin stepped away. She still touched him, held him, and he kept her in an identical grip.

"Dini, I—"

"Nope." Her voice, like his, thick with everything she was too afraid to hear right now. "No important talk before food."

"Right."

"And, to help"—she lifted her head and spoke over his shoulder—"Alexa, playlist House Music," bringing to life a big band orchestra in the Bluetooth.

"I don't think this is what the kids call house music."

"I'm not a kid, and this is my house."

With only three tortillas left to cook, Dini transferred Quin's responsibilities to both the rolling and the cooking while she busied herself crumbling and cooking chorizo into a pan on the second burner and cracking eggs as it sizzled.

"I hope you like this," she said, whisking. "I wanted you to have one last taste of San Antonio before you go."

"I totally trust you." He took a tortilla from the freshly cooked stack, tore it, and offered half to Dini.

They ate and cooked, each humming along as a different instrument until they were finally seated at the little table, a plate of *chorizo con huevos* and a stack of tortillas between them. Individual plates were incidental as they served themselves from the center dish, making tacos, and silenced for a bit with the satisfaction of heat and flavor. Their conversation remained inconsequential: he talked about his rambling, whip-smart family—a mass of sisters and husbands and nieces and nephews, with Quin the bachelor uncle who could be depended on to give the noisiest, most questionably age-appropriate gift on any occasion. She countered with stories of her unusual childhood, realizing that many of these were memories she'd been carrying around for years but was voicing for the first time. How she'd learned to fold herself up so her father could cut her in half, how it was her job to make sure her mother wore the right shoes and stockings to match the spring-loaded feet when it was her turn in the box.

"I think that's why I never thought anything really bad could ever happen to my mother—to either of my parents. When I was told they'd been killed, I thought it was another trick."

"I'm so sorry," Quin said. "Confession? I googled your parents' accident. It's so hard to understand why God allows things like that to happen."

"I had a hard time with that myself. We never went to church or anything even remotely close to that when I was growing up, but then when Arya took me in—I wouldn't know God at all if it weren't for her. And it's been harder since I've been on my own to really keep up. Church always seems more geared to families, you know?"

"I know. I think that's why I let myself get pressured into getting married before I was ready, to someone I didn't totally love. It was just. . .expected. The next thing to do in life so I could keep fitting in. So I have to work hard to keep my faith intentional."

"Like finding a church when you're out of town?"

"Exactly. And finding the right scriptures to back up why we can't believe in ghosts."

"Right." Dini took the empty dish to the sink and came back with the carafe of coffee, refilling their cups.

"So, I guess that means it's time to talk about Hedda now?"

"The big stuff." She brought a small tray with her butter dish and sugar bowl to the table. "But one last snack to top it off."

"I am going to have to spend the next three days in the gym to work this off," Quin said, following her example of dipping the back of the spoon into the softened butter, spreading it in the middle of the still-warm tortilla, and sprinkling the top with a sugar and cinnamon mixture.

"You have an eight-year-old's birthday party tomorrow. Same

amount of calories burned in a bouncy house."

He lifted the rolled tortilla in a toast. "To glitter ponies."

"To glitter ponies."

"Now," she said as she watched him thoroughly enjoy his breakfast dessert, "I know we both think we have something, but I'm going to start. I don't think Detective Carmichael ever solved this case."

"What makes you say that?" Only, he was eating, so it sounded like *Whamakshoosayzat?*

"I noticed something in his notebook. He dated the top of the pages whenever he started a new investigation and then dated it at the end, near the bottom. *But*, he didn't just write the date. He also cut the bottom corner off the page so he could easily find the first page of the next case. He didn't cut the page on this one. I feel like he *almost* knew. I feel like *I* almost know, but there's something missing—"

"There is—"

"—and something probably so obvious—"

"—it is—"

"—like right under our nose—"

"—or, like right *behind* your nose."

She was about to take a bite but let her hand drop. "Behind my nose? What could possibly be behind my nose?"

He pointed with his bitten stub of a rolled tortilla. "You. You've had the key your whole life."

Chapter 20

Excerpt from
My Spectral Accuser: The Haunted Life of Hedda Krause
Published by the Author Herself

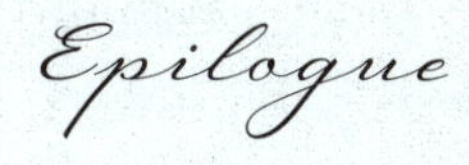

I am known, affectionately, as the Lady in Residence. Some of the old-timers, the ones who have been around almost as long as I have, still call me by my name. Though, of all the people I knew from my first night here at the Menger Hotel, only Bert remains. Mr. Sylvan died of a gentle stroke behind his desk not long after the end of the Second World War. I witnessed it from across the lobby. He was simply writing in his ledger, looked up, sent me a rare friendly smile, and then dropped behind the counter. We had long since mended our feud—partly owing to the weekly payment I made for my room, and partly to the visitors who came to hear my story.

For my part, I had abided by my promise not to go to the press with my story. But the hotel was full of guests that night who had been questioned by Detective Carmichael. They left, taking the tale far and wide, and many brought it back. They'd whisper to Mr. Sylvan, *Is the woman who was robbed by the ghost of Sallie White still here?* And he would nod in my direction if I happened to be reading in the lobby or knitting by the light of the fire.

Because, Reader, as you know unless you purchased this book by pure happenstance, I never left the Menger Hotel after that night. Quite literally, for nearly the first year. I opened my bank account via written correspondence, followed by coffee in the Menger dining room with the bank president to reassure him of my existence and situation. All that time, Mr. Sylvan's truth rang in my ears, and I feared he would toss out my things if my person passed the threshold. The next year brought the Spanish influenza, giving me more reason to embrace my reclusive status. I watched the seasons change through the brief moments of the front door's opening to the street as guests came and went.

And I simply stayed.

The same allowance that, while I was married, afforded me every sort of luxury—new hats, new furnishings, elaborate luncheons and garden parties, and box seats at our theater—only promised to meet my needs from one month to the next, with a little saved up in case the boys ever found out and put a stop to it. Since that night—the night I chose to live alone with my clean conscience and unapologetic freedom—David Thornhill has faithfully deposited the rightful amount in my account, and some bank employee has faithfully delivered my envelope of cash for whatever incidentals I might chance upon.

There were times when I was at my loneliest, my heart its emptiest, my days long and my nights longer, that I wished I had chosen differently. There had been time. I could have caught him in the street, had I chased him. I could have sent an urgent note to the police station, asking them to contact him on my behalf. He'd told me he lived within blocks of the hotel; I could have spent a series of spring days knocking on each door until I found him. But make no mistake: the woman he left behind, the tragic victim of her choices as some might paint me, was completely and utterly whole. Something within me came to life the moment I opened the envelope he had left behind.

I was, for the first time, free.

Young readers, with all the advantages of modernity, cannot imagine what it meant to be a woman simply allowed to live. Independently. I was not kept by any man, nor was I in any danger of falling into poverty or degradation for lack of one. I had come to San Antonio with vague expectations of rebuilding the life I lived with my late husband, hoping that with enough charm and enough promise, I would fall into the circumstance as I had before. Mutual companions, mutual caretakers, mutual rescue. I had lived three weeks in the whirlwind courtship of Irvin Carmichael, my heart nearly bursting with love for him every moment of every day. That night, in the dark of the Menger Bar, with Bert watching in the shadows, I stood behind a closed door, choosing not to open it.

I had no model to follow in this course. Men, I understood. All my life—and, Dear Reader, it is without an ounce of exaggeration that I use the word *all*—my survival has depended on the lust-driven generosity of men. Early on, men who ensured my mother's keep. But too soon, the responsibility fell on me, and I quickly learned my value. I'd been loaned out, sought out, and sold time and again. My late husband rescued me, Irvin Carmichael loved me, and now I had the means simply to exist. Not with money that originated in my husband's death, but with the same he had given me in life. I recalled what I learned during my time going to my husband's church. I had a value far beyond rubies and a Father in heaven who saw past my faults and would loosen the pain that bound me.

While some might define my life as one of leisure, my conscience pricks at the idea of perceived idleness. Opportunities abounded for me to fill my hours and occupy my hands as well as my mind while doing some good for a world that had, ultimately, been so good to me. I rolled bandages and knit socks during the Great War, though I pity the poor soldier who had to wear my first efforts. Later I knit hats and mufflers for the "Bundles for Britain," sometimes working here by the roaring lobby fire, but other times with groups of women in church basements. There I came close to forming friendships, though I bristled at questions regarding my circumstances. It seemed the only way to avoid speculation and judgment was to keep to my own company. Occasionally I did agree to a dinner, even spending a vivacious evening with a certain undisciplined baseball slugger. Most of my outings, however, were with gentlemen I knew from my days before the robbery. These were the men who knew me at the peak of my beauty, and what a comfort they were to reassure me that it hadn't faded. I saw the Menger nearly burn to the ground and then swell to twice its size, the bar moved to a place where I'd have to navigate a sea-sized lobby to have my occasional brandy with Bert. But my life, my room, my memories remained small.

Through all of this history—disease, depression, destruction, and war—I heard not a word from Detective Irvin Carmichael. And so I carved out a place for myself, vowing never again to measure my worth by a man's words. Not that I would have turned him away, had I kept my power to bewitch him back to my side. Since the night all was taken from me, I wore only the ring given to me by my late husband, letting myself be haunted by the ghost of respectability.

As for that other haunting, I cannot say that Sallie White ever left me completely. I never abandoned the habit of listening for her in those moments of darkness between shutting off my light and drifting off to sleep. Like other guests, I have seen shadows, felt brushes against me, experienced the flickering of lights and the persistent sound of doors opening and closing, but I'm not so quick to attribute them to a phantom presence. Our hearts like to tease our minds and make our eyes see what will bring a rush of feeling—both in love and fear. In the dullness of life, I sometimes longed for the terrible jolt of seeing Sallie White.

Bert remained my constant companion, and once I'd decided my reputation was my own to determine, I visited him several evenings a week, running down the news of the world while enjoying a glass of wine in the summer or a hot toddy in winter. I teased him over the years, as my hair turned gray and the skin on my neck found new folds, he remained nearly unchanged. A bit of salt in his close-cropped curls, but hadn't it always been there? His face softened with familiarity, and every time I walked in to see him standing behind the bar, I felt instant comfort and release. Once a year, on Valentine's

Day, after the bar closed, he cooked up the supper he'd made for Carmichael and me and we'd talk about that night. Over the years, the more my encounter slipped into memory, the more my irrationality became apparent. We could laugh, Bert and I, about my scream-filled run through the halls, my erratic moves through the lobby.

"You could have been one of those actresses on the screen," Bert said, though for all I knew he'd never been to a motion picture. I didn't care for them myself. I always preferred the stage, seeing flesh and blood characters brought to life right in front of me. Films disconcerted me, knowing the men and women on the screen were actually existing in another place in time. But I knew what he meant. My exaggerated expressions—all in an attempt to convey the overwhelming realness of my terror.

"I should not have left my room," I said. Ten years had passed since that night. It was nearly two o'clock in the morning, the last of the romantic couples chased away. I looked forward to this night all year—my celebration with the one person I counted as family. This was the only time I talked about the night, the only time I gave the memories free rein in conversation. Oh, I *told* the story to strangers, but there is a gulf of difference between telling a story and sharing a story. With Bert, my words found a soft landing. We could laugh and not feel offense; he could wonder and not question. On this night in 1925, I finally hit upon the perfect alternate history. "If I'd simply stood in my doorway and screamed for help, the robbery would never have happened."

"Might have taken some time for anybody to hear you."

"You would have heard me." Of this, I was sure.

"Might never have met that detective. . ."

"Or had my heart broken. . ."

"Or found your money." This was always his favorite part of the story because my allowance kept me here. "God brings people in and out of a life. Or in and out of a place. Guess He wanted you and me to stay."

"Like Sallie?"

He shook his head and chuckled. "Just when I thought you was coming to some senses, there you go."

I touched his arm and reassured him that I wasn't going anywhere, neither in matter nor in mind. I finished my meal, and he walked me to the door, dropping a kiss to my cheek as too was our annual custom. A woman must be allowed to feel like a lady all the days of her life.

I walked through the darkened hotel—a path I could have taken with both eyes blind. We say such things, but in my later years it has proven nearly true. I was still young then—not quite forty—and full of a good meal washed down with an equally good drink, and all the comfort of conversation on a cold night. The lobby was deserted, the only sound being "Good night, Mrs. Krause," spoken by the man charged to run the desk overnight. I wished him the same and began my ascent, unable to explain the niggling of dread within me.

I heard her before I saw her. She was humming a tune that would take years for me to track down: "The Old Rugged Cross." The notes were soft and uneven, and they stopped the moment I turned the corner to my hallway.

The way she stood at my door made me feel like she'd been standing there for hours. I knew—every part of me knew—this was Sallie White. *My* Sallie White. My personal phantom. However, tonight there was no translucence. No levitation. No blurring of her face. She waited, every ounce of her form as solid as my own. Yes, I wasn't just seeing Sallie White, I was remembering her—all those times my mind played its trick, holding on to the idea of the dead come back to life rather than the living come to steal and to kill.

"Mrs. Krause?" Her voice was thick and deep, though nothing like the strangled, abrasive sound that had called my name from beyond the door.

"I know who you are." I choose not to use her name in this book, as I have little more than speculation. Though, on our next Valentine's Day, I offered it to Bert and thus confirmed a suspicion he'd held all along. When I asked why he'd never told me, he said, "Answers are only true if you find them for yourself."

She didn't speak another word. She didn't budge either, and I might have remained standing in my hallway to this day if I hadn't stepped toward the door. I moved as if I could walk right through her, imagining her to be the shadow of the photograph, the mist of that night when she flew. I stopped before I touched her, studying every feature, matching it to memory and fear. Then I felt her hand—cold and dry—her fingers curled around mine, opening them. Something hard and small dropped into the middle of my palm, and my fingers closed again. She moved her face even closer, until I could no longer see her features but could feel her breath—living, warm breath—in my ear.

"I've been ruined since that night, Hedda Krause." Here was the tortured vocal of my nightmare, though when I drew away, I saw her smile. No warmth there, though. It was broad and menacing—the kind of smile that one assumes after playing a trick. And, oh, the trick she'd played on me.

I knew Bert was downstairs, and the night clerk, for all the help he'd be. I could scream loud enough to wake the dead and bring them running to my side. Instead, I watched her walk away, feeling the heaviness in her step, knowing the coat she wore would do nothing to protect her from the cold of the night waiting outside. I held my breath as she walked right past the stairs and went to the little sofa on the landing where she nudged at a bundle that unfolded itself to become a little boy. She picked him up, his arms wrapped firmly around her neck, and disappeared down the stairs.

Not until that moment did I open my door and turn on a lamp to bathe my little room in amber. I stepped over and held my hand beneath it, knowing what I'd find. My earring. Amethyst rimmed in tiny diamonds. Come back to me at last. Carmichael held the other. I went to my bed and—fully dressed—curled up beneath the covers. I had no feelings for Sallie White—no anger or remorse or pity. For her, I was as cold as I believed her blood to be. My only thoughts, as I brought the jewel so close to my eyes that I could see only it and my palm surrounding, was a longing for a reunion with its partner. To see him again. To take him if he'd have me.

Thus, my answer. When the curious, the romantic, the thrill seekers and amateur detectives ask me: "Why do you live here? Why do you stay?" I tell them—I am simply waiting for that which I have lost to be found and to make its way home where its partner is buried beneath a new foundation. My soul is at peace in this world and will pass on in peace to the next, where I will seek the true Sallie White and take her in my arms to give her the strength and comfort she was never afforded here. Until that day, however, I continue to wish her good night as I usher each day into darkness. And when the sun comes up, I watch. I wait. I reside.

Chapter 21

Hold that thought," Dini said. "Remember, the idea is uninterruption for the important stuff."

"What could possibly interrupt us?" Quin looked around as if anticipating a secret waitress to come from around the corner.

"You have obviously never been given the care of a cast iron skillet. Five minutes to clean it out, or everything will stick and—you don't want to know." She charged him with pouring each of them a fresh cup of coffee, ignoring his startled look when she instructed him about how much of the generic nondairy creamer to add to her cup. Then she sent him to wait in the living room while she ran water into the cooled iron skillet and scrubbed it clean with her bare hand, rinsed it, then wiped it dry with the good paper towels bought expressly for this purpose.

All the while, her mind raced. What could he mean, she'd had the solution all her life? Part of her buzzed with anticipation to hear his theory, while the rest of her silently grumbled at the idea of having this stranger—totally new to the entire legend—come with a solution she'd never conceived.

Dini washed her hands thoroughly, using three pumps of the foamy, lemon-scented soap and scrubbing up past her wrists, wanting to rid herself of the slick feel and savory scent of the sausage and eggs. She rinsed, smelled, and, satisfied, went into the living room, dropping the tea towel on the back of the chair while ordering,

"Alexa. Volume down."

Quin was sitting on her couch, looking entirely at home. Not lounging, exactly, but not *perched*, either. He had one leg crossed casually over the other, his coffee cup resting on his knee. Dini had a choice: the vintage-print accent chair on the other side of the coffee table or the sofa beside him. She stood, never before so indecisive about where to sit in her own home, and then she noticed her mug sitting on an animal-print coaster. He took a sip and set his mug right next to it. He might as well have patted the cushion beside him.

"I hope you don't mind," he said as she settled in, a good half a cushion between them. "I went ahead and took the tour."

"Did you? Without a guide? How brave."

"I absolutely don't want you to take this in any kind of a wrong way, but your house is adorable."

She laughed. "Why would I take that the wrong way?"

"I don't know if it's a thing to call a person's house 'cute.' But it is. It's cute."

"That's Realtor talk for small. Which it is. So. . ."

"Just one question. What do you have locked up in that room? Do you have a secret first husband that went mad after you brought him here from Barbados? Is there a crazy Bernie locked up in there?"

She swatted him with a llama-embossed throw pillow. "No. That's where I keep all of my stage stuff. Costumes and trunks and—everything. All the tricks of the trade. I keep a combo lock on it for whenever I AirBnb the house. It means I can only rent it out as a single bedroom, but that's okay. It means no kids, right?"

"Do you rent it out a lot?"

"Not really. Sometimes I'll take a gig out of town, and I'll just hang out and explore for a week or so. If the Spurs make the playoffs? Or like at Christmastime? I can make a few bucks. And then, I've worked a few cruises, so I'm gone for months at a time there. Arya takes care of the business end of it."

"Back up." He leaned in closer. "Cruises? Like *Love Boat*?"

She clutched the llama pillow in front of her, both to defend herself and to create a barrier to remind her not to launch across the distance between them. "Yes, Quin. Exactly like *Love Boat*."

"Did you—did you mend marriages through magic? Ever help a guy out by pulling an engagement ring out of your hat so he could propose in Puerto Vallarta?"

"Oh my gosh. How do you know so much about *Love Boat*?"

He shrugged, uncrossed his leg, and turned his body fully toward her. "I dated a girl who was obsessed with classic TV."

"Tell me, Quin Carmichael. How many of your stories begin with 'I dated a girl. . .'?"

"Oh, I don't know, Dini Houdini. How many of your stories begin with, 'That summer I traveled with the carnies'?"

"I only spent two summers with carnies." This was true. "And they are lovely people." This, unfortunately, was not.

They'd been inching closer to each other throughout the banter. In a single move, Quin grabbed the llama pillow, tossed it behind her, and closed the gap, wrapping his arm around her waist, sending his glasses clattering to the table, and bringing her into a kiss that both took her by surprise and made her think, *Finally*.

Her sweater was bulky and she wore her cami beneath it, but the combined powers of both garments could not camouflage the feel of his hand splayed across her back. She felt the pressure of all five fingers plus his palm, while his other hand wound itself in her curls, holding her face close to his, as if she would ever consider pulling away. She ran her hand the length of his sleeve, then snuck beneath it, her other braced against his chest, feeling the pounding of his heart matched to her own. She wondered if he knew how her body roiled within, like one of those wind sock men you see at car dealerships, bowing and rising within her. His hand moved, his fingers grazing her calf, and the jolt that ran through her explained why those Victorians kept their legs hidden beneath miles and miles of fabric. She pulled away and touched his face, feeling the lingering ghost of his beard on her skin.

His eyes were closed but fluttered open. He looked down to where his thumb stroked the knot of her scar.

"This looks painful."

"It was," she said, pulling herself away from his reach.

"I think we need to talk about important stuff, Dini."

She ran her hand through her curls, tugging them to bring her senses back in line. "I think you need to tell me why you texted me ninety-seven times this morning."

"Ninety-seven might be an exaggeration, but okay." He took a deep breath. "I think you have something that belonged to Hedda."

"A few things, actually. My mother was always on the lookout. I have a rhinestone brooch."

"I don't mean that." He took her hand—gently, with no expectations—and ran his thumb across her knuckles, stopping to rest on the silver spoon handle ring on her first finger. "I spent all day yesterday looking at your hands. While you were driving, eating a burger, during your show. The way they move when you talk. And that ring—"

"My witch's heart ring—"

"And thinking about that story. The girl at the inn. . .I remembered—" He reached for the book and flipped immediately to the back, reading: " 'Not that I would have turned him away, had I kept my power to bewitch him back to my side. Since the night all was taken from me, I wore only the ring given to me by my late husband, letting myself be haunted by the ghost of respectability.' " He looked up. "That's the legend of the ring, right?"

"But surely she was just speaking in general terms. Bewitching with her body, or her—I don't know—magnetism."

"In the next sentence she talks about a ring. I know it's a stretch, but she's often pretty cagey with details, right? The way these three pieces just fell together in my head. I think there's something there."

"That ring was a gift from my grandfather. How would it have come into his possession?"

"Hasn't your family been here forever? She—whoever the robber might have been—could have pawned it anywhere. Trust me—the coincidence factor here is high, but I don't believe in coincidences. Sometimes God just opens our eyes at the right time—"

"Stop." She took her hands away and covered her eyes, appalled at the sting of tears. "I've read this book a million times. A million and one counting last night. I've never seen that connection." She moved her hands away and noticed he'd put on his glasses again.

"Maybe it's like when officers have cold cases, and it takes a new detective to look at the evidence to put things together. Please, indulge me for a minute. Your ring? Go get it."

"It's too random."

"Please?"

She complied, needing a moment to catch her breath, to come to her senses and clear her mind already too clouded with his kisses to be of any reliable use. The ring waited in its case in the top drawer of a tall bachelor dresser, the furniture piece itself on casters so she could easily roll it into the locked room when the house was rented. She slipped it on her third finger, and in doing so, realized a flaw in Quin's logic.

"One thing," she said, walking back into the living room and being struck—again—by the comforting feel of having him waiting there, "this wasn't always a ring. It was a brooch. The clasp was broken, so I had it turned into a ring because, I mean, when would I ever wear a brooch?"

"Interesting," he said, sounding preoccupied as he scanned the detective's collection of bits and pieces of a case.

"Plus, Carmichael made a list of everything that was stolen, remember? To take to pawn shops and the like. I think I would have remembered if he listed a witch's heart ring."

"Maybe. . ." Quin picked up the notebook and turned to the back. This time he did pat the cushion next to him. Close. She sat, and he held the notebook between them. Carmichael's meticulous list took up half the page. *Pearl earrings, drops. Jade bracelet. Silver hammered cuff.*

"Wait." Dini brought her finger to touch the page. "*Green stone amulet.* This could be it. Maybe she didn't know it was a peridot?"

"Or my great-great-grandpa didn't know how to spell it."

"And it might have been worn on a string at one time." She held her hand up close between them. "Or a thin chain. See? Between the little prongs in the crown. It could easily have been turned into a brooch the same as I turned it into a ring."

"And she wouldn't have called it a 'witch's heart,' right? Not that evening, when she was already trying to explain how she was blaming the whole thing on a ghost."

"Weird enough to use the term *amulet.*"

"I dunno." Quin took her hand and studied the ring. "Rattled as she was, she was still in full-on flirt mode. *Amulet* sounds interesting—more interesting than. . ."

"Pendant," Dini said, finding his lost word. "And it makes sense that the Sallie White thief would have kept it, especially if she knew its legend. Even today as an antique, the jeweler I took it to valued it at around two hundred dollars. It's a cool piece to keep, not an advantageous sale."

"One of your ancestors might have bought it in some pawn shop."

"I don't think so." She couldn't explain it, the way this newly opened door seemed to corral the story into closer confines.

"Do you ever wonder who she was?"

He was looking off and away, maybe studying the series of vintage River Walk photographs on the wall behind her, which was a good thing, because that meant he didn't see Dini roll her eyes. A sarcastic remark sat on the tip of her tongue. *Nope. Never even crossed my mind.* But she knew Quin was musing out loud, his question purely rhetorical, so she came back to it from another angle.

"There's never been any way to know."

"Why do you think she didn't just come out and say it? Give up the woman's name and clear her own? All those people who thought she was crazy or that she lied."

"All those people?"

He sighed. "You think she was writing to an audience of one? He died before the book came out."

"But he was still known to be connected to the case. The Christmas picture was mailed to him from someone who didn't know he'd left the city."

"She might have obtained a second copy and mailed it to the police station, knowing they would forward it. The message written on the back is pretty much what she says to Sallie when she confronts her."

"No, the message is what Sallie says to her." Dini was already reaching for the envelope and tipping it to drop the photograph into her hand. She studied it, feeling the same chill as she did every time she read about it in the book—a chill that ran deeper and colder than seeing the photo itself, because she felt its impact through Hedda's eyes. She turned it over and read the faded note.

This night began my ruin.

Something—some new, explosive knowledge—began to crackle at the base of Dini's brain. "Hedda didn't write this."

"How can you be sure?"

"First, Hedda wasn't ruined from the picture. If we believe what she wrote, and there's no reason *not* to, nobody even knew about the photo for sure except for the photographer and the woman posing as Sallie."

"Maybe Sylvan?"

"Maybe, but he didn't send it either, and we couldn't have been completely sure without this." She traded the photograph for the detective's notebook and turned to the page with the three questions. "It's not her handwriting. Look at the *T* in *This* and *Tennessee.* Not even close."

"So," Quin said, "this tells us, maybe, that the Sallie actress sent the picture—"

"—or, the photographer."

"Yes, but I lean toward Sallie, since this is marked"—he held the envelope close—"January. . .something. . .1925."

"A month before that final meeting between she and Hedda." Dini stood and began pacing the limited length of her living room, hoping the action might mitigate the near explosive pressure in her head. All of this now felt like a giant, fuzzy knot, and she need only find the perfect place to pick it all apart. "And both of these—mailing the photo and the meeting—are like confessions of sort. To the investigator and the victim. Almost, but not quite, turning herself in."

"Yes. More like a show of remorse."

"A confession to the universe."

"Or," Quin said, "to God. We can't always go back and undo our sins, but we can restart. Maybe she was trying to start over."

"A kindness. Trying to put their minds at ease and give back what she could."

"Right. But it still does nothing to tell us *who* took on the role of Sallie White."

Dini stopped in her steps. Her back to Quin, she twisted, moving as spontaneously as her Ugg boots would allow. The electricity in her head was nearly unbearable; her own pulse rang in her ears. The knot brazenly displayed its first vulnerable loop. "You keep saying that. Things like that."

He dropped the Christmas ghost photo casually on the table. "Things like what?"

"The *role* of Sallie White. The *actress* who played the part."

"Well, it's obvious somebody did. Posing for the double-exposure plate. Filmed for that Haunted Mansion trick."

"Pepper's Ghost," she corrected automatically. "It was an actress."

"That's what I've been saying!"

"No. She was an actress-actress." Dini ran (shuffled, really) around the table and stopped in front of him, taking his face in her hands and planting an enthusiastic kiss on his lips while the rest of her filled with unfurling ribbons of delight. "And you know what?" she said, pulling away and jumping out of his range of recapture, "my great-great-grandfather is in this story too. At least, I think so. I might be a descendant of none other than J. P. Haley."

"Wait. What?" He looked so confused, so adorably confused, that every moment he'd spent nine steps ahead of her vanished in a *whoosh* of affection. His claim that her witch's heart once belonged to Hedda still stung a little, but that was a matter of fresh eyes. This—*this*—was a detonation that could only happen with the right flame touched to the right wick. This was the final three cards in a game of Clue—only instead of the weapon and the killer and the room, the three elements needed here were the book, the notebook, and the contents of the box.

She picked up the book and held it to her heart. "Just like Hedda wrote: the only true answers are the ones you find for yourself. So, I tell you today, that if we were casting the role of the spectral Sallie White for the film adaptation of *My Spectral Accuser*, she would be played by"—she paused to build anticipation and smiled as he scooted closer to the edge of the sofa—"Thalia Jean Powers."

The sound of a tenor sax, recorded half a century ago, filled the silence as Quin remained—somewhat deflated—sitting. "Who?"

Not exactly the burst of enthusiasm she'd expected, but the overwhelming relief of finding the final piece of a puzzle that had been sitting—unfinished—at the edge of her consciousness for most of her adult life would not be tainted just because she had to lead Quin a little further. After all, this was relatively new to him.

She handed him the book. "Turn to chapter 3. When Hedda goes to the theater and has her first photograph taken by J. P. Haley. See the name of the actress starring in the play?" She watched his eyes skim the pages and wanted to rip the book away to find it for herself, but patience. . .patience.

"Thalia Jean Powers." He looked up over the rim of his glasses. "But—"

"And Hedda mentions mingling with the crowd after the show. The two might have met each other. I can imagine Hedda angling for an introduction, can't you?"

"Hedda doesn't mention meeting her."

"Plus, I'll bet the thin assistant helping Haley with the Christmas pictures was Thalia too."

"With a beard?"

"Fake beard and tiger eyes. By the time Hedda writes her book, she knows it was Thalia Powers. And she chose not to disclose her identity."

"And why do you think that is?"

"Because, no matter what her past, at her heart Hedda was a good and kind woman. Thalia suffered enough." She looked at the assembly of items from Detective Carmichael's box and saw each in a whole new light. "Of course," she said, coming around and sitting down with the movie magazine in her hand. "She must be in here." For all she knew the next few minutes, Quin might have dissolved into the carpet, or disappeared behind the paint. Her full attention was given to every page of the magazine. Every advertisement for hair crème and perfume. Every story of Hollywood scandal and gossip. Every profile of new starlets—and there she was. Her hair a mass of pinned curls, her eyes heavy with kohl. She was posed on a chaise lounge—not seductively, but definitely inviting, in a seamless sheath dress that fell to reveal all the peaks and valleys of her body. The text around her told the tale of this "exotic beauty" with "dark eyes that reached past the screen into the very soul of those poor suckers in the seats just waiting to fall in love." She was "a chameleon." A "goddess from ancient time."

What Dini hadn't noticed the first (or tenth) time she thumbed through this magazine the other night—because she hadn't thought to look for it—was the way this particular page was bent along the spine's margin. This magazine had been folded to stay open to this page. And the bottom corner had been ripped away. Neatly. Like it was a page in a detective's notebook.

She handed the magazine gently over to Quin. "There she is."

He looked, and a low, appreciative whistle came through his lips. "She is gorgeous." He looked up. "Look, I don't want to slow your mojo here, but wasn't Sallie White African American?"

Dini nodded. "So is, was, Thalia Powers."

One eyebrow arched over the top of Quin's glasses. "I don't mean to be. . .but she doesn't look—"

"Technically she was biracial. Which, being born around 1890, meant black. But she wanted to be an actress, and so she took advantage of her skin tone. She. . .*passed*, is the word. And while she wasn't successful on stage, she starred in a few motion pictures. Until somebody—probably some actress who lost a part to her—blabbed to the studio executives. She was set to star in a romance. A black woman and a white man—they wouldn't be able to get it into theaters. But she was still under contract with the studio, so after a couple of good roles, she was bumped to playing housekeepers and slaves." A new thought took root. "Hold on," she said, jumping off the couch.

"How do you know all of this?" Her house was small enough for the question to carry. She was still in her bedroom, unplugging her laptop when she answered.

"Once, my mother and I watched this movie, *Imitation of Life*. Have you seen it? It's about a young black woman who passes as white, much to the heartbreak of her mother. I loved that movie, and Mom told me about Thalia Jean Powers. And *she* knew about Thalia Jean Powers because her great-grandfather was in love with her. I think her great-grandfather was J. P. Haley."

"You think? You've never heard his name?"

She held a finger to her lips, shushing him, then kept it aloft as a reminder for as long as it took to open her laptop and click on the YouTube icon. She typed "Thalia Jean Powers" in the search bar and scrolled down to what looked like a period piece: *The Rebel Was a Maiden*, a Civil War film. "Come watch." She brought her feet up and angled her body so he could see the screen. He draped an arm along the back of the couch and moved in close enough that she felt him braced against the length of her back. She tapped the arrow to play the video and paused it on the third title card. "There: 'Photographed by J. Preston Hale.' " She twisted to face him. "That's my great-great-grandfather. His real name. We've always been a show business family."

She instructed Alexa to stop playing music in order to listen to the instrumental overlay of the flickering images on the screen. Quin shifted, handing her the reasonably warm cup of coffee, and took up his own. From what she could tell, *The Rebel Was a Maiden* was a story about a Union soldier in love with the daughter of a Confederate general, with all the difficulties such a relationship entailed.

"This is 1922," Dini said. That magazine is dated, what, 1918?"

"Mm-hmm," Quin affirmed. "So, this is after the fall from favor." She felt his response in every vertebrae and considered posing one question after another just to feel him speak.

They watched the couple on screen fall into a kiss behind a rosebush by the door. "And to think," Quin said, his breath against the back of her neck, "those people are dead now."

"I had no idea you were such a romantic."

He laughed, and everything within her liquefied to the consistency of her coffee. Propriety, she supposed, demanded she move away. But, glancing at the clock on the bottom of the screen, they had little more than an hour left to be together. Bad enough they had to spend it watching B-rated silent film actors on YouTube.

Then she and Quin let out a simultaneous gasp.

There she was, standing on the back porch, oblivious to the couple canoodling behind the rosebush. She paused her comically furious sweeping to holler for the boy, then placed her hand on her hip, waiting.

Dini paused the video.

Quin leaned closer. "Are you sure that's the same woman?" He leaned over, picked up the magazine, and held it next to the laptop screen. "She looks. . .darker."

"I think," Dini said, choking past the unexpected tears forming in her throat, "she has makeup on. They put a black actress in blackface to make sure she was black enough for the role." She paused the movie at a moment where Thalia was midshout and said, "Hand me the Christmas picture?"

Quin handed her the magazine and reached for the photograph. This too they held next to the screen. The clothing was nearly identical—drab, nineteenth-century calico and apron, though Sallie wore a white cap and Thalia's character, a dark kerchief. But the resemblance was unmistakable. The blurred phantom in the photograph, the starlet in the magazine, and the actress on the screen were all the same person.

"Do you think," Quin asked, "that's what she meant when she said her life was ruined from that night?"

"Like she'd been cursed for her crime? Punished in ways other than prison?" Dini closed her laptop and moved away, creating breathing space between the two of them. "Her visit to Hedda was a couple of years after this film. Not only did she have to watch her career die because of racism, but the man she loved had to watch it die too. That had to have been humiliating."

"I don't know if I can feel sorry for a man who didn't stand up for his wife."

"They probably weren't married. It wasn't legal yet. But if I put this together with what Mom told me, that child was my great-grandfather, whom I never met. I've only ever known the grandfather who lived in this house—and he's barely a memory—from my mother's family. And nobody from Dad's. I guess I'm just a sad little orphan, all alone in the world." She hadn't meant for the final sentence to sound so mournful and pathetic, but apparently it did, because Quin reached for her and took her to him, her head cradled on his shoulder.

"I don't ever want you to feel alone, Dini." He touched the bottom of her chin and raised her face to meet his. "And I don't know exactly what that means, but I know I hate the fact that I have to leave and I won't see you tomorrow."

"I hate that too."

"Mostly, though, I hate leaving you with all of this. It's so much. How are you feeling? About. . .everything."

"Good," she said, and with the next thought, reached for her laptop again, opening it and typing "IMDb" in the search bar. From there she typed in "J. Preston Hale Photographer." "I can't believe I have to go to a website to learn when my own ancestor died," she said, attempting levity before looking at the date. "Wow. Just a few months before Sallie—Thalia—came to Hedda."

"Does it say how he died?"

"No, but it could have been. . .anything. Hedda was right not to name her. She'd been through enough. And Carmichael too."

"Maybe he didn't put it all together."

"I think he did. Maybe he didn't cut the corner in his notebook, but he did in the magazine. And, maybe. . ." She stretched for the notebook, hating to leave the cocoon of Quin's embrace, but wanting to check a final detail. Finding the page with the list of Valentine's party attendees that night, she saw that most were marked out, a few were left blank, and two had a tiny star etched beside them.

Thalia Hale

John Hale

"He knew." Dini showed him the list. "Why do you think he didn't say anything? Do anything?"

Quin took out his phone and began to scroll through, finally stopping and tapping on a picture, which he showed to Dini. "It's the family Bible. Remember? This shows when he was married. April 12, 1921. By the time he got the Christmas picture in the mail, he had a wife. Maybe even a kid. He wasn't going to go back to Hedda Krause."

"But he kept everything."

"Kept it *away*. All wrapped up with a bow. Literally."

"And never recorded another case in his notebook."

"Case closed." He touched her cheek.

She turned her head and kissed the center of his palm. "Case closed. Do you want to watch the rest of *The Rebel Was a Maiden*?"

"Ah, no. But"—he picked up the magazine—"it would be cool if we found some footage from her leading lady days. Just to—" He stopped short, taking off his glasses and bringing the magazine closer.

"What is it?" Dini inched forward, but he kept the page angled away as he took out his phone, opened the camera, and held it over the image.

"Oh man," he said, then moved closer. The image on his phone had zoomed in on a thin ribbon of silk edging the neckline of Thalia's white dress. And there, right at the deepest point of the V, an unmistakable jewel.

"My witch's heart." She held out her hand. "She kept it."

"They probably sold everything else off to get themselves out to California."

"But this made its way down to me. I don't know what to do now. I need to find a new obsession."

"You could try being obsessed with me." He spoke with his chin tucked under, like a shy child sure of his rejection. "Because I am with you, Dini. Everything about you. And not in that creeper stalker way—"

"If you were a creepy stalker, you wouldn't tell me."

"I just—my head tells me that it's way too soon for me to feel like this. It's crazy, isn't it? To fall in love in, what, a week?"

"We've only seen each other three days. So, yeah. It's ridiculous. You know if we lived in the same city, if we didn't have this stupid countdown, you wouldn't feel this way."

"I don't think that's true. I know what it's like to know someone my entire life, and I never had five minutes feeling about her the way I do about you. I'm in love with you, Dini."

Her heart longed to say that she loved him too. She was *allowed* to love him because she didn't know any better. He had ignited parts of her that she thought were too damaged by loneliness and grief to ever come to life. Surely she would recognize those stirrings again. Quin had been the first to access them, but that didn't mean he would forever be the *only* one.

He was waiting. Not expectantly, but not seeming to be in any hurry to fill the silence with any other sentiment.

"I might love you too, Quin. I mean, I do—I probably do. But that might be because I don't know what else to feel. I've never been this close to anybody. I've never had my time be so consumed by another person. But we don't know each other's worlds. We've just started to belong in each other's lives. I can't imagine you anywhere but here. I've only seen you in the Menger, in my car, the Sidecar, and in my house. Other than the picture of you with the ducks, I have no proof that you exist away from me. You're like a refrigerator light."

"Wow." He ran his hand over his beard, as if trying to wipe away his words. "That might be the most wisdom-packed rejection I've ever heard."

"It's not a rejection. I don't know what it is, but it isn't that."

"I'm just afraid, I guess. Like you said, that this is all going to disappear when I leave. Like a broken spell."

"There's no such thing as spells," Dini said. "I should know. I'm a magician. There's no magic to any of this. It's just our minds playing tricks, making a few days seem like. . .more. Showing us what we want to see, making us feel what we want to feel."

Another silence, a long one this time. The atmosphere still and heavy like a summer night before a storm. They didn't move, they didn't speak, they didn't touch—but in every way it felt to Dini like their most intimate of moments. There were no words left to say, there was nowhere to go, and the consequences loomed certain if they dared to touch.

"I think I'm going to call for a ride." He opened his phone, and she noticed his lock screen was a photo of the empty Menger Bar.

"It's early, isn't it?"

"Yeah, but I think maybe it's time."

He stood and she followed, looking around the room as if she might find something that could entice him to stay. "You want to see my gig room?"

"Car's on its way. Seven minutes, so maybe next time?"

"There'll be a next time?"

"I hope so." He bent and kissed her cheek. "My bag is still in your car. Want to wait outside with me?"

"Of course." She took his hand and they walked outside. It was chillier than she'd anticipated, but she resisted the urge to wrap her arms tightly around herself. Instead, once Quin took his bags from the back of her car and set them on the driveway, she allowed him to hold her and protect her from the breeze.

He made a frustrated groan. "I just don't want to end up like Hedda and Irvin. I don't want to walk away and never see you again."

"But maybe you'll meet a modern version of your great-great-grandmother. Have a little Irvin the Sixth." She felt his laugh roll through her and lifted her head for a kiss.

"First of all, disgusting. Second of all, I don't want you to be like that girl at that inn and pine away for me until you die."

"Text me from the airport. And text me when you land. And text me when you're home. And, if you don't text me, I'll send men on horseback to find you."

"Promise?"

"Promise. I'll make them drag you back."

"Why can't we be like J. Preston and Thalia? Heading out on an adventure together? Loving against the odds."

"Because they were jewel thieves who ruined a woman's life before he died making Thalia a washed-up single mother."

He laughed and tugged her closer. "Isn't there a single happy ending in that book?"

She thought for a moment and stepped away, cradling his face in her hands. "Yes. Hedda and Bert. They were friends for the rest of each other's lives."

She pulled him down for a final kiss, thinking of the one and only shared between the lifelong friends. How it had given her courage to face every fear, how it had been given and received with no hint of expectation and no promise of another to come.

They kissed until the crunch of tires on a silver Toyota Camry brought them apart.

"I think I might be finished with Hedda," she said.

"Good," Quin said, reaching for his bag, "because I don't want to be Bert."

Chapter 22

Like the other passengers on the crowded flight, Dini turned on her phone the moment the plane's tires touched solid ground. As they scooched through the landing, Quin's message tone played over and over.

Q: Have a safe flight.
Q: Text me when you land.
Q: I love you.

This last one she had answered with I love you too. The sentiment came easier with every message and had wormed its way into video chats throughout the spring. She texted her safe landing, with a message that she would call when she got back to the house, wanting to be phone-free at baggage claim. When her Lyft arrived, she climbed in the back seat and immediately put in her earbuds, trading music for conversation on the familiar ride.

She'd been gone for two months, taking a decent-paying job as a crowd-warming act at a regional theme park. "*Another set of stories about the summer you spent with the carnies*," Quin had said, thinly masking a disappointment at canceling their plans to spend part of the summer together. Or at least, in the same town. Instead, they'd watched the entire *Little Dorrit* BBC miniseries one episode at a time—she in a shabby motel room, he in his cozy bachelor apartment—making sweet, snarky comments on FaceTime throughout. But even that level of togetherness disappeared under a punishing show schedule. Now she was touching down, going home, for two blessedly empty weeks before a string of gigs in New Braunfels for Oktoberfest.

Her heart sank a little at the sight of Arya's Escalade overtaking the small patch of concrete in front of her house. Not that she didn't love her friend or appreciate all she'd done to keep extra money rolling in, booking the house consistently, but Dini was looking forward to uninterrupted silence and solitude.

She thanked her driver and declined his offer to take her luggage to the door. Arya appeared the minute the trunk slammed shut, ready to help.

"Sweetie," she said, after a surprisingly restorative hug, "you look terrible."

"Always good to come home to a friendly face," Dini said, taking the handle of the largest of the three cases.

"Sorry." Arya held the door and followed, rolling the two smaller bags. "But I do have a fresh deli pizza and Dr Peppers in the fridge, and there's some cookies in the Gladware in your breadbox. And"—she held up a bottle—"wine for later. Plus, I had the whole place cleaned top to bottom yesterday. So welcome home."

Dini immediately regretted her flippant remark. "Thank you for everything, and I'm sorry I was such a snot. It was a three-plane-ride day. I just want a hot bath, a ton of good food, and to watch the entire *Real Housewives of New York* season in one sitting."

"Well, may you be blessed with all of that," Arya said, planting a kiss on Dini's forehead. "I'll get out of your way, but maybe let me come back tomorrow and help with your unpacking and laundry?"

"Let me guess—need to get away from Bill for a while?"

"You can't even imagine." She paused at the door. "How are things with the nerd?"

"You're going to have to learn his name sometime, Arya."

"Really? Why? Because he's sticking around?"

"Yeah," Dini said. "At least I hope so."

Her friend dispatched, Dini texted Quin: HOME. WILL CALL YOU LATER! thinking that of all the things she loved about him, maybe the most was that he would not call her until given clearance to do so.

She set the oven to preheat and took a quick shower to wash off the day spent with strangers. After, her wet hair wrapped in a towel, she drew herself a bath, telling Alexa to play her favorite music while she soaked. Love songs, one after another, the lyrics of each conjuring pictures of Quin. While she loved Arya for stocking her fridge with a favorite soda, bath time called for a chilled glass of wine, poured in a plastic cup for safety.

She supposed she should be happy. The exhaustion currently wrapped around her muscles was a symptom of success. This was the life her parents led, only on busses and trains instead of planes and rideshares. She was doing what she was born to do, fifth generation in the business of dazzle (as her father liked to say). He—her father—would have been so proud of her, as he was always consumed with procuring the next big booking. And her mother would have been here, filling in the quiet moments, padding them with bits of comfort meant to simulate a home. She'd done her best, making sure Dini always had her own bedding, her own special shampoo and soap, her schoolbooks and travel case of little tricks, packing and unpacking a normal life from town to town. And, really, if asked, especially in the long conversations with Quin late into the night, Dini had been happy. That was her life. That was her normal.

The difference—and perhaps this explained the emptiness after returning from what was arguably her most financially successful run of shows—is that all that time, all that travel, she'd been with a family. Tonight, as affectionately as she kicked Arya out of her bungalow, she felt the weight of loneliness descend. To combat it, she scrolled through her phone, holding it safely above the water, catching up on social media posts. Through the intimacy of Facebook and Instagram, she had been introduced to Quin's entire family—parents and sisters

Lauren, Cassie, and Jill—virtually attending the glitter ponies birthday party, and a few others since. She video-coached an eight-year-old nephew through a magic trick for his end-of-school talent show. Every post that featured this rambling family gathered in lakefront rentals and campsites got a *like* with a side of envy. Summer gone, she scrolled through all of their back-to-school pictures, one slideshow beginning with an adorable pigtailed, freckled girl heading to her first day of kindergarten, and ending with twenty-nine-year-old Quin ready for his fifth year of teaching. He stood on the same redbrick porch (must be the sister's house), holding the same slate with his year written in chalk. Dini couldn't even imagine that sort of commitment to tradition, and blamed the weird tears pricking at her eyes to a day of travel fatigue and the now empty glass of wine.

Food would help.

She dragged herself out of the tub and put on a thick terry cloth robe. She took the cheese pizza from the refrigerator and was about to cover it with the sliced Roma tomatoes and fresh basil Arya thoughtfully provided, when her phone sounded Quin's text tone. Her stomach flipped exactly as it had during their first week together, and while that same stomach was grumbling with hunger, she abandoned her pizza and opened the message.

Instead of the usual blue conversation bubble, she found an image of a handwritten message. Tapping the picture to fill her phone's screen, she needed less than a second to know what she was seeing. The color of an unripe peach, cadet-blue lines. It was a picture of a blank page from Carmichael's notebook, and on it, in Quin's neat, utilitarian handwriting, a simple message:

Come to supper.
Car should be there at 7:30

Next came a selfie, the rich, dark tones of the bar surrounding him, Teddy Roosevelt peeking over his shoulder. Her hand trembled, the tiny keyboard blurring in her hand. How was this possible? How could he have concocted this kind of surprise? How was she supposed to feel? She texted only:

D: How?

But his response was nothing but a repeat of the summons. All of their talks, their texts, their messages and memes were peppered with Hedda and the detective, so she texted: ARE YOU BACK FROM TENNESSEE? before jumping into the action of getting ready.

It was after seven already. Her mind buzzed with unanswered questions, but the fatigue that seemed ready to turn her bones to powder repurposed itself as nervous invigoration. She turned off the oven and put the pizza away. Her hair was still damp when she took the towel off, so she used a few precious minutes to scrunch her curls under the diffuser until it was *mostly* dry, using her free hand to put on enough of a face to camouflage a fourteen-hour day in recycled air. Alexa added to the excitement by playing "Midnight Train to Georgia," and Dini sang every word.

Her favorite jeans, washed to butter-like softness, hadn't made it into her suitcase, so they waited in her closet to be paired with a cute top and wedge sandals.

"What do you think, Hedda?" She spoke to the image hanging in the midst of her starry sky—the photograph of Hedda, messy and content, which Dini had enlarged and printed on canvas. "I'm going for cute and casual. Did I get it?" A quick twist in front of the mirror affirmed that she had, and as a last addition, she grabbed the witch's heart ring from its box and pushed it onto her first finger. "Because, you know. . .he came back."

The first person she saw when she walked through the door was Gil, who clutched her fingers and held on to her hand a bit longer than necessary after their high five.

"Look at you," he said. "Haven't seen that color on your hair in a long time."

"It's the real deal," she replied, tugging at the curls. "Is he here?"

She followed Gil's eyes, spotting Quin at the foot of the steps leading up to the second level. The minute she did, she regretted her choice to wear the tall wedges, because her shins disappeared, and she couldn't manage a single step. But then, she didn't have to, because within two heartbeats, Quin crossed the room and took her in his arms, lifting her off the ground in an embrace that brought an appreciative *awwww* from the crowd scattered among the tables.

Dini buried her face in his neck and breathed in the scent she'd been guarding in her memories for the past seven months. Nothing before ever felt as perfect as this moment, her body suspended, his voice in her ear saying her name. When her feet were once again on the floor, he took her face in his hands and kissed her—properly and appropriately for their public display.

"I have a table upstairs," he said, taking her hand and leading her. She grabbed a glass of water from Gil on the way up and resented the creak of every step, because it seemed to delay the moment when they could greet each other again in the privacy of a dark corner.

"How are you here?" she asked, once her breath and lips were free for conversation.

"I had to see you, and I didn't want to see you anywhere but here."

"Don't you have school?" It was a Thursday night.

"I took a couple of days off. I figure I worked during my spring break last year. Tell me about your travels."

"You know about my travels."

"Tell me anyway."

"Are you stalling, Quin? Is there important stuff to talk about after the food gets here?"

The minute she said it, Gil appeared with two plates of chopped steak, peppers and potatoes. He set them down, saying, "It's off menu. You got to have connections in the kitchen."

Dini's stomach, empty save for the Kind bar she had on the last flight, growled as if on cue, and she dove in the minute Gil left, wishing, "*Bon appétit*."

"What a guy," Quin said, attacking with equal gusto. "You know, they should put this on the menu. Call it the Hedda Carmichael plate."

"Or the Tennessee dinner," Dini countered.

They ate and they talked, falling into an easy rhythm of family stories (from Quin) and theme park shenanigans (from Dini). They had the entire second level to themselves, which limited the number of times the staff would make the journey to check on their needs. Finally, their dishes cleared and drinks refreshed, Quin handed their waitress a twenty-dollar bill and promised he would holler down if they needed anything else.

"It's like the night we met," Dini said, taking in their solitude. "But I've been lugging bags around all day, so I don't have any cards to do a trick."

"I don't want you to do a trick," he said, his voice suddenly taking a turn that transformed their table into an island that stranded them in the midst of all that kept them apart. All of the distance, all of the days—*whoosh*, like a coin up a sleeve.

"Why are you here?" It was the first question she'd ever asked him, and now it came with a tiny tug of fear. There had been no mutual agreement to fall into a relationship. But the intimacies they had shared—not physical, of course, but the dreams and memories and silly moments—would call for a mutual ending. She hadn't given the possibility even a thought until now. What she knew of Quin, what she loved about Quin, pointed to a guy who would not break up via text. "Why did you come all this way?"

"So—" He took a sip of his drink and adjusted his glasses, his one nervous tell. "I found all of that stuff cleaning out my great-great-grandfather's house, remember?"

"Do I remember the 'stuff' that led me to find my ancestry linked to the actress who gaslighted Hedda Krause into thinking she was robbed by the ghost of Sallie White? Vaguely."

Quin took a deep breath before continuing. "Anyway, I gave a bunch of clothes to my school's drama department for costumes and such. Stuff from all decades and in really great shape."

"I would have loved to have gotten my hands on some of that," Dini said, imagining the accessories.

"Right. Well, the department is putting on a production of *Our Town*, and a couple of weeks ago the drama teacher comes to my room and says she feels guilty keeping some of the items." He took out his phone and opened it to his photo gallery. "Look," he said, bringing her to sit beside him.

She did, wondering about the grim set to his features.

Quin held the phone between them. She saw a small leather case, and when he scrolled to the next picture, saw that it held a detective's badge. He scrolled and narrated: "His cuff links, an FDR campaign pin, a pocket watch, a wrist watch, an ornate fountain pen. And then, this."

Quin scrolled one more time, and Dini gasped, tears pooling instantly as her throat burned beyond speech. It was sitting on a folded white square—a handkerchief with the initials *I C* monogrammed in the corner. The stone was a deep, rich purple, set in gold, with three gold beads clustered at the top. The amethyst earring. "He kept it," she said at last.

"He did."

"I always pictured them as teardrop," she said, speaking more to the image. Then she looked over to see Quin studying her in a way he never had before, like he was holding her up the way he did when he first greeted her downstairs, and to look away would be to drop her and lose her forever. "You came all this way to show me?"

"I wanted to see the look on your face."

She smiled, the tears now free and harmless. "Was it worth it?"

As an answer, he kissed her. "Let's go." Dropping his phone in his jacket pocket, he stood then descended the steps, remembering her preference for who led who down narrow stairways. He called out his room number to Gil to charge the food and drinks, then took her hand as they walked, not stopping until they were in front of the black marble fireplace, surrounded by the glass-enclosed antiquities of the Menger Hotel. Quin gestured for Dini to sit on one of the leatheresque sofas, but he did not follow suit. It was like they were moving through some sort of fog, like they were the ghosts projected in this room, because the air had gone out of it the moment Quin's knee hit the floor.

They'd had countless conversations about the fate of the earring Sallie White returned. It was never accounted for in any of the writings about Hedda after her death, so they took her at her word that it was somehow buried beneath this foundation. Even if she had been rehomed during the times of major renovation, she may have strolled over and tossed this bit of stone among excavated rubble. Or into the concrete. Or behind the marble slabs of this fireplace. They concocted scenarios where she'd embedded it in the bar, with Bert's help, or beneath the surface of the pool.

"Do you remember," Quin said, an almost imperceptible quiver in his voice, "what answer she gave when people asked why she stayed?"

She looked up and away; somehow the words on the page came clear in Dini's mind. *"I am simply waiting for that which I have lost to be found and to make its way home where its partner is buried beneath a new foundation."* When she looked at him again, he was holding a small box, and a gasp came from a group of ladies rounding the corner from the Victorian lobby.

"I don't want to be haunted by you anymore, Dini Blackstone. I don't want to keep you in my memories, I want to keep *you.* With me. When I hear your voice, I want it to be because you are next to me."

"Quin—" The room, her world, her past disappeared behind this moment. Her pulse raced in her ears, and it was just as Hedda described the moment she was face-to-face with the specter of Sallie White. Fear, lodged in her throat, pressing her into place.

"I took some liberties," Quin was saying, "because I knew nothing else could be as perfect." Then he opened the box, revealing what she knew would be inside. The amethyst earring—no, now the amethyst ring, released from its case and held out to her.

The band was thick, perfectly proportioned to the stone. She held it in her right hand, seeing it and the witch's heart together. This ring was not intended to be worn on her first finger, she knew that. It was not a distraction or meant for any kind of conjuring. Its past was buried, gone forever, and here it lived a new life. A new design. A new purpose. She slid the ring onto its intended finger, and everything fell into place. No illusion, nothing magic, but a moment so inevitable it must be true.

"I love you, Dini."

"This is crazy."

"I know."

"I love you, Quin. But I don't want you to think you're somehow. . .I don't know. . .*bound* by some kind of past honor. Would you love me if you weren't—you know—who you are?"

"I wouldn't have met you if I wasn't who I am. Think about it: God set our paths toward each other a hundred years ago." He took her hands, kissed her pulse, and stood, bringing her to her feet.

"I don't know how to share my life," she said. "I don't know how to be with another person."

"We've been sharing our lives from the moment you spelled my name with the cards."

Entwined before they met. "It's like the setup for an illusion," she said. "All of the planning and rehearsing means nothing if the timing isn't perfect. If the angle isn't just right. It seems so effortless, meeting you and just. . ." She wished she had a flash paper. What a moment to expel a harmless bit of flame.

Instead, Dini snapped her hand, the way she would if she'd drawn a coin from Quin's ear, and let the amethyst catch the lobby light.

"Will you marry me, Dini?" His question was simple, leaving no room for her own. Like where would they live? Or how would she work? Or whether or not his niece was limber enough to fold herself into a box. All of that would be worked out later. If Hedda and

Carmichael taught no other lesson, it was that some questions need answers in the moment, while others could be solved over the course of a lifetime.

She kissed him before saying, simply, "Yes."

Those who witnessed the moment—and there were many—did so through the lenses of their cameras, capturing each kiss, each gaze. Quin on his knee, Dini and the ring. They exploded in familial joy and approval, posting to their Instagram and Twitter accounts (@Dini-Blackstone, #Proposal #MengerHotel).

Later, much later, that night as she texted a final good night to Quin, she lay beneath her sky of twinkle lights and scrolled through her phone, tapping red hearts and replying, "Thank You!" to a world of well-wishing strangers. She zoomed in on the pictures, looking for the tiniest blur, the most minuscule orb—anything that might have hinted at other unseen well-wishers. But the spirits of Sallie White and Hedda Krause haunted only her heart. She looked at the ring, the stone fathoms deep in the darkness, forged in a broken past. It hadn't come back to the Menger. It came home to her hand—a hand that would hold another and spin its own worthy tale.

Author Note

A confession: I love a good ghost story. Do I believe in ghosts? No, at least not in the restless spirit of the dead variety. Ghosts are memories. Stories. When I hear stories about a "haunted" house, I don't care about the current bumps in the night; I want to know the story of the person behind those bumps and why the story has lived long after the soul.

The story of Sallie White is true, and the details of it as depicted in *The Lady in Residence* fall in line with the newspaper accounts of the time. If you take the Sisters Grimm Haunted History Walk in San Antonio (which I highly encourage!), you will stand on the sidewalk where she was murdered by her common-law husband. That's where I first heard her story, and while it might have disappeared into the thousands of other historical tidbits I carry in my brain, instead it haunted me for two reasons. First, the murder of a chambermaid impacted the owners of the Menger Hotel—easily one of the most prestigious hotels in Texas at the time—enough that they paid for Sallie White's funeral and burial. The entry in their financial ledger is proof of their compassion. Rarely would that kind of attention be given to such an employee. Second, the most often reported haunting of Sallie White is a brisk two-knocks sounding in the middle of the night. Nothing terribly frightening or ghoulish. Something that associated her with the simplicity and mundaneness of her life. (Also, something super easily explainable if you've ever spent a night in a hotel.)

Still, I didn't want to write Sallie's story, because there's no happy ending there. But I wanted a story of a haunting. There's a Russian nesting doll structure to *The Lady in Residence*. Sallie haunts Hedda. Hedda haunts Dini. I tried to bridge the idea of haunting and obsession: obsession can lead to a certain self-destruction, but a haunting? Think about all those times when you speak out loud to a lost loved one, or the times when a memory is so bittersweet you can't really tell if you're crying from joy or loss. Think about the biographies of men and women who inspire you to work for change—either in yourself or in the world. Think about the lessons you learn from knowing the mistakes others have made. All of that is *haunting*. I tried to bring all of that into the stories of Hedda and Dini. I wanted them to break free of a past that haunted them. I wanted them to look to the stories of the women who preceded and learn. What is the opposite of a woman murdered at the hands of the man she trusted? A woman who could forge a life without needing to trust a man. But then, what is the opposite of choosing to walk away from a lifelong love? Choosing to run right into it.

I can't tell you enough how beautiful the Menger Hotel is, but there is a *heaviness* to it too. I would love for everyone who ever reads this book to make a pilgrimage to San Antonio for a stay, but don't let its reputation for being one of the most haunted hotels in America be the reason for your visit. The place is just historically exquisite. It has been expanded and renovated through the years, but you can still book a room that (with the welcome additions of air-conditioning and Wi-Fi) is exactly how it was at the time of construction in 1859. Creaking floors, tiny rooms, antique furniture. I booked one of these rooms last summer, needing to really make sure the halls would accommodate my Pepper's Ghost plot point, as well as Hedda's world. The COVID-19 shutdown delayed my research trip, as the hotel was completely closed, but I was there the first week it reopened. I, along with maybe twelve other guests. I stayed the first night with my husband but opted to stay alone a second night so I could really get some work done. The place was massive and empty. There was literally one employee working as a makeshift bartender, food server, and room-service runner. I roamed the halls—every hall, at all hours—without encountering another human being. My air-conditioning unit had a sharp little *knock* sound at the end of each cycle, which brought me out of a dead sleep the first night and kept me wakeful from that point on. The second evening, I heard conversations outside my window and looked down to see the ghost tour crowd. That's when I realized my room was directly above the spot where Sallie White was murdered. I was all alone that night, so—yeah, I prayed and read until the wee hours and slept with a light on.

Both Hedda and Dini, of course, are women crafted purely from my imagination. And I promise I included a line about Hedda knitting during World War II long before my research uncovered hotel guests claiming to see a woman in a blue 1940s-style dress sitting in the lobby, knitting. If you find Hedda a bit unreliable as a narrator, that's fine. So do I. Lots of authors will tell you that their characters speak to them, but that's not usually the case for me. I tend to keep my characters on a pretty tight leash. I know what the story is and how it's supposed to happen. I tell them what to say and they (with a few exceptions) say it. Dini, in fact, sounds a lot like me. She tells some of my jokes. But not so Hedda. Of all my heroines, she is the first to come with her own voice. I heard her almost audibly as I typed. Even as I wrote her, I questioned—is this true? Did this really happen? Are you lying to me, Hedda? But then I wrote it anyway.

On the final morning of my stay at the Menger, I was in its massive lobby—again, all alone—working on my edits. The space was filled with swoony big band music, and my mind began to wander, thinking about this same place during the previous months when night after night after night after night there was nobody. Not a single living soul (as we say). And then I thought about all the *living* souls that passed through these halls, walked up and down the stairs, drank in the bar, ate by the fire in the dining room. All the lives and all the stories—all of them ghosts spread far and wide. Generation to generation. And right there, in that moment, I was among them, separated only by time and space and breath.

Allison Pittman is the author of more than a dozen critically acclaimed novels and is a four-time Christy finalist—twice for her Sister Wife series, once for *All for a Story* from her take on the Roaring Twenties and most recently for the critically acclaimed *The Seamstress*, which takes a cameo character from the Dickens classic *A Tale of Two Cities* and flourishes her to life amid the French Revolution. Allison lives in San Antonio, Texas, blissfully sharing an empty nest with her husband, Mike. Connect with her on Facebook (Allison Pittman Author), Twitter (@allisonkpittman) or her website, allisonkpittman.com.

More from Doors to the Past Series...

Hope Between the Pages (Coming April 2021)
by Pepper Basham
Clara Blackwell helps her mother manage a struggling one-hundred-year old family bookshop in Asheville, North Carolina, but the discovery of a forgotten letter opens a mystery of a long-lost romance and undiscovered inheritance which could save its future. Forced to step outside of her predictable world, Clara embarks on an adventure with only the name Oliver as a hint of the man's identity in her great-great-grandmother's letter. From the nearby grand estate of the Vanderbilts, to a hamlet in Derbyshire, England, Clara seeks to uncover truth about family and love that may lead to her own unexpected romance.

Paperback / 978-1-64352-826-7 / $12.99

Bridge of Gold (Coming June 2021)
by Kimberley Woodhouse
Underwater archaeologist Kayla Richardson is called to the Golden Gate Bridge where repairs to one of the towers uncovers two human remains from the late 1800s and the 1930s. The head of the bridge restoration is Mark Andrews, who dives with Kayla, and a friendship develops between them. But as the investigation heats up and gold is found that dates back to the gold rush, more complications come into play that threaten them both. Could clues leading to a Gold Rush era mystery that was first discovered during the building of the bridge still ignite an obsession worth killing for?

Paperback / 978-1-64352-957-8 / $12.99

See the series lineup and get bonus content
at **DoorsToThePastSeries.com**